'TWAS ONLY YESTERDAY

A Life Remembered

Years ago, he started
writing stories of his childhood,
this man now of more than eighty years.
Stories of a simpler time and place:
before TV, before cell phones, before the internet
blared constantly the violence of the world,
a time of self-reliance,
when if you wanted something done
you had better learn to do it yourself.
Where children roamed,
where dangers were more known,
where neighbors watched each other's kids
but gossiped endlessly as well.
Where kindness and bookless minds
circumscribed the small town where he grew.
As a child he longed to leave,
and escape he finally did,
but if you want to know the elder man,
his stories are the way inside.

– Margaret Porter
October 18, 2024

'Twas Only Yesterday

Life Stories by an Old Man from Missouri

James Dan Knifong

Hat Publishing

Title: *'Twas Only Yesterday: Life Stories by an Old Man from Missouri*
Author: James Dan Knifong
Editor: Rahima Baldwin Dancy
Layout: Ann Erwin
Cover: Photograph from *Gerald Massie Photograph Collection MS 192*, with
        permission from Missouri State Archives, Jefferson City, MO

Published by Hat Publishing, 1654 Yellow Pine Avenue, Boulder, CO 80304
Manufactured in the United States of America
ISBN# 979-8-218880-68-2

Contents

Foreword

I WOULD LIKE TO TAKE A MOMENT to share what this collection of stories means to me personally. For most of my adult life I have been embarrassed that my writing wasn't as good as I felt it should be. So I was hesitant when in the late '90s my therapist, Joe Mancini, suggested I write about my childhood. I finally decided to take his advice, and in 1999 I enrolled in a writing workshop at the Writer's Center in Silver Spring, Maryland. I had two goals in mind: to improve my writing skills and to explore my psyche. I was determined to use the experience to learn to write well. (I was less sure it would help my psyche.) Although I hardly noticed, ever so slowly my writing became more polished.

I have been reluctant to believe, and accept as real, the praise that has come of late from readers of my stories. It has taken much prodding from friends and family for me to agree to collect these stories into a book. I am like a fat man who slims down to a normal weight, but who continues for years afterward to think of himself as being too fat. There are still times when I am unsure that I am writing well enough for others to find it even tolerable to read, let alone enjoyable.

Regardless, over time, I have begun to enjoy writing, and as I look back on these stories, I realize that the retelling of them has indeed played a cathartic role in helping me come to peace with my childhood. Other stories have offered me an opportunity to gain insight into how I came to be the person I am today.

I hope that none of this will matter and that, you, as a reader, will simply enjoy the stories as much as I have enjoyed writing them.

Introduction

ROUGHLY TWO-THIRDS of the following stories are set in an often-overlooked part of rural America—Milan, Missouri—where I was born and where we lived until I was fourteen years old. The other stories are from later in my life. The events in all the stories actually happened—as my memory recalls them, though I have changed many of the names of people who might otherwise be disconcerted to find themselves mentioned without their permission.

The Milan stories offer the reader an opportunity to live vicariously the adventures of a young Missouri boy who enjoyed the freedom to roam the town and countryside while being watched over by a whole community. Since most of us now live in urban areas, there are few youngsters today who know the freedom that I took for granted in my youth. The later stories are accounts of a country boy who chose to live in a much larger world than he imagined as a child.

The stories are not in strict chronological order, in part because I don't remember how old I was at the time. Some stories span early childhood to adulthood and I had to choose where I thought they best fit. Because the town of Milan plays such a prominent role in the collection, I have included a brief sketch about the town and Sullivan County in the Appendix.

1
Before

*I remember clearly a time before retirement and grandchildren,
before loves and losses, before school and career—even before sisters.
It was a time before struggle, before triumphs, before defeats.*

I AM SUDDENLY AWAKE. It's early morning; the light is dim; all is quiet. I lie looking at the ceiling, slowly stretching, yawning, and moving my arms and legs, happy just to be.

Time to stir. I roll over, grab the upright rails, and stand looking about the spare room: a curtained window, brightly painted wooden blocks on the floor, an oak dresser with mirror, a door standing ajar. For a moment I pause. It is all fresh and interesting. But too quiet.

Time to make things happen. I shake the side railing and try to push it lower so I can climb over and out. It doesn't move. I've seen it move for Mama. But she reaches for something underneath, out of sight. Crouching, I reach through the side rails. After groping, pushing, and pulling, there's a satisfying clang and the railing drops to its half-height position. In a heartbeat I have a leg over and am lowering myself to the floor—to freedom!

Running to the door—I never just walk—I squeeze through, and run to the next door, squeeze through it, and run to the bed. Grabbing fistfuls of blanket, I climb up, crawl across Mama's ankles, and move up the valley between her and Dad. At the head of the bed, I squirm beneath the covers, nestling between the large warm bodies, which are now beginning to stir.

I hadn't noticed I was wet, but it feels wonderful when Mama changes me to a fresh diaper. That done, the three of us cuddle, holding and hugging one another. I wonder at Dad's whiskers and their rough and sharp feel against my skin. I squirm when he nuzzles my belly. Soon the three of us are tickling each other and laughing. Then, as Dad lies on his back, I start to climb on top of his belly. He catches me with his hands and tosses me to arms' length, up and down, up and down. I squeal at the fun of it. After a bit, Dad sits up against the head rail and draws his knees up, forming a gentle slope with his shins. He sets me on top of his knees facing away from him and releases me. I slide down his shins, immediately turning back for more. And still more. We do this slide game again and again. It is good to be alive.

Eventually our play ends. The three of us rise. Mama heads for the kitchen, Dad to the bathroom to shave. I wander through the rooms of our house, eager for the day that is to come—eager for the life that is to come.

And life did come.

And now life is going.

SIMPLY BEING EIGHTY-FOUR, my body has a way of reminding me daily that death is near. There is the constant parade of physical failures: Muscle strength goes, eyesight blurs, and chronic disease, in my case Parkinson's, sets in with a vengeance. I can no longer run. I just barely manage to walk, but only in a most awkward sort of way. I've had a good life over the years, but now life, like all other things is ending. But not quite yet.

And so, I sit writing this book of short stories—memories from an ordinary life lived to its fullest.

Young Jimmy

2

The Man of the House

GRANDMA HAD POTS boiling on the stove. The green beans and potatoes gave the kitchen a humid, warm odor that quickened my appetite and reminded me it was near suppertime. Jane was on her back in the playpen, already having her bottle of warm milk. Being four-and-a-half, I was playing with my toy trucks under the blond oak kitchen table. Aunt Esta was not yet home from her job at the Courthouse as Mom came through the door, tired from her day at Thelma's Beauty Salon. It was Friday evening and she was pleased to be home, done with the day and nearly done with the week—Saturday would be a half day. She spoke to Grandma, gave me a hug and kiss, and was leaning over Jane, about to pick her up.

"You have a letter from J.B. It's in on the dining room table," Grandma said.

Leaving Jane with her bottle, Mom left the kitchen while Grandma continued preparing supper. Grandma told me it was time to set the table.

I positioned the plates and glasses and all the knives, forks, and spoons beside each plate, just as I had been taught. I got the salt and pepper from the cabinet, placed them on the table, went out on the side porch and fetched the butter from the oak icebox and then, with nothing more to do and Grandma still busy with her cooking, I wandered into the dining room, and from there I could see Mom in the living room beyond. She was sitting on our green hassock, her back to me, letter in hand. There were no lights on in the living room, and the light that came through the windows was dim from the fading evening sky. She didn't make a sound, but I knew she was crying—something was wrong.

Going to her I placed my hand on her back. "What's wrong, Mommy?"

At first, she didn't answer, then she wiped at her eyes and without turning to me, she said, "Oh, nothing. It's okay. Run along and play."

I didn't move, but stood there with my hand on her back. I didn't know what was wrong, or what to do. Mom was troubled and it bothered me to see Mom so distressed. I wanted to do something to make it right.

Finally, hearing Aunt Esta enter the kitchen, Mom refolded the letter, dabbed a second time at her tears, and stood up. Reaching down she put a hand on my shoulder and said in an upbeat voice, "Don't worry about it. Let's go say, 'Hi' to Aunt Esta and see what Grandma has for supper." We walked back into the warmth, the

Dad in Navy uniform somewhere aboard a ship at sea

light and the bustle of the kitchen, each of us bearing our own private worry.

Over dinner, Mom related the contents of her letter. As it turned out it carried no bad news, other than Dad's general loneliness: *Dad is healthy; he sends his love; they are feeding him well; and he usually doesn't know where he is.* Of course, the Navy wouldn't let him say even if he did know his location. As it turned out, all he knew was that he was in the middle of the ocean with nothing but water as far as the eye can see. Not a tree in sight. It must have been hard for a Missouri farm boy who had grown up among Sullivan County's green hills, fertile fields, and trees. He had never seen an ocean until he was drafted to fight in WWII.

THE NEXT DAY WAS SATURDAY, and after a lunch of Campbell's tomato soup, grilled cheese sandwiches, and milk, Grandma announced that it was naptime. Being just over a year old, Jane never gave Grandma trouble about naptime. Being three-and-a-half, I thought for myself, and I simply didn't see the point of sleeping in the middle of the day. Besides, this afternoon I was going to get my hair cut at Joe's—a special adventure. I whined that I wasn't sleepy, but it was to no avail.

Of course, we kids were not the only ones who needed a nap. Grandma had been watching over two small children all morning, and as an old woman who was lame from a stroke, she was feeling the weariness of her years. Today, eighty-one years later, I am more sympathetic to her than I was at the time.

After I woke—I did drift off in spite of myself—Grandma helped me put on my best outfit: short pants, a light jacket, and a cap, all in matching gray wool. I looked sharp. It was Saturday and Mom and Aunt Esta would finish work early. After work, and after my haircut, the family—Mom, Aunt Esta, Grandma, Jane and I—would be joining Milan's weekly promenade around the Courthouse Square.

Moving slowly, Grandma dressed Jane and loaded her into the baby buggy. She then wedged her walking cane in the buggy's frame beside the basket. She would be using the buggy to steady her walk, but she never liked to go anywhere without her cane. We set off for the southwest corner of the square and Thelma's Beauty Salon. It was slow going uphill, but we had only to travel three-and-a-half blocks. Like an eager puppy I ran ahead, fell behind, and explored a range of interesting rocks, bugs, trees, and an old torn baseball lying in the gutter.

THE BEAUTY SHOP was on the second story of the First National Bank, through the main door, up a long flight of wooden stairs and down a hallway with wooden-framed, frosted-glass doors on

The bank building with its cupola. Thelma's Beauty Shop was on the top floor, Joe's Barber Shop was in the basement.

either side. Each door, except one, led to an office. The special door opened to Thelma's. When Grandma and I arrived at the bottom of the stairs, I was permitted to race ahead and tell Mom that we were coming.

Although I could not yet read, I had no trouble choosing the right door. While still in the hallway, I could already smell the perfumes, powders, hair sprays, shampoos, permanent wave solutions, and burnt hair from the curling iron. And I could hear a half dozen women chatting among themselves, sometimes loudly whispering semiprivate confidences, all over the noise of radio music and two large, beehive hairdryers operating at full blast. I went in.

Light from two large windows flooded the room and was backed up with mirror lights and a hot spotlight at each workstation. With my hand still at head height on the door handle, the chatter abruptly stopped as the women paused to take in the newcomer. Then it began again, but refocused in my direction. The women began to fuss over me, saying to Mom, "What a fine boy you have there, Fay." "My, isn't he the handsome one in his gray suit. He looks just like J.B." "Look at those curls, what many a girl won't do for curls like that." And saying to me, "How are you, Jimmy?" And, "Come here and let me look at you, Jimmy," as if they couldn't see me perfectly well as I stood by the door. I didn't go near them; if I got too close, they would be likely to pinch my cheek or try to hug me.

Mom left her station and came to my side. Ignoring the chatter of the ladies, I told her that Jane and Grandma were at the bottom of the stairs, and she left to help them negotiate the climb.

As Mom left the shop, I saw the magic wand leaning against the wall near one of the workstations. It was really just a magnet on a stick that could be moved about the floor—sort of like a lightweight golf club. My job when visiting the beauty shop was to pick up the dropped bobby pins that were strewn around the floor, half hidden and mixed in with cut hair. It was my first experience with magnetism, and I found the device fascinating. And, since the task was also an important and useful duty, I took it on with the seriousness it deserved. By the time Mom returned with Grandma and Jane, I was engrossed in my job, and it was easy to ignore the new fuss made over my baby sister.

Soon, Mom put the lady she had been working on under a hairdryer. She then used her break to walk me downstairs to Joe's Barbershop. Mom gave me a quarter, which I put in my pocket to pay for the haircut. To reach Joe's we had to leave the building and re-enter the half-basement shop from the sidewalk. On the way, Mom stayed beside me until I started down the half-flight of concrete steps. She then stood on the sidewalk and watched as I opened the screen door and entered the barbershop alone.

Being a hairdresser, and given that quarters were hard to come by, Mom might well have cut my hair herself at home, or even in the beauty parlor. But I would have none of it, although years later, I often asked her to cut my hair and she did so gladly. But back then I was just beginning to be aware of my male role in life. So Joe the barber cut my hair, not Mom the hairdresser.

BIG JOE AND HIS CAST IRON, nickel-plated chair, which he could pump up and down, dominated the barbershop. The chair was a wonder to behold. It was covered with ornate scroll work and sported both a headrest and a footrest. It could be made to recline and, with white porcelain enamel, it was appointed strategically in the center of the shop. Its padded leather cushions promised comfort and luxury. The chair and corpulent Joe himself, with his balding head and rimless glasses, were framed by a wall-long counter lined with various colored hair tonics and backed by an equally long mirror. Against the opposite wall, facing the barber and his chair, was a wooden bench rescued from a country church.

Joe laughed, told stories, and gossiped while, on a shelf above the mirror, a radio played ballgames broadcast from Kansas City,

130 miles to the southwest. An audience of three or four old men—the young men were all gone to war—sat on the bench. Some of the men were rolling and smoking (no one smoked ready-made cigarettes—too expensive), others were chewing and spitting, and one was glancing through a magazine. All were joining in the conversation. The room was warm and the fan next to the radio swung back and forth mixing the manly odors of hair tonic, talcum, tobacco and sweat.

I entered and took my place on the bench, feeling reassured as I touched the quarter in my pocket. The men turned to see who had entered. In quiet good humor one of them spoke, "Howdy, Jimmy ... Come to get a haircut, did ja?" Another asked, "How's your daddy doing in the war?" Not knowing what to say, I only nodded my head *yes* in reply.

Nobody really expected more, and after the greeting I was left to sit, and listen, and wait my turn. The men returned to their talk about baseball, crops, the war, and the weather. Although I didn't always understand what was said, I was comfortable. These men did not gush over me, pinch my cheeks, or comment on my curls. I was accepted as simply belonging there among them.

Although there were three or four men in the shop, when Joe finished with the man he was working on, my turn was next. The others were just there to pass the time of day. Joe placed a well-worn, wide board across the arms of the chair, and I climbed up and sat on it with my feet on the seat of the chair. With a practiced flourish Joe draped a large white smock over me and the chair, fastening it close around my neck. I felt the soft upward jerks as Joe pumped me up to a convenient height, as he asked me, "How do you want your hair cut, Jimmy?"

I replied, "I don't know. Just a regular haircut I guess."

"Well, we'll trim the sides and take a little off the top. How does that sound?" Without waiting for a reply, he took up his clippers and, working them rapidly with a practiced squeezing motion, he closely trimmed around my neck and ears. Then, using his scissors, he cut the longer hair covering the rest of my head.

It didn't take long, and when finished, he dipped his horsehair whisk in a tin of talcum powder. While he brushed away the hair from my neck and face, I sneezed. He then rubbed my hair with one of the perfumed tonics, gave it a combing and carefully checked his work. This final treatment left my hair with the slick, just-been-cut look much prized at the time. The breeze from the fan at the back of my new-mown neck felt cool and fresh. I paid Joe the quarter, climbed down from the chair, and headed back up the steps to Thelma's.

In the beauty parlor, Aunt Esta had arrived, and Mom and Thelma were just finishing their tidying up before closing the shop till Monday. With the last hair clippings swept from the floor and the last counter wiped, Grandma, Aunt Esta, Mom, Jane and I descended the long flight of wooden stairs in anticipation of our Saturday afternoon tour of the shops ringing the Courthouse Square.

I SUPPOSE TIMES HAVE changed in and around Milan, as well as elsewhere, and I know Saturday afternoons aren't like what they used to be during the '40s and '50s. Because we lived in town, we had electricity, a radio, a telephone and neighbors next door. But in the surrounding countryside there were no phones—party lines or otherwise, there was no electricity, the roads were rutted mud lanes. There was precious little entertainment so folks looked forward to the Saturday afternoon promenade and Sunday church. Everybody referred to the promenade as an opportunity to "do a little shopping," and people did shop, but it was as much a social event as it was a commercial one.

Families would clean up and dress special before arriving at the Courthouse Square. They would stroll around the square, stopping in the various stores, greeting people they met, and occasionally pausing to chat through open car windows with those sitting in their cars. After this first circuit, they would then take their turn to sit in their cars to watch neighbors, friends, and relatives parade past—chatting with those who stopped. Saturday afternoon was an opportunity to catch up on community happenings and to share judgments about those events. One might easily overhear, "I told Sam it was too early to plant corn. He went ahead and done it anyway. Now half of his crop is ruined. He'll be lucky to get his seed money out of it."

AS WE EMERGED FROM the bank building directly onto the square, we paused to assemble ourselves for our stroll. Mom and I would be in front, with Mom pushing Jane and me walking on the outside. Grandma and Aunt Esta would follow behind. Our formation was not by chance. In spite of her being something of a tomboy most of her life, Mom believed that there were proper roles for ladies and gentlemen. Early on she made it clear to me that I was going to learn to be a "proper gentleman." When we were walking together on the sidewalk, I was to walk on the outside. When we

Sullivan County Courthouse in Milan, circa 1955

came to a shop, I was to hold the door for her. If we stopped at a soda fountain, she would give me money, and I was to pay for the sodas.

We had made two small purchases at the Rexall Drug store, greeted several friends and had just started down the second side of the square when we met the bank president, Mr. Caywell. He smiled broadly as he came toward us in his wool suit appointed with a gold chain arching across his vest. After greeting the adults, he leaned over and shook my hand and then squatted down to look me in the eye.

He first asked, "Have you heard from your daddy? Is he winning the war?"

I replied, "We got a letter ... He is on the ocean and he doesn't know where he is. There aren't any trees."

He chuckled at my reply and next asked, "How are you and your mom managing with you daddy gone?" Then without waiting for an answer he went on, "With your daddy gone, you are the man of the house now. That's a big job. You have to take care of your mother, you know. Can you do that?"

I nodded my head *yes* in response; I didn't know what else to say. With that, Mr. Caywell smiled, stood up, and began talking with Mom, Aunt Esta, and Grandma. We all stood there on the sidewalk as shoppers passed by. With the adults talking over my head, I was left alone to ponder about the burden of the responsibilities being thrust upon me, and I wondered at how I, as only a boy, was ever going to meet them.

IT HAS BEEN EIGHTY YEARS since that day I met Mr. Caywell on the Courthouse Square in Milan. I am amazed at how our culture has changed, and how I have changed with it. I am also aware that, at some deep level, that life is still a part of who I am—and who we are as a people.

3

Poulet de Grand-mère

THE TWO OF US were to have dinner alone at a nice restaurant in celebration of my birthday. Margaret and I arrived exactly on time. The *maître d'* greeted us, and when he stepped aside to present our table, I was startled with a chorus of

"SURPRISE! HAPPY BIRTHDAY!"

There was a table of friends laughing at my shock and gently poking fun at me for being an old man of sixty. "How does it feel to be older than dirt?"..."Were you surprised when Columbus discovered America?"

It was a typical Washington, D.C., gathering in one of my favorite restaurants, *Le Vieux Logis* (The Old Inn), a replica of a French provincial inn. In addition to my wife, a government lawyer, there were scientists, an analyst, administrators, and fellow professors—all old friends collected during my twenty-five years in the Washington area.

After I had recovered from my surprise and things had settled a bit, the waiter started taking orders. When it came my turn, I ordered *poulet la grand-mère avec haricots verts à la Niçoise et pommes de terre au beurre* (grandma's chicken with green beans and buttered potatoes). It sounded good, and I was tired of steak. The food arrived and halfway through dinner, someone began discussing her recent decision to become a vegetarian. "I had many reasons, but I guess I just don't like the idea of killing animals...whole countries eat vegetarian...it's good for you." Someone else took up the discussion, "But we have canine teeth as well as molars—we are designed as omnivores...."

As the urbane dialog batted genteelly back and forth, I struggled to join in. It was no use. My mind was drowning in a flood of childhood images, images of picking beans, digging potatoes, catching chickens, and plucking feathers.

I took a sip of wine and retreated into silence as my mind wandered to another time and place.

—— *1946* ——

THE EARLY MISSOURI MORNING was already warm as Mom worked at the sink, cleaning up after her breakfast with Dad. Although both kitchen windows and the back door were wide open, there was no breeze; and the left-over smell of coffee, fried eggs, bacon, and dishwater lingered in the room. The yellow box of Cheerios stood on the blond oak table next to a bowl and spoon laid ready for me.

Mom and I chatted as I poured the cereal and patted it down with the palm of my hand. I added two heaping teaspoons of sugar to the cereal, and then, realizing the milk was missing, I headed for the oak icebox on the side porch. A spring pulled the screen door shut with a bang as I returned with the glass milk bottle. Pouring milk on the cereal washed the sugar down to the bottom and gently lifted the Cheerios. I patted them down again, making the rounded, floating cereal level with the rim of the bowl before I began to eat.

At first, our chatter was light, but as I finished my cereal and dug into the milk-soaked sugar at the bottom—always a special treat— Mom led the discussion to more weighty business.

"What are you planning to do today, Jimmy?"

Although Mom often asked me this question it always caught me unprepared. It presumed that I might have made plans, and, as a five-year-old boy, I never made plans. Plans were for grownups.

Not seeing the trap until after I spoke, I admitted, "Oh, nothing. Just play around. I guess."

Of course, this is what Mom had expected me to say. She had just wanted it clearly established between us that *I* really didn't have any plans for the day before she brought out *her* plans, plans she had no doubt been forming since she'd gotten up that morning.

"Well, you can play this afternoon. This morning, I need you around the house. You can help Grandma in the garden and with the chickens. Your Aunt Reva and Uncle Ike are coming to town to do some shopping. They'll stay for supper before going back home. I thought we'd have fried chicken. We'll also need some green beans, potatoes and other things from the garden, and we might as well get started on it this morning before it gets too hot."

Although Mom had neatly substituted her morning agenda for my lack of one, "helping Grandma" was actually a relief to my ears. I dreaded "helping around the house," which could mean dusting, cleaning, sweeping, and doing dishes—chores I did often enough, but chores I hated. It is true that I also hated most garden work. But gathering green beans and other vegetables wasn't nearly as bad as hoeing and pulling weeds. And I had found the chickens sort of interesting ever since Mom brought them home as baby chicks.

DURING THE WAR many foodstuffs were rationed and people were encouraged to plant "Victory Gardens." This governmental urging might have had a real impact in the cities, but in small, Midwestern farming communities like Milan, it made little difference. Nearly every household before, during, and after the war kept a large garden and put up vegetables for the winter. True, Mr. Gray's A&P on the Courthouse Square did a small trade in canned beans, corn, and other vegetables, but these items were always talked about in the most disparaging tones by the women of the town. "I suppose those store-bought canned goods are 'all right' if you are a bachelor and can't put up your own.... They probably won't make you sick, but I just don't feel right about 'em. You don't know where they come from or who has had their fingers on 'em...." Fortunately for Mom, the house we rented from Mr. Baker on the corner of Fourth and Painter had a large lawn, a large garden, a storage shed, a barn, and barnyard. Following the local tradition, we always put in a sizable garden.

And we kept chickens. Grandma had lived all her life in the country, and she had always kept chickens for eggs, for egg money, and for meat. Well, that is, she had always kept them until her stroke made her lame on the left side, and, just as Dad was drafted in the war, she came to live with us in town. During the war, meat and eggs were rationed, so it did not take much urging from Grandma before we started raising chickens, a practice we continued after the war.

I CAN STILL RECALL that early spring evening when Mom first brought home a flat cardboard box from the farm store down on the levee. It had nickel-size holes around its perimeter and she handled it very carefully as she set it on the kitchen table. There was something mysterious inside—something moving and making small, scuffling sounds. I was awash with curiosity and wonder.

Mom had me catch Old Moe, the cat, and Scotty, the dog, and put them outside. She then placed the box on the kitchen floor and urged me to open it. I was surprise and amazed to see twelve yellow balls of fluff strutting and pecking about at random. When I picked one up, I marveled at the delicate softness of its feathers and how its tiny beak tickled my hand as it continued its instinctive pecking.

That night the baby chicks stayed in their box on the kitchen floor, making soft chirping sounds, but the next day we cleaned out the chicken coop built into the side of the barn. I helped string a simple chicken-wire fence between the storage shed and the barn to make a pen about ten feet square. Mom ran an extension cord from the house to the barn using a bent nail to hang it above our heads. This powered a heat lamp for cold nights. We scattered cracked corn in a shallow cookie sheet and without hesitation the chicks waded in, bumping into one another, walking on their food, pecking, scratching and chirping. From that day on, I tended chickens, and, when they were old enough, I gathered eggs.

WELL, ON THIS SUMMER morning Grandma came into the kitchen just as I finished my cereal. After she finished her coffee and toast, I went to the barn for a shovel and basket while she walked to the garden. When I met her in the garden, she was leaning on her cane in a long plain white dress that hung on her frame like a drape. She also had on her black lace-up shoes with wide, solid heels, which she always wore. It was a strange getup for gardening, but then, I was the one who would be doing the digging.

She started me on the potatoes, and even with her guidance I still managed to slice a number of them with the shovel. Their startling white flesh glistened as they nestled in the black earth still damp from the morning dew. Finally, I had loosened enough ground to pull the rest up with my hands. After the potatoes, she pointed me at the carrots and onions. Then, she watched as I picked a mess of beans, three or four large cucumbers and tomatoes, and three green peppers. Finally, with the basket nearly full, we cut a dozen stalks of pie plant (rhubarb) which grew near the fence at the edge of the garden.

One of the reasons I hated gardening was that, of all the stuff we had gathered, only the potatoes and the rhubarb interested me. In my mind, all the other stuff fell under the general classification of vegetables, and I didn't care much for vegetables. Potatoes went well with meat, which I liked, and rhubarb would be made into pie— I liked pie of most any kind.

Grandma followed behind me as I lugged the basket to the well on the side porch. Once there, I pumped water and washed the dirt from the onions, carrots and potatoes.

Mom brought out some large bowls and Grandma and I settled in to snapping beans and generally cleaning the rest of our harvest. With the vegetables in good shape, Grandma sent me to fetch a washtub from the basement and place it next to the storage shed. Mom and I then carried steaming buckets of hot water that had been heating on the stove to fill the tub. We would need this to clean the chickens. While Mom and I finished with the water, Grandma, leaning on her cane, moved over and stood beside the chicken yard. When I joined her, she raised her cane, and pointing over the fence to one of the chickens said, "Jimmy, go get me that one right there."

Opening the fence where it was attached to the barn, I stepped inside with the chickens. It took me a while to corner the one Grandma wanted, but finally I made a successful grab and brought it to her. She had moved back into the open barnyard away from the chickens and waited patiently. When I handed her the chicken, she hung her cane over her left forearm and nestled the chicken in the same arm. She used her right hand to pet it, until it settled and felt comfortable being held. Then while still petting it she slowly placed her right hand over the chicken's head and lightly cupped it in the palm of her hand.

Suddenly, before either I or the chicken had any idea of what was happening, she pulled the bird from the cradle of her left arm and swung it in a fast, full arc over her head, then down and forward. The motion was almost exactly the one used by practiced softball pitchers just before releasing a fast underhand pitch to the batter. The only difference was that at the end of their swing, pitchers release the ball, but at the end of my Grandma's swing, she hung on tight to the chicken's head and gave it a quick snap of the wrist. Of course, that was all the difference in the world to the hen.

The chicken went flying horizontally across the barnyard about three feet off the ground and hit the side of the barn before falling to the ground. Upon landing, it regained its feet and took off in a fast run. Thinking it might get away, I started to chase after it, but with a motion of her hand Grandma cautioned me to be still. After moving her cane back to her left hand to steady herself, and with the chicken still running about the barnyard bumping into things, she said, "Come 'ere Jimmy." When I was close by, she slowly opened her right hand. I stood in wide-eyed wonder looking at the chicken head with its closed eyes in the palm of her hand where she had originally placed it while cradling the bird in her arms.

I marveled at how a crippled old woman could swing a bird with such power and grace—and, how the headless bird insisted on running around the barnyard, bumping into things it could no longer see. Of course, after a while, the bird grew weak from the loss of blood and lay still. When it was done, we dunked the chicken in the hot water tub and plucked feathers. There is nothing quite like the smell of hot wet feathers clinging to your hands. It is an odor that one remembers for a lifetime.

Grandma Byrd, Jimmy and Great Aunt Ida

—— *2001* ——

BACK TO MY BIRTHDAY PARTY: Margaret had noticed my disengagement from the conversation. I had also stopped eating. Touching my arm lightly, she whispered, "Are you alright?" The touch interrupted my reverie and brought me back to the restaurant. I took a bite of chicken and sip of wine. As usual, the food was excellent.

The discussion moved on from vegetarianism to the virtues of tofu. "It is so versatile. It takes on so many flavors," someone said. I added, "Of course. It has hardly any flavor of its own. Now if something could be done for its rubbery texture...." Gradually the conversation left food and turned to the foolishness of the current White House occupant. I easily joined in the skewering and roasting of "King George of the Shrub." It was only later, on the quiet drive home, that I had time to wonder at how, even after a man has grown "older than dirt," one's childhood continues to cling like hot wet feathers.

4

"It's Your Machine"

I COME FROM A LONG LINE of poor Missouri dirt farmers, with the emphasis on "poor" and "dirt." At one time or another, my father, grandfather, great grandfather, great, great grandfather, and my great, great, great grandfather were all Missouri farmers, as were all my aunts, uncles, and cousins as well.

Dad tried his hand at farming during the spring of 1931, his sophomore year in high school. Perhaps he was not thinking too clearly when he figured that farming would be a lot more profitable than staying in school. So that spring he quit book learnin' and planted corn. He was thinking he'd be a rich man when he harvested the fall crop.

The weather was favorable, and he had a good, shoulder-high crop in July. Then disaster struck. A swarm of locusts came through the countryside and in a single day they ate his entire crop down to the ground. As far as the eye could see, there was absolutely no vegetation left standing. Every leaf, ear and stalk were gone. He told me later that all that remained of his corn was a neat row of white dots across the field where the stalks had proudly stood. He recalled that it "looked like someone had walked along and pushed rows of new, shiny quarters into the black dirt."

The experience changed Dad's thinking some about farming as a career. He figured there had to be a better way to make a living than growing corn for hungry locusts. It was just after the start of the Great Depression, and like millions of other young men, he left home and rode the rails in search of work. Later he worked with the Civilian Conservation Corp (a government work program set up by the Roosevelt administration). Later still, he found employment as a day laborer with a company that was digging a basement for a large building in Chicago. He was assigned to the business end of a hand shovel.

IT WAS DURING THE '30s that motorized diesel equipment to move earth was just coming into common use. One of the most prominent of these early machines was the cable-controlled bulldozer. These first dozers could only move earth that the front blade had scraped and pushed in front of itself. The blade couldn't be pushed downward to dig into the earth, nor could it lift dirt above the ground.

Certainly, using a dozer was better than the previous method of digging with a horse or mule. To dig earth with a horse required a man to walk behind a horse-pulled "slip-scraper." (It's kind of like a wheelbarrow with two handles but no wheel.) Unfortunately, both the bulldozer and horse-drawn methods can only scrape the ground, removing just a thin layer at a time. Hence, the hole being dug must have gentle sloping sides. Using a dozer to dig a vertical-walled basement leaves quite a bit of shovel work to be done by hand before a foundation can be laid.

WHILE DOING THIS SHOVEL WORK, Dad noticed that the operator on the dozer wasn't very good at his job. He kept jerking the machine this way and that to no effect; and he often stalled the dozer by trying to push too much dirt on one pass, and then on the

A slip-scraper for digging

A horse-drawn slip-scraper in action

A cable-operated dozer pushing dirt

second pass he would pull the blade so high that he would hardly move any dirt at all.

One day at quitting time, Dad went to the foreman, and said, "I can run that dozer better than the man you have on it."

The foreman looked up at the impertinent, Missouri hillbilly and asked him, "Where did you learn to run a dozer?"

Dad replied, "Why do you care where I learned? I can do a better job than the man you've got on it."

Apparently, the foreman had also been noticing that his dozer operator wasn't very skillful. He replied, "I'll give you a chance tomorrow. We'll see how you do."

From that day onward, Dad was an equipment operator making fifty percent more an hour than the laborer he had been the day before.

THE WAR MOSTLY TURNED out well for Dad—if you overlook the time he spent aboard a Liberty ship that served as target practice for German U-boats. Later, he served in a similar role, helping sharpen the skills of the Japanese submariners. As it turned out, the Japanese skills were already pretty sharp. Once, in the South Pacific, Dad's ship was hit by a torpedo. Fortunately, the torpedo-quality-control skills of the Japanese were not up to the same level as their aiming skills. The torpedo hit the ship, leaving a deep dent in its hull, but it didn't explode.

The war did end the Depression, and the GI Bill provided guaranteed loans to veterans who wanted to start a business. Although he was only a barely-literate Missouri farm boy, Dad was able to borrow money to buy what at the time was a very expensive (think of the cost of a house), newfangled kind of dozer called a "front-end loader."

Like a typical dozer, it could dig by pushing dirt straight ahead, but it also had a hydraulically articulated bucket in place of a dozer blade. It could lift the dirt overhead and place it in a truck or carry it to another part of the job site. Because of this bucket, which is common today, an end loader can dig flat-bottom basements with straight vertical walls—perfect for the concrete workers who had to pour the foundations and form the basement walls. No hand shoveling required!

THINGS WENT WELL that first summer as Dad set about digging basements, ponds, and trench silos for the farmers of Sullivan County. People would come to watch Dad dig a basement and stay for hours. The word spread quickly about the new machine which was like a bulldozer but that could dig a basement under an existing house! Dad dug several such basements under farmhouses, carrying the dirt in the tractor's bucket up a ramp that would later become an outside stairwell entrance to the finished basement.

That first summer there was lots of work and plenty of money. But all too soon winter arrived and—as it does every year—the ground froze solid, effectively putting Dad out of work until the spring thaw. To make matters worse for his business, the paperwork, loan approval, and so on had taken longer than expected, and the end loader was not delivered until June—mid-season for an excavator. Try as he might, Dad had not had time to build a cash reserve for the winter months. We had enough to eat. Mom kept a large garden, and she had "put up" enough canned goods to feed half of Milan, but money was scarce, and the monthly mortgage payments on the machine were huge.

Dad could not make his December payment and notified the bank of his situation. When he missed January's payment he got a harsh call from the bank demanding payment. Dad again explained his situation, that is, he didn't have the money the bank was demanding, nor did he have any way to earn the money until the spring thaw. As much as he wished it were not so, he simply could not dig frozen ground. He tried to reassure the banker by pointing out that he had several jobs lined up, and that come spring, he would make up his back payments and earn enough during the warmer seasons to make his payments through the next winter.

Dad digging a farm pond east of Milan, 1954

This didn't satisfy the caller who pushed a bit too hard, suggesting that Dad either make his payment or the banker would have to repossess the machine. To this threat Dad replied in a matter-of-fact tone, "If you want money, I can get it for you in the spring. If you can't wait, the end loader's sitting out there on the Johnson farm. You can come and get it whenever you like. It's your machine."

When Dad put the matter that way, the banker paused to rethink his situation. He realized he liked being a banker; he did not actually want to own the machine, and he certainly didn't want to change careers. The idea of being an excavator or even the salesman with a used end loader for sale was sobering. During the pause he also remembered that because the federal government had guaranteed the loan, there was no way the bank would lose money on the deal. Maybe waiting a couple of months for the spring thaw was a better idea after all.

That was the last of the calls from the bank.

The spring did come and the ground did thaw, and as soon as he could, Dad started once again digging ponds and basements. He made up his back payments, and during the summer he earned enough to make it through the next winter. His business was firmly launched.

OVER THE YEARS Mom, who kept the books for Dad's business, constantly complained that if *Dad would just work for someone else, he'd have regular hours, a regular paycheck and fewer headaches.* And he'd make more money! Mom was usually right about such things, and no doubt, all this may well have been true, but being his own boss suited Dad well. He liked doing quality work the way he thought best, and he liked not having a boss urging him to hurry and possibly cut corners. Once his business was launched, he never considered another path.

Later in life I often reflected that by becoming a university professor I managed to fulfill both of my parents' dreams. Following my mother's desire, I had a steady, salaried income every month. And yet, reflecting Dad's desire to be his own boss, I had autonomy. Both in the classroom and in my research I was free to pursue my own path.

5

The Nuts and Bolts of Learnin'

I WAS SIX when I watched Dad having trouble loosening a nut on a rusty bolt. When the wrench slipped a second time, I was surprised to see Dad pick up a hammer and chisel. Placing the sharp end of the chisel at the base of the nut, he swung the hammer and cut the nut free in one blow. I was impressed!

I was so impressed that one afternoon a week later, I rummaged through Dad's tools, found his hammer, picked out his sharpest chisel, and went looking for my own rusted bolt. I found lots of prospects on a discarded farm tractor that had more rust than paint. After clearing away some weeds and a huge black and yellow spider on its web, I chose a bolt that was at the perfect height and angle for me to swing a hammer. Holding the sharp end of the chisel to the base of the nut, I swung the hammer as I had seen Dad do. To my great surprise, the nut and bolt remained unscathed. But the chisel broke!

Feeling bad about ruining one of Dad's tools and not understanding what had happened, it was with some trepidation that I waited for him that evening to return from work. When I showed him the chisel and explained what I had done, Dad laughed and said, "Of course it broke; that chisel is meant for wood. It won't cut steel."

Dad had used a cold chisel to cut his bolt. Not knowing any better, I had used his woodworking chisel to try to cut my bolt. (Cold chisels are made of tougher, less brittle steel, and are specifically designed for the "cold" cutting of softer steel and other metals, and sometimes brick, stone, and concrete. Their cutting edge is typically more blunt and not razor sharp like a wood chisel.)

WORKING WITH DAD DURING the summer vacations, I tried hard to be careful and responsible, but like most young people I made a number of mistakes at his expense. I cannot recall a single time he got angry with me. Instead, he would survey the carnage and comment, "Well, at least you won't do that again." And, by and large, I didn't.

Because Dad didn't get angry with me for doing something "wrong," I didn't try to duck responsibility for my mistakes and wasn't afraid to continue exploring. By not repeating my mistakes (too often), I gradually learned Dad's way of being with the physical world, and I learned to be careful with tools. I also learned that, when exploring the mechanical world, the worst that would likely happen was that I might break something and must repair or replace it. Only if I was outright careless might I hurt myself or others.

⸺◆⸺

DAD WAS SMART, but as a youth he had made a bad decision. In his sophomore year of high school, he dropped out of school to plant corn. It turned out to be disastrous mistake. The corn did well, but then a swarm of locust found his field. The next day all he had was an empty field of barren earth.

Although I didn't realize it until it was too late, he carried a hidden shame about having not pursued more education. Earning his living as an excavator, he did most of his own repair and maintenance work, and he became an excellent, self-taught mechanic. (This is despite half-believing some of the myths he heard along the way. He once told me, "Metric bolts ain't as strong as them English ones," but he said it in a way that was more of a question than a statement.) Having gone to college myself, and then on to graduate school, it never occurred to me that he felt ashamed of his lacking a formal education. I always thought of him as smart and knowing nearly everything about earth-moving—it was just a different kind of knowledge than I learned in school.

By the time I had learned plane geometry in high school, I could take measurements to calculate the number of cubic yards of dirt that needed to be hauled away to level a small hillock. Dad would scoff at my "educated" approach, glance at the hillock, declare that "twenty-seven yards ought a do 'er"—and he would be right! In general, he didn't need more formal education than he had, and he held a low opinion of engineers who, relying too heavily on their "book learnin'," didn't see that their plan "obviously won't work. Just look at it!"

I have come to understand this difference as that between a blacksmith and a metallurgical engineer. The blacksmith looks at heated iron and knows when it is soft enough to bend. The engineer measures the temperature to know. They both "know" when the iron is hot enough to be soft, but they come to that knowledge in different ways.

IF I RAN INTO TROUBLE dismantling a piece of equipment or putting it back together, Dad typically would stand aside and thoughtfully watch me struggle. I am not sure he was aware of the advantage this gave him, but by not engaging directly, he had space and time to reflect on why I was having so much difficulty. After a bit, when he had figured out the best way to proceed, he would say with a mock swagger, "Let me show you how to do it." When he, likely as not, was successful, he would then comment to whomever was about, "You send them off to college, and they come back and don't know nothin'." Such statements never bothered me. I knew Dad was proud and pleased that I was in college and that he was equally proud and pleased that I was learning to be clever with mechanical things. For me, the comment was an assertive statement of his greater knowledge of, and skill with, machinery—a fact I readily accepted.

AS A YOUNG ADULT, I thought I knew Dad well. I was thoroughly familiar with the high value he placed on being a skilled mechanic, but I completely missed the significance he placed on being "college educated."

I came home one spring break to find Dad in the equipment yard replacing the exhaust manifold on an old 1950 Studebaker dump truck. Because the wheel housing crowded in close to the engine, he could not get a wrench in the right position to loosen the last of twelve nuts on the manifold. This last nut had to come free from the engine block to remove the exhaust system. Completely unaware that I was copying his behavior, I stood back and studied his dilemma as he tried to get the wrench to turn that last bolt. When I had worked out how to remove the nut, I said, as I had so often heard him say, "Let me show you how to do that." With my smaller hands I was able to position the wrench deeper in the maze of pipes, hoses, struts, and other clutter blocking its path. I removed the nut in a flash. As the manifold fell free, I was feeling proud of my accomplishment, and while looking for the nut that had fallen to the ground, I said, "That's what a college education will do fer ya."

As the last of the impish phrase escaped my lips, I was smiling when I glanced up at Dad. Suddenly I wanted to swallow the words back in my throat. The humiliation and embarrassment that flooded his eyes still haunts me today. I was the cocky son, full of pride at finally mastering his father's game, but I had cut him to the quick with my careless attempt at a joke. It had all come out in a single breath, and like a barbed arrow, the words had plunged deep into his heart. There was no way to lessen their impact, and there was nothing to say that would pull them from the wound without causing even more damage and pain. I didn't even try.

It was a small thing that was lost between us that day. Dad never again joked about my having a college education, and still "not knowin' nothin'." And I never again joked that I had learned a thing or two by attending college.

I HAVE LONG KNOWN that I was fortunate, but only of late have I become grateful. Dad encouraged to me to gain a working man's knowledge of nuts and bolts—a type of knowledge that can only be learned by breaking a few chisels—and at the same time, he was proud to support me to go to college and learn from books. Both ways of knowing are good by themselves, but together they make a powerful combination that has served me well. I regret that I became aware of Dad's contribution to this duality too late to thank him.

6

Parallel Parking

THE NOVEMBER DAYS were growing short, cold, and often gloomy. Coming home from school—I was in second grade that year—I stepped through the back door into the kitchen. Before I could think, Mom reminded me of my chores. It was my job to clean cinders out of the furnace every afternoon and spread them on Painter Street—it was really more of a dirt alleyway—that ran alongside the house. After hauling the ashes, I then had to re-stoke the furnace with enough coal to last until bedtime when Dad would bank it for the night.

That done, I begged a couple of peanut butter cookies that Mom had baked and washed them down with a glass of milk. I then headed to my toys in the dining room. With bedrooms upstairs, the two-story house had three main rooms on the first floor: living room, dining room and kitchen. All were in a row with a bath added later, off the side of the dining room, and a bedroom where Grandma slept off the other side of the living room. Since we usually ate in the kitchen, I was allowed to keep some of my toys in the dining room rather than upstairs in my room. Their special place was in a wooden wagon that served as a toy box. I was to keep it parked along the dining room wall between the hutch and the China cabinet—a small space that was out of the way, if not quite out of sight.

Grabbing the wagon handle, I turned the front wheels of the wagon to the left and pulled the wagon and its contents smoothly from its nook. Navigating around the dining room table, I pulled the wagon through the open archway into the living room where I unloaded an Erector Set, a top, Tinker Toys, Lincoln Logs, assorted trucks and cars and other miscellany on the rug. I especially liked my Erector Set, which provided an abundance of small nuts and bolts, pulleys, and shiny steel trusses. Soon I was absorbed in trying to build a crane that would lift Lincoln Logs into my truck.

After an hour or so, the cookies and milk had faded into the distant past, and I began to notice the warm dampness of boiling water and the smell of baking meatloaf coming from the kitchen. It was getting near suppertime; Dad would be home soon.

THOUGH IT WAS GETTING LATE in the season, as an excavator, Dad was still able to work the ground with his new Allis-Chalmers HD-5 front-end loader. Missouri farmers around Milan had done well with their harvests that year and they were keeping him busy digging foundations, ponds, trench silos, and basements—some even under existing farmhouses. We all knew that once the ground froze, it could not be worked until the spring thaw. By then the farmers would be busy with planting and have little time, or money, for construction projects. It was better to have the earth work done in the fall so any building could be done by the farmer during the slower winter months.

Mom often said Dad brought half of Sullivan County with him when he came home. She kept a chair beside the kitchen door so that he could remove his outer clothes and boots without tracking mud through the rest of the house. True to his routine, I soon heard the kitchen door open, chair legs scrape, boots clump on the linoleum floor, and Dad's voice as he greeted Mom and they began their usual discussion of the day's happenings.

After a bit, Dad came padding through the dining room in his white socks and underwear carrying a bucket and teakettle, both filled with hot water. Mom followed close behind with another large, steaming pan. The bathroom had been added to the side of the house off the dining room before we moved in, and it had only cold running water. The hot water for Dad's bath had to be boiled on the kitchen stove.

I was just thankful that we lived in town where we had city water and an indoor toilet. My aunts, uncles, and cousins all lived on farms and had to depend on hand-pumped wells and outhouses—our next-door neighbor still used an outhouse. I knew from visiting relatives overnight that the first feature, no running water, meant more chores for a boy my age, and the second meant freezing half to death in the winter in response to nature's call. Not having hot water from the tap was only a small inconvenience for a boy who didn't care all that much for baths in the first place.

Dad wasn't long in the bath before Mom realized that she had forgotten about me and my toys in the living room. Raising her voice so it would carry through to the front of the house, she shouted, "Jimmy! Time to get ready for dinner. Put your toys away. When your dad gets out of the bath, go in and wash your hands."

Absorbed in my project, I was a little slow to answer.

She shouted back, "Young man, did you hear what I said?"

"Yes, Mom."

"Get those toys up. Your dad's going to be ready to eat in a minute, and we're all hungry. I don't want to have to wait on you."

Realizing that I, too, was hungry, it didn't take me long to load my toys in the wagon and pull it to its parking space in the dining room.

Without thinking much about it, I steered the Radio Flyer head first into its space beside the wall. But I then noticed that the rear of the wagon was sticking out of the space at an awkward angle. I reached down, lifted the rear wheels slightly, and scooted the wagon over, flush with the wall, like I had found it before I first pulled it out.

WITH MY TOYS AND WAGON now put away, I might well have gone on to supper, but for some reason I was distracted. Remembering earlier when the wagon had rolled smoothly from the wall, I realized that something was amiss. Grabbing the handle,

I pulled the wagon from its place as I had earlier, and just as before, it rolled away smoothly. I took the wagon around the dining room table, approached the wagon's parking spot and tried again. As before, I steered it in head first, and as before the back end was left sticking out. I lifted it into place next to the wall for a second time, and this time I understood what was bothering me: If the wagon could roll smoothly out of its space, why didn't it roll smoothly into its space?

After puzzling some more over the parked wagon, I pulled the front wheels sharply to the left and, for the third time, rolled the wagon from its place. However, this time, just as the wagon pulled free, I stopped and backed it into its place. Success! Both the front and back of the wagon moved effortlessly into their proper positions against the wall.

Radio Flyer wagon

Pleased with my discovery, but to be sure it wasn't an accident, I again pulled the wagon from its place, made the circuit around the dining room table, and, approaching, I pulled just a little beyond the allotted space. Then, reversing direction, I backed the wagon into its position. Looking at the result, I felt the satisfaction that comes from having solved a difficult problem. In fact, I was so pleased that I made another trip around the table just for the enjoyment of practicing my new skill.

During all this time, I was only vaguely aware of Dad standing in the open bathroom door while he buttoned his shirt and combed his hair. When Dad moved past me through the dining room and entered the kitchen, I overheard him say to Mom, "We got us a smart boy. Jimmy just figured out parallel parkin'."

"Huh? What are you talking about? Do you want coffee with dinner?" was Mom's only reply.

Mom may have been distracted, but the mention of my name got my attention. I forgot about washing my hands as I stood and listened for more.

"Yea, that'll be fine," Dad said, referring to the coffee.

Then he went on to explain what I had been up to with the wagon, and I became aware that he had been watching me for much longer than I knew.

I heard Mom's voice say, "Here, hold back that meatloaf while I pour off some of the drippings. I can use it to fry potatoes for breakfast in the morning." Then, after a silence followed by the clanking of a pan, she said, "Yea, I guess he's smart enough. There aren't many people in this town who would know the first thing about parallel parking—no need for it. I wonder where he learnt it? He's never seen it around here. He was too young to notice it when we were in Chicago."

"I don't think he learned from us. I watched him. He just figured it out on his own," Dad said.

"Yeah, I've seen him do that with other things," Mom said.

Then she realized I had still not shown up for supper and called out, "James Dan. Get your hands washed and get in here this very minute. It's time to eat. Right now. Do you hear me?"

This question was launched in a stern tone that would have been clear to a deaf man. She meant business.

"Coming," I shouted as I hurried to the bathroom and splashed water on my hands and ran to the kitchen.

Dad had begun to fill his plate by the time I took my place in front of a tall glass of milk and an empty plate, Mom asked, "Did you wash your hands? Let me see."

I held them up, showing her that they were wet.

Satisfied, she asked, "Do you want meatloaf?"

"Yeah," I said, reaching for the bread and butter while she lifted a slice onto my empty plate.

The rest of the table conversation that night was totally uninteresting grownup talk about the day: who did what in town and how Dad's work had gone.

LYING IN BED, I felt wonderfully satisfied with my achievement, even more so because I had overheard my parents' admiring remarks as they spoke to one another with complete sincerity, utterly unaware of my presence.

7

Dancing Sunlight

FROM MY SEVEN-YEAR-OLD point of view it was shaping up to be an all-too-typical late June day. The sunny and warm morning would soon turn hot, just as it always did in Missouri until September brought the coolness of fall and a return to the classroom. As typical, Mom had a gazillion chores for me to do before I would be let free. Not that I ever knew what to do with that freedom, not in Milan, not in 1948. It seemed to me that the town must be the most boring town in the whole world, and my life the most boring life a boy ever had to endure. This summer day, however, was to be worse than boring. It was to be the most tragic, the most devastating, the most god-awful day of my life—the single day in my whole seven years that I wanted not to live—or so it seemed at the time.

The early morning showed no hint of the coming calamity. The only change in routine, and a very minor one at that, was prompted by a recent rain. The grass had grown, and Mom gave me a choice: I could either cut the grass or help her and my sister Jane, four at the time, with the daily dusting, cleaning, and mopping of the house. It was a tough choice. I disliked mowing as much as house cleaning—and still do—even though mowers now have motors to do most of the work for you.

In the end, I figured that if I agreed to one big job like mowing it might be easier to make my break for freedom when done. On the days I took on a list of small chores, Mom had a way of always finding just one more that "...wouldn't take you a minute, and then you can go play." And that one minute seemed to give her all the time and encouragement she needed to think of another, which led to another, and another, and so on. Some mornings those "minutes" felt like they might stretch on until the day itself was gone.

Another reason for working in the yard was that I would be less likely to get roped into taking care of my youngest sister, Becky. She was a year-and-a-half-old toddler that summer, and into everything. Mostly Mom kept her close by, but if I wasn't careful, I'd be assigned to watch Becky while Mom ran upstairs, downstairs, to the shed, to the garden, to wherever—again, "just for just a minute."

I did try to negotiate with Mom over exactly how much of the yard I had to mow, but I wasn't very successful—I had to mow it all. "It'd look pretty funny if half of the yard was mowed and the other half wasn't, wouldn't it?" *No*, I thought, *it'd look just fine to me*. But I kept my thoughts to myself. I wasn't that dumb!

Jimmy and Jane holding Becky, circa 1948–1949

SO, IT WAS WITH A HEAVY HEART I trudged to the outbuilding where we kept the mower, hauled it out, and began pushing it through the grass in a square pattern, starting with the outermost edge of the back lawn. Even before I'd made the first pass, my mind began to wander. I couldn't stop thinking about how much better mowers worked when their blades were sharpened and adjusted and their gears were well oiled. Of course, the mower I had in front of me that morning was sharpened and adjusted, and well oiled. Still, faced with the whole lawn to do, the idea was distracting. When the fourth pass around the yard brought me near the house, I diverted the mower to the yard near the side porch and returned to the outbuilding for a pair of pliers, a screwdriver, a file and an oil can. Time for a tune-up.

Returning with my tools I noticed Becky chasing bugs in the yard. Jane was standing with Mom, who was chatting with my Great Aunt Ida, who lived two doors up from us on Fourth Street. She had a neat cellar in her backyard that formed a small hill that was fun to play on. After saying a polite "Hi," to my aunt, I turned back to the mower. Adult talk could be really boring.

The easiest way to work on those old "push" mowers was to turn them upside down, exposing the rotating reel where it lightly contacted the blade. I had seen my Great Uncle Mike work on his mower that way. I knew how to go about it.

In too short a time I was done. I had filed the blade sharp; I had tinkered with the adjustment so it was set just right and the gears were literally dripping with oil. To check the blade adjustment, I grabbed the reel and gave it a strong spin. The high-pitched click, click, click, click sounded just perfect. As it slowed down, I grabbed the reel and gave it another spin; click, click, click, click. I really did not want to go back to mowing.

Concentrating on my task, I didn't notice Becky as she came close, fascinated by the flashing sunlight dancing off the spinning reel. Nor did I see her hand reach out to touch it.

Instantly she was wailing. I heard her cry out, but it had happened so fast. The first thing I saw was blood spotted across the front of her dress. Hearing her cry, Mom ran to her side and was soon wrapping the hand in Becky's own dress.

I sat astonished, motionless, mouth agape. What had I done? Had I cut off my sister's finger, maybe her whole hand? In a heartbeat, Mom had bundled Becky into the car and driven the two blocks to Dr. Simpson's place. Jane and I remained behind with Aunt Ida. After they'd gone, my head drooped, my shoulders slumped; I just sat on the edge of the porch fearing the worst.

I was still lost in grief in front of that up-turned mower when Mom and Becky returned. As Mom lifted Becky from the car, I saw a large, white bandage covering her entire left hand. But she was no longer crying, and when she squirmed to be let down, she immediately took up where she had left off—chasing bugs and exploring the yard.

Seeing my long face, Mom came over, sat beside me, and put her arm around my shoulder. "Don't worry, she'll be all right. It just caught the tip of her finger."

It wasn't until then that I realized I had been crying. I moaned, "I didn't see her. I didn't even know she was there."

"I know, I know…. Don't worry about it. It wasn't your fault. It wasn't anyone's fault. Put the mower away and come in the house. You can finish tomorrow. Everything'll be alright."

And, with time, it pretty much was alright. Becky's finger healed quickly, and over the years she grew into a good natured, good looking, matter-of-fact kind of woman. Still, I am sure she would prefer to have her whole finger, including that tip, but she was never the sort of person who would pay that sort of thing much mind.

I RECOVERED MORE SLOWLY. As a youngster I knew adults who had lost body parts. A friend of Dad's had a missing right hand; Uncle Bud, an auto mechanic, had lost a finger working on a car engine, and Uncle Ike had lost a leg in a farming accident. It wasn't until the bandage came off, and I could see the limited damage with my own eyes that I fully believed Mom's reassurances.

Then too, there were all those thoughts that began with "if only...." Mom said that it wasn't my fault; she meant it; I believed her; and nobody blamed me. But still today, when I think of that morning, it's my hand I see, spinning that reel, making the sunlight dance, as I foolishly believed that all days pass more or less the same—not yet knowing how everything can change in an unguarded instant.

8

Saying Goodbye to Grandma

IT WAS 1949, Dad was back from the war, and we were just finishing dinner in the kitchen when the phone in the corner of the dining room rang. (Our phone number at the time was "4.") Mom left the kitchen, and I watched through the doorway as she picked up the long black ear piece hanging from its brass cradle on the side of the phone. She then picked up the rest of the phone and spoke into the mouth piece, "Hello." She listened to the caller.

It wasn't but a few brief seconds when we heard, "Oh, no! We'll be right there." She came back to the kitchen and told Dad, "Mom's had another stroke and is in a coma."

Dad, Jane (my younger sister) and I helped clear the table, putting the remaining food in the oak icebox on the porch and stacking the dishes in the sink to wash later. Mom wiped Becky's hands and face (she was still a toddler), got her down from her highchair and changed her diaper. We then all piled into our 1939 Ford and headed for Aunt Reva and Uncle Ike's farm ten miles east of town. Grandma (Foster), who had lived with us since her first stroke, had gone to the country to visit her youngest daughter for a few days.

It was a black night in the countryside. On the hour-long journey over rutted dirt roads—today the trip takes only twenty minutes on smooth blacktop—we didn't see another car. As we passed farmhouses, barking dogs leaped to greet us and run along beside the car, but we hardly ever saw light, other than the stars above and those of our own headlights. Although Aunt Reva and Uncle Ike had just gotten a handsome, wall-mounted, oak phone installed on the wall of the kitchen, it would be another two years before REA, the government's Rural Electrification Administration, came to rural Sullivan County.

45

As we pulled into the farmyard, we saw a bright light coming from the living room window and a softer, barely noticeable glow coming from the kitchen. There was nobody on the porch to greet us, but by the time we reached the side door, Uncle Ike, on his crutches—he had lost his left leg in a farming accident—swung the screen door open. Carrying a kerosene lantern to light our way, he led us in through the kitchen to the living room where Dad and we kids stayed while Mom continued alone into a side bedroom. I could hear Aunt Reva's low sobs as Mom opened and then closed the door. Uncle Ike and Dad sat in the overstuffed living room chairs near each other with serious faces, exchanging a few quiet words. Becky had gone to sleep on the couch.

As Jane and I milled about, I became fascinated with the gasoline lantern, the first I had ever seen. It gave off a brilliant, white light—as bright as the electric lights we had in town. I asked Uncle Ike how it worked, and—patient as always, and perhaps relieved to have something to do—he showed me how to pump up the gas under pressure with a little plunger that jutted out of its side.

After a while, Mom came back to the living room, crying. She told Jane and me that it was time for us to say goodbye to Grandma, and she ushered us into the side bedroom. The way Mom had presented us with our duty, I expected to have a conversation with Grandma like I had often had with people leaving on a car trip. Instead, Grandma lay silent and still on the bed in her white nightgown. A bedside kerosene lantern filled the room with a "close" smell, its soft, orange glow lighting her face. She looked like she was asleep—peacefully resting.

With Aunt Reva and Mom softly weeping, Jane and I stood beside the bed, not knowing what to think or say. Finally, at Mom's prompting, I awkwardly said, "Goodbye, Grandma," and Jane repeated the words quietly in her own small voice. Grandma gave no sign of having heard us. She never revived from her coma, but died in the night, sometime after Mom had put Jane and me to sleep in the upstairs bedrooms. Though I loved Grandma, I was too young to understand what this meant about my own eventual fate, nor did I feel much grief. I only felt wonderment at the solemn occasion, an occasion that so disturbed the adults.

TWO DAYS LATER, BACK HOME on Fourth Street, Mom was still sober with grief, but the house was in an uproar. That morning, Mom, Jane, and I engaged in a house-cleaning frenzy. Everything except Scotty, the dog, and Old Moe, the cat, got dusted, wiped, or swept. The animals were made to stay outside until the operation was over—though they really weren't interested in being around such activity.

By afternoon, the pies started arriving. Today, nearly eighty years later, I know there must have been main-course dishes and side dishes of vegetables, but all I can truly remember from that day were the pies: cherry, apple, pumpkin, peach, blackberry, mincemeat. The neighbor ladies brought more pies than I had ever seen gathered in one place, before or since. As the pies lined up on the kitchen counter at eye level, I delighted in anticipation of our evening meal.

After an early, somber supper—I stuffed myself with two helpings of pie and snuck part of a third when nobody was looking— friends and family members started arriving for the wake. Although he still needed his crutches to move about, Uncle Ike wore a suit jacket over his blue denim bib overalls and his artificial leg for the occasion. It was the only time I ever saw him wear the leg. People sat on the couch in the living room and on the straight-backed chairs lined against the wall in the dining room. Grandma Knifong sat next to Grandpa, who placed an empty coffee can on the floor to use as a spittoon.

The house was stuffed full of mournful adults. Nobody really had anything much to say, and they just sat shifting from side to side, avoiding eye contact. After a bit, Grandpa, Dad, Uncle Ike,

Uncle Bud—Mom's brother—and some of the other men drifted outside to stand by the Ford. With nothing better to do, I followed. They smoked, and in the darkness, someone produced a flat, pint bottle of Old Crow. Away from the house and the women, the men spoke in quiet tones: "Byrd Foster was a good woman." "Byrd was a good cook." "Byrdie kept a clean house before her stroke, neat as a pin." "There warn't no better woman than Byrdie."

After some time had passed, the comments turned to more common topics: the weather, the outlook for the crops, the future for hog and corn prices. Then, there was a low quiet chuckle. One of the men had told a story with a mildly racy turn. I had heard the story and didn't understand it—and, I knew enough not to ask or I'd risk being sent back to the house.

THE NEXT DAY WAS overcast and drizzly as Mom, having gotten Becky ready, inspected me in my Sunday-go-to-meetin' outfit. After licking her hankie and rubbing at a spot on my cheek, she then turned her hankie on Jane, and then finally on Dad. Satisfied with, or at least accepting of, our appearance, she headed us all to the Ford, and we drove up the hill to the corner of Fourth and Market. There stood the redbrick Baptist church with its steeple. I had spent many a Sunday morning in that church. Grandma used to take Jane and me to church so that Dad and Mom would have an hour or so to themselves. This day, hardly a pew was empty, but the front had been roped off for family. Grandma herself was in an open mahogany casket in front of the pulpit.

The service opened with a hymn, then a prayer, then a Bible reading, then another hymn, then another prayer, and finally the main event: a sermon. Familiar phrases still float through the recesses of my memory—some of them sung, some spoken: "The old rugged cross, where the dearest and best...." "I go to prepare a mansion for you in my Father's house...." "You shall not die but have everlasting life...." "But believe in the Lord, Jesus Christ...." "I walk in the garden alone...." "I am the resurrection and the light...."

The whole ceremony was devoted to two messages. A hopeful one: Byrd Foster was a good Christian woman who had not died, but has "gone to a far better place." (This confused me. We could all see her lying in her casket, dead as a doornail.) And the sterner one: If you are a lost sinner, you had better declare your soul for Christ, be saved and join the Baptist church before it's too late. If you don't, you'll be headed to the other place.

After the sermon, the preacher stepped down from the pulpit to stand beside the coffin with his Bible in hand and a sorrowful look on his face. We all rose and filed past the open casket, the adults crying into their handkerchiefs. After the whole congregation had looked in at Grandma's face, the casket was closed, and the pallbearers carried the casket down the center aisle, through the main door to the waiting hearse. As it slowly pulled away, we followed in a single line of cars, each car burning its headlights in the middle of the day, so that the purpose of our mission was clear to all.

THE OAK GROVE CEMETERY stood on a knoll about three miles east of town. A light, misty rain started as I stood next to Mom, holding her hand. The wooden casket was placed in a second, reinforced concrete casket, and its heavy lid was fitted in place. The whole affair was then moved over the grave in preparation for lowering into the ground. Sheltered by a dark green awning, the minister held another, shortened service, as if the first one hadn't quite gotten through to everyone. Mostly he repeated what he had already said back at the church. As he began to ramble a bit, the undertaker, Mr. Shadow, leaned over to Mom and motioning to the casket, perhaps seeking to comfort her, he spoke in hushed tones, "That concrete vault is guaranteed for fifty years."

After he had straightened up and was again listening to the preacher, I looked up at Mom and asked, "How long is fifty years?"

"It is a long, long time, Jimmy," she replied through her tears.

Byrd Foster on her wedding day,
December 1906

—— *Afterword* ——

IN THE STORY, I refer to the undertaker as "Mr. Shadow." I recall hearing the undertaker's name spoken by adults—he lived near us on Fourth Street, but I don't recall ever having seen it written. Recently, while looking over some Milan material, I ran across the family name "Shato," which, depending on how it is pronounced, may rhyme with "Shadow." As a child I may have confused the two words. Or maybe I didn't.

9

"Good as New"

I DIDN'T KNOW IT when I woke that morning, but it was to be the first day of a rewarding, life-long hobby. Mom announced over breakfast that Jane, my younger sister, and I would be spending the morning cleaning house—we could play after lunch. She had a way of ruining otherwise beautiful summer mornings with mundane chores. I hated cleaning house as a child and haven't grown to like it much better with age. This particular morning, I was assigned the bathroom while Jane got the dining room.

After finishing my Cheerios, I grudgingly found a rag and cleanser under the kitchen counter and headed for the bathroom. As I sprinkled Bon Ami on a mostly dry porcelain sink, I saw water trickling from the tap. A rust stain had formed on the porcelain under the faucet. I reached to stop the leak, but even though I turned the faucet with all my strength, the water wouldn't completely stop.

"The faucet won't turn off. It keeps dripping water," I yelled to Mom, through the open door.

"I know," she replied. "I've tried to get your dad to fix it, but he's always busy." This was true enough. Since Dad started his excavating business, he left the house before I got up and didn't return until darkness forced him to stop working.

Stepping into the bathroom to look at the problem, Mom added, "If you'll fix that faucet, I'll finish your cleaning chores. It probably just needs a washer."

"I don't know how," I replied.

"Just pull it apart and take it up to Poole's Hardware. They'll sell you what you need."

51

I HAD NO IDEA what I was getting into, but I figured it couldn't be as bad as housework. I went looking for a screwdriver and one of Dad's monkey wrenches. Back in the bathroom I applied the wrench to the large nut at the base of the faucet—really the only nut in sight. As I turned the nut, the handle also turned. Soon, water started gushing from around the nut as well as the spout of the faucet. This wasn't going well.

I called out to Mom, "How do I stop the water from pouring out?"

She called back, "Turn off the main shut-off valve in the basement."

I had never heard of a "main shut-off valve," but in the basement I found a valve, and, hoping it was the right one, I shut it off. Back in the bathroom, I again turned the large nut. This time I was able to remove the faucet stem without gushing water.

At the stem's base was a rubber washer held in place with a brass screw. The rubber was seriously grooved. Surely this was the washer Mom had been referring to. Wrapping the stem in a rag, I stuffed the whole thing in my pocket, got a dollar from Mom, and headed uptown on my bike for Poole's Hardware on the southwest corner of Courthouse Square.

ALTHOUGH POOLE'S HARDWARE had bright morning sunlight pouring through a full glass front, it was dark and dingy inside. A counter ran the length of the store, front to back, separating the customer area from shelves of goods. In the middle stood a wood-burning iron stove with chairs scattered around. Clem had been sitting in one of the chairs with his head slumped forward, apparently dozing. He jerked up when the jangling bell, attached to the door, sounded. Rubbing his face with his right hand and, without getting up, he smiled and asked, "What can I do for you, Jimmy?"

"My faucet leaks," I said, drawing the stem from my pocket.

Studying the stem, Clem said, "Looks to me like you need a new washer." Rising and going behind the counter, he produced a box of various sized rubber washers. Choosing one, then another, he found a washer that was the same size. Then, turning to me he said, "Now, you see that screw in the middle? Get yourself a screwdriver, and take it out. Remove the old washer, and replace it with this one. Then put the screw back, and it will be good as new. "That'll be 5 cents," he said, putting the washer in a brown paper bag.

I paid him and was soon on my bike headed home, thinking, *This was easy stuff and much more fun than cleaning house, and I get to ride my bike.*

A valve stem that screws tight against the seat
when the handle is turned

AT HOME, I REASSEMBLED the faucet with its new washer, and thinking success was at hand, I went to the basement to turn on the main.

In the bathroom I turned the faucet on full. After a bit of belching and burping, the water flowed smooth and even. I then shut the water off. It almost stopped—and it was better—but like before, there was a slight drip, drip, drip that wouldn't quit, even when I cranked hard on the handle. This was clearly not "good as new."

Thinking perhaps I had done something wrong, I turned off the main a second time, disassembled and reassembled the faucet. This time, I carefully studied each step to see where I might have caused the problem. But turning the main back on, the faucet still had a slow drip.

Not finding where I could possibly have erred—there was only one way the parts fit back together—I was stumped. Because I had managed to slow the drip, I thought the problem must surely have something to do with the washer. After some thought, I decided that the rubber washer was too hard. Maybe Clem had a softer one. Stuffing the stem back in my pocket, I once again got on my bike and headed to Poole's Hardware.

I WAITED WHILE CLEM FINISHED talking about the weather with Mr. Morrison. When he turned to me, I asked if he had any softer washers. He laughed and said, "I don't think so. What's your problem?" I explained that I couldn't get the water to stop dripping. He again examined the stem and its new washer. "There's nothing wrong with that washer. The water has probably cut a channel in your brass seat. Now, if that happens, even when the washer is turned down hard against it, the water has a bypass channel and won't shut off completely. There are two solutions: One is to buy a tool and grind the seat smooth. However, since this is an *American Standard* faucet, you can replace the seat."

Once again, he went behind the counter, this time finding a small box containing round brass seats with holes in the middle. Taking one of the seats from the box, he said, "I am pretty sure this is the right size for your faucet. When you get home, look down the throat of your faucet. You'll see a seat just like this one, but there

*Valve seats – one new and one with
a channel cut by water*

will be a small cut in it made by the water. They make a special wrench that fits the hole in these seats, but if you have the right size screwdriver you can use it to unscrew the seat. Put this new seat in its place and everything should be good as new. The seats are 48 cents. You'll need some thread sealant or it'll leak around the threads. That'll cost 27 cents." When I asked, "What's thread sealant?" Clem unscrewed the cap and squeezed out a small dab of stuff on his finger and rubbed it into the treads. "Now ya load up your threads with this stuff all around before ya screw 'er down tight and she won't leak." For all the world, the sealant looked like gray, oily mud from a creek bed, which, I learned much later, it essentially was.

AS I CAME IN THE BACK DOOR, I was surprised to find mother putting out baloney sandwiches for lunch. Jane was already at the table finishing hers. Mom said, "Sit down and have lunch. Where have you been? Since we couldn't turn on the house water, we had to pump water from the well." Caught up thinking about the faucet, I was not much interested in lunch. I replied, "I had to go for another part at the hardware store. Let me see if this works. I'll eat when I am done."

If asked earlier, I would have argued strongly that it was not possible for water to cut brass. Yet, once I removed the old seat and was looking at the two brass seats lying side by side in my hand, it was just as Clem had said: There was a channel in the old one clearly cut by something, and the only thing it could be was water. This was neat stuff!

Reassembling the faucet was a breeze. In no time I had turned on the house main and was trying the faucet. This time, it truly worked "good as new." I was pleased with myself to no end—and I was hungry.

Over lunch I eagerly related the morning's saga to Mom as she made a fresh batch of chocolate chip cookies. Later that afternoon, when alone, I realized I had spent far more time working than my sister, but it hadn't felt like work. Instead, it had become such an interesting puzzle that I had even put off lunch to solve it!

—— *Afterword* ——

FROM THAT DAY FORWARD, I have avoided routine work by volunteering to tackle jobs that I have only a general notion of how to do, but must figure out during the process: from faucets to heating and cooling systems, to electrical fixtures and, more recently, to computer systems. I find it more fun to figure out how a thing works and then try to fix it. Many people are more than willing to do my share of routine tasks in exchange for my troubleshooting their malfunctioning devices. And, even though I have aged a bit, I still appreciate chocolate chip cookies at the end of a successful repair.

Poole's Hardware hasn't changed much, except for the newer model cars out front.

10

Only the Horses Dance

FOR ALL I KNEW AT THE TIME, that first week in April of 1951 was completely unremarkable. I had ten years' experience being a boy, which, I have come to realize, is long enough time to master most any career. I felt confident that I had figured out how to deal with routine childhood challenges. Of course, it would not be long before the shock of adolescent hormones would cause me to rethink most everything, but that was yet to come.

In the rural Missouri town of Milan, I knew each of the sixteen boys who were in my fourth-grade class, and I knew most of their brothers and sisters. I knew which kids I was friends with and which ones I fought with. I knew what it was like to be in school during the winter and to be free in the summer. I knew how to deal with teachers and other adults: what would earn me praise, what would get me in trouble, and what I could probably get away with—if I was careful. And I thought I knew how to deal with my parents.

As far as I could tell, Dad pretty much didn't have rules, plans, or expectations for me—that was Mom's department. And Mom seemed to make enough plans and rules to suit Dad just fine. In fact, Mom's general plan for me resulted in a good many rules. She recited this plan often when I did something she didn't like: "Whatever you choose to become doesn't matter, but you're going to learn how to be a proper gentleman." As a growing boy the first part suited me just fine. It gave me latitude to fit in with the other boys in the town, as long as—and there was always a second part—I had to "clean up well."

It was this second part of Mom's plan that motivated many of her admonitions, admonitions that always seemed to start with, "We may be from the farm, and we may not have much money, but...." This handy phrase could, and did, introduce a variety of prohibitions: "*We don't eat peas with our knife.*" "*We don't wipe our mouth on our sleeve, we use a napkin.*" "*We can at least be clean.*" And so on...and on, and on, enough to make a boy weary. Of course, adhering to such rules was only annoying when I was around the house. When I was out of Mom's presence, these warnings didn't seem that important. Nor were they of special importance to Dad, who allowed me to mostly ignore Mom's rules, but then he didn't seem to care much if people knew he was from the farm.

COMING HOME FROM SCHOOL that Wednesday in April, it was the "gentleman" part of Mom's plan that I had to deal with. After dumping my books and sitting down to a glass of milk and a peanut butter and jelly snack, Mom, while working at the kitchen counter with her back to me, casually mentioned Mrs. Hendrickson. "Some other mothers and I met with Mrs. Hendrickson today. She drove over from Kirksville. She is a very nice lady."

Barely paying attention, I took another bite, and thought, *So what.*

"She runs tap dancing classes over in Kirksville.... Jane wants to learn, and I signed her up."

Why did I care if my seven-year-old sister wanted to sign up for some dumb girl thing? This news didn't mean anything to me. I reached for my milk.

"Mrs. Hendrickson said she was taking boys, too. Do you have any interest in learning to tap dance?"

I nearly sprayed the table with a mouthful of milk. This got my full attention! After forcing my milk down, with only a little dripping from my nose, I managed a casual-sounding reply. "Nah, I ain't interested in no dancing."

Turning, Mom said sternly, "*Aren't!* You *aren't* interested.... Don't say 'ain't,' and don't say 'no dancing.' You're not interested in dancing."

"I'm not interested in dancing," I repeated, fully caught off guard by the harshness of her reprimand.

Turning back to her work, and once again in a sweet, pleasant voice, she said, "That's okay. You don't have to if you don't want to, but there will be other boys there."

"Nah, that's okay."

I had *maybe* once seen tap dancing at the Saturday afternoon movies, but I wasn't sure. Mostly I watched cowboy movies. Nobody danced in a cowboy movie, except sometimes the horse, when the hero wanted to show off what a good horse he had.

What really worried my mind about dancing was the thought of being teased by the other boys in town. They'd call me "sissy," and they'd make up nicknames for me like "Jumping Jimmy," or "Twinkle Toes," or whatever. We'd have to have a fight, probably several fights. It was not that I really minded fighting, but I knew it would not stop the teasing. And why would I ever want to dance anyway?

Well, that Wednesday afternoon it was easy enough for me to dismiss any further thoughts on the subject: Mom had said I didn't have to take lessons if I didn't want to, and I certainly didn't want to. I had said so, and Mom had heard me. My thoughts turned to more important things: "What're we having for supper?"

"I fixed chicken, and we'll have some carrots and potatoes, but that's still two hours away. You just finished a snack.... You're not hungry already, are you?"

"Nah, I was just wondering," I said as I drifted from the kitchen with no particular purpose in mind.

TWO DAYS LATER, as we all were finishing a Friday night supper of meatballs and spaghetti, Mom said to me, "Jimmy, tomorrow is Saturday.... I'm taking Jane to Kirksville for her dancing lesson. Then I'll do a little shopping. You don't have to take dancing if you don't want to, but I'm not leaving you home alone. You'll have to go with us. You can wait while Jane has her lesson."

"Aaahhh, do I hafta? That's not fair."

I knew I couldn't win this fight, and my automatic response lacked much real passion. The fact is, I didn't mind going shopping in Kirksville—though the idea of sitting around for Jane's lesson didn't sound so hot. Maybe Mom would let me buy a new comic book.

Dad was no help. He just grinned and said, "What's the matter Jimmy? Don't ya wanna chance to get close to them girls? Some of 'em might be pretty."

Mom shot a look at Dad that would have stopped a blind elephant.

"J.B., don't! ... If he doesn't want to dance, he doesn't have to. But he is going to Kirksville."

Although Dad had been warned he was treading on dangerous ground, he couldn't stop thinking it was all a bit funny, and he added, "I always liked gett'n' close to girls."

But no more was said. The issue was settled. Supper was over, and Dad, who had never cared one way or the other, rising from the table, drifted toward the radio in the living room. Jane and I began arguing about whose turn it was to wash the dishes and whose turn to dry.

THE NEXT MORNING we were almost to Kirksville when Mom said in a light chatty voice, "Jimmy, have you ever seen tap dancing?"

"I don't know...."

"Well then.... When we get there, you might want to go in and see what it is all about."

"Uh-huh, I guess."

Privately—very, very privately—Mom was sort of right. I was curious. That is to say, I was curious in an *I-might like-to-watch* sort of way. I was definitely not curious in an *I-might-want-to-try-it* sort of way.

"Mrs. Hendrickson is a very nice lady, and she is looking really hard for boys. When I signed Jane up for classes, she asked if I had a boy. I said I did have a boy, but I didn't know if he would want to join or not. She said that if you weren't interested in dancing that was fine, but she'd like to meet you sometime, if you ever came along with Jane."

When we stopped in front of a plain brick building on Elson Street, south of the main business district, I could see "HENDRICKSON DANCE STUDIO" on the front glass. There were people inside, but I could not see much more. I figured I'd go inside and look around.

Pushing open the door, we were blasted with "She'll Be Coming around the Mountain" coming from an upright piano in the far corner. It was being played to a strong beat. In the middle of the room was an old lady—maybe thirty or so—dressed in a white blouse, black shorts, and black high-heeled shoes with taps on the toes and heels. She was leading a line of kids through their steps. Mothers, toddlers, and other children sat in folding chairs near the door, waiting for the class to end.

Mom must have kept a sharp eye on her watch to have timed our arrival so well. We waited only a minute or two for the class to end. When the students filed off the floor, Mrs. Hendrickson approached the new arrivals. Smiling warmly, she greeted each of us and listened to learn our names. When she heard my name she said, "So you thought you'd like to come and see what it was like after all?"

"Uh-huh," came out in a mumble. It was all I could think to say.

Mrs. Hendrickson accepted my response as adequate, smiled at me once more, and then, stepping to the middle of the empty dance floor she just stood there looking at us and thinking. Finally, she called a girl to come to the middle of the room and stand just so. Then again, Mrs. Hendrickson just stood in the middle of the dance floor, looking at us and thinking. She seemed to reach a decision. She walked over to us and, placing a hand on my shoulder, she looked back at the girl standing on her own in the middle of the room. "Jimmy, you are about the right height, why don't you stand next to Mary?"

With her hand on my shoulder, she guided me to the middle of the room and had me, too, stand just so.

After that, she quickly called the remaining boy and two girls. We would be a line of five. After some rearranging, she started showing us what to do with our feet.

Time flew by, and as the class ended, I was surprised to notice the waiting area filled with a new batch of kids my sister's age. Being our first class, Mrs. Hendrickson explained to the mothers what kind of tap shoes we would need and where we should go to buy them uptown. Then, before she started her next class she spoke directly to me. "I was glad to see you, Jimmy. You did very well today. Did you like it?"

"Uh-huh, it was okay." Her eyes faded just a bit. I knew more was expected from me. "Yeah, I liked it. It was fun."

And I meant it, sort of. It wasn't as bad as sitting in school all day. But it wasn't as good as recess either. It was in between. It was just all right.

"Well, you'll be coming back next week then?"

"Yeah, I guess so. If Mom'll bring me." At least that's what I said with Mrs. Hendrickson standing right there in front of me, Mom standing to one side looking on, and both smiling broadly as I said the right thing. Privately, I was less sure. Next Saturday was a whole week away, who could predict such distant future events?

"Fine. Well, get your shoes over at Bermann's, so you'll be all set. We have a good class. We'll have fun. I'm glad you decided to join us."

Mrs. Hendrickson smiled, quietly pleased with her new acquisition.

AFTER JANE'S LESSON we stopped at the downtown dime store for lunch and Mom gave me a quarter for a couple of comic books. We also stopped at the IGA for groceries and at Mullen's to see what clothes were on sale. By the time we got to Bermann's, I had forgotten about the boys who might tease me.

After choosing shoes that seemed to fit, Mr. Bermann had me stand with my toes in a slot at the bottom of an amazing machine. The top of the machine had three viewing ports. When he flipped the switch, we all looked inside. Just like Superman's x-ray vision, I could see my toes through the shoes. I wiggled my toes. After choosing shoes for Jane, Mr. Bermann used small nails to attach aluminum taps to the toes and heels of the shoes. We were all set.

On the way home, I was content: Eating in the restaurant had been a rare treat, I had two new comic books to read, Mrs. Hendrickson did seem nice, and there *was* another boy in the class. There were girls in the class too, but I didn't have to actually touch any of them. The dancing had been OK. And, best of all, no one else from Milan was there to tell the gang how I had spent my Saturday morning.

THE FOLLOWING SATURDAY morning I woke with a different point of view. My apprehensions about engaging in such a girlish activity had returned, and I figured I had better things to do with my Saturday mornings. Over breakfast, assuming as much casualness as I could manage, I announced, "I've decided I'm not going to take any more dancing lessons after all."

Mom's reaction was swift and ominous. She looked at me as if she had Superman's x-ray vision and could see inside my brain. "What do you mean you're not taking any more dancing lessons?"

I had skated onto thin ice, and I didn't know how to turn around. "If I didn't like it, you said I don't have to do it. I decided that I don't like it."

"I did say that, but I watched you up there last week and you did like it.... And, more to the point, you told Mrs. Hendrickson that you were going to be in her class. Now she is counting on you to be there. And you let me spend fourteen dollars on those patent-leather shoes. Now you're telling me you're not going to wear them?"

"But I don't want to."

"Maybe not, but it's too late for that. Besides, every gentleman needs to know how to dance. There's going come a time in the not-too-distant future when you'll want to know how to dance. This is as good a time as any to learn.... Now, finish your breakfast, we've got to get ready and get out of here or we'll be late."

I wasn't the least bit persuaded by Mom's appeal to becoming a gentleman or my keeping my word, or by Dad's suggestion I might enjoy being close to pretty girls. But the matter was clearly, and firmly settled: I would learn to dance. I pouted for a while, but as the car headed east out of Milan, I forgot about my anger and began to look forward to the day, dancing and all.

THOSE SATURDAY LESSONS continued for four years, until the family left Milan and I entered high school in West Chicago. After that, I never tap danced again. But Mom was right, there were several occasions when I wanted to be on the dance floor with a date or spouse. Learning to tap gave me confidence and made the transition to social dancing easy. And, most important at the time, I was able to keep my Saturday activities hidden from the guys in Milan, except on one occasion.

Like many other dance instructors, Mrs. Hendrickson, like to show off her students' talents. During those years, it seemed she scheduled us for every community event in northern Missouri that would have us. Typically, there would be three or four shows a year. As I grew older, Mrs. Hendrickson saw an opportunity to play off

Our first dance line: Jimmy on the right

my bashfulness with girls. She paired me with Carol, a girl my age who wasn't the least bit bashful. We danced a routine based on "Ma, He's Making Eyes at Me."

From an adult point of view, it was all very cute and a real crowd pleaser. We were a hit as we toured the countryside, and of course, eventually, the summer just before we moved to Illinois we played in Milan.

Knowing that I was leaving town somewhat calmed my fears about being teased. Still, when the Milan show finished, I waited nervously for Mom and a ride home. Worried that my secret was out, I tried to hide among the crowd of adults as they slowly left. It was with real dread that I saw Arthur, one of the guys I sometimes fought with, coming directly toward me.

As he came close, he said, "You did good up there. You were great." There was even a hint of respect in his tone and manner. I was so prepared for a fight, I only mumbled a reply.

IT TOOK WEEKS before Arthur's compliment sank in. It took only a year or so for me to appreciate Dad's comment about "getting close to girls." But it wasn't until many years later, when I saw grown men awkwardly stumbling about on the dance floor, or watched as others refuse to leave their chair beside the wall, that I slowly came to appreciate what Mom had done for me.

Jimmy Dan and Carol

11

My Uncle Ike

LET ME TELL YOU about my Uncle Ike. He was a Missouri farm boy. Movie-star handsome. Tall, rugged, muscular. Square jawed with a twinkle in his eye, a ready smile—and smart. Born, raised, and lived all his life in Sullivan County ten miles east of Milan. Joined the Army in WWII and was lucky; he spent his time serving as an airplane mechanic near Warrensburg, barely a hundred miles from home. He had hardly seen an airplane before he joined up, but they made him an airplane mechanic. That's the Army for you.

Shortly after enlisting, he came home on leave to marry my mother's sister, Reva, the youngest of the three Foster girls. After the war, Ike came back to Milan, to his wife Reva, and to their new son, David, and, true to his roots, he started farming.

Now, Sullivan County farming in those days meant diversified farming, that is, a farmer would raise cattle, hogs and sheep, and probably keep a horse for riding—after the war, no one used horses for draft anymore. In addition, he would grow alfalfa and hay on the hillsides and corn and beans in the bottomland—soybeans that is, though everybody just calls them "beans" and you know they aren't talking about green beans from the garden. Speaking of which, the farmer's wife would put in a large garden, half of which she would put up in jars for the winter. And she would also keep a cow for milk and perhaps a few ducks, a goose or two, and chickens for eating and for eggs. If there were enough eggs, they provided pin money when sold to Mr. Gray's A&P in town.

When he returned after the war, Ike followed in his father's footsteps, setting himself up as a typical Missouri farmer. However, what happened a year later made Ike anything but typical. I was only five, and I wasn't out on the farm the day it happened, but

I remember overhearing my parents and relatives talk about it at the time.

IT WAS MID-AFTERNOON on a dry, summer day. Ike was about a mile from the house, mowing hay so that it could dry before stacking. His black and white terrier, Spot (Missouri farmers don't waste much effort on dog names), was sniffing at mouse holes in the grass.

Finished with the hay, Ike had unhitched the mower from the John Deere, climbed back on the tractor, and headed down to Yellow Creek. He planned to use the tractor to run over to the other side of the creek to see about a sagging fence. When he got near the shallow water, there was a barbwire gate that had to be opened to let the tractor through to the next field. So Ike set the brake and started to climb down off the seat.

Ike's Farm

NOW IF YOU DIDN'T GROW UP around those old John Deeres, it might help to pause here and explain a bit, so you can make sense of what followed. Made in Waterloo, Iowa, they were always green and the kind of tractor that you think of when you picture the typical, old-fashioned farm tractor. They had high wheels in the back and two little wheels in front set side-by-side and toed-in at a funny angle. The Deeres gave a farmer so much height—to reach over the crops—that they were easy to tip over backward if you headed straight up on those Missouri hills. Many a farmer did, and many a farmer died. On the steep hills, it was safer, though more awkward, to back up.

The engine was a two-lung affair, that is, it had only two cylinders. However, those cylinders were about as big as coffee cans and packed a wallop every time they fired. The farmer sat straddling the transmission, his left foot operating the clutch down low on the left side, and his right foot operating brakes to the rear wheels. A short stick shift with a Bakelite knob rose straight up from the transmission between the farmer's knees.

Directly below the seated farmer, and sticking horizontally straight out the back of the axle hub, was a splined, six-inch steel shaft. It provided rotating power to a mower, a spreader, or other implements pulled along by the tractor. It was always turning in rhythm with the engine whenever the engine was running—whether the tractor was in motion or not.

NOW THAT DAY Ike was wearing a brand-new pair of bib overalls. Later, there was some speculation that things might have turned out a good deal differently if those overalls hadn't been so new. I don't believe it myself. OshKosh B'gosh denim is tough stuff, even with some age on it. But be that as it may, the overalls were new.

When Ike got to the barbwire gate, he stopped the tractor. Thinking he would be only a minute, he set the brake, left the engine running, and started to climb down. But as he swung his left foot down, the loose end of his pants leg got caught in that spinning power takeoff.

Later, he could never remember what happened. He just remembered waking up with Spot whimpering and licking his face. Sprawled on his back, his head on the hard ground, he was looking up through the tall grass at a blue, cloudless sky. Other than the dog, everything was quiet. When he looked at the tractor, it was no longer running, and he saw his left foot sticking off to one side at a peculiar angle and his left pant leg wrapped tightly around that power takeoff shaft, a shaft that was now above his head.

He couldn't get up. He couldn't crawl away. And he couldn't unwrap his leg. There was no use calling for help, there was no one to hear; and he wouldn't be missed till suppertime, three hours away.

There wasn't much pain, not at first, nor much blood—just shock. As his head cleared, the leg began to throb, then to ache, but the real pain would come later. He had to get that pant leg free, and he groped in his pocket for his knife. It was a damn awkward reach, but he was able to cut the denim free of the shaft. Of course, that allowed his leg to fall and hit the drawbar which rode below the shaft. That hurt, and he nearly passed out from the pain. His leg, now free, was still above his head, though not so high as before. Finally, using his arms and his right leg, he managed to stand, and lift his broken leg free from the bar. After a brief standing rest, he used his arms and good leg to climb back up to the high seat of the tractor, his left calf and foot dangling in the air.

He now faced another problem. Quite aside from the pain, his lower left leg was totally useless. How could he get the engine started and put the tractor in gear without using the clutch, which was low on the left side of the transmission and completely out of reach by either hand or his functioning right foot? On the one hand, he could start the engine in neutral, but then, with the gears turning, he wouldn't be able to force them to mesh without the clutch. And they had to mesh to power the wheels. On the other hand, he could put the transmission in gear before he tried to start the engine, which he tried, but the starter wasn't powerful enough to turn the engine and move the tractor forward at the same time.

The tractor wouldn't start. But it had to start if it was going to take him to the house where he could get help. Fortunately, he had carried a posthole digger with him when he headed to fix the fence. Putting the transmission in neutral, he started the engine and then used the digger's handle to push the clutch pedal and shift the tractor into gear. With the tractor in gear and moving, and with Spot trotting alongside, he headed for the house.

His leg had been bleeding a little from the first. Now that he was sitting upright with the leg dangling below, it began a slow, steady flow. With the loss of blood, and the pain that came with every bounce, he was near fainting. Approaching the first barbwire gate between him and the house, he knew he couldn't stop. He ran straight through that first gate and then a second one. The gates could be repaired another day; his leg would not wait.

Pulling into the yard next to the house, the tractor was still dragging locust gate posts strung with barbwire. Some of the wire had wrapped itself around the rear axle. It made a hell of a clatter, but it hadn't stopped the tractor. When he was well into the yard near the house and still rolling, he killed the engine. There was a loud backfire and the tractor came to a stop. He dropped his head to the steering wheel and waited for Reva to find him.

IKE COULD NEVER RECALL much about the next five days. By the time he was awake enough to understand what was happening, he had undergone two operations and numerous blood transfusions. The first operation was below the knee; however, penicillin hadn't made its way to rural Missouri yet. Two days later, when gangrene set in, the surgeon had to operate again, this time well above the knee. Ike left the hospital with a twelve-inch stump where his strong left leg had been.

Well, being young and otherwise healthy, Ike was soon standing vertical on his size thirteen right foot—even if the left one was missing. The doctors sent him home on crutches. Bored, and with chores aplenty that needed tending, he was soon farming much as he had been before. It was what he knew. It was what he had always wanted to do. And, as he would tell me later, "There weren't nothing else I could do." At the time I believed him, though with time I realize that wasn't entirely the case. He was an able fellow, and he could have done most anything he set his mind to. Of course, what he had always set his mind to was farming. The fact never seemed to occur to him that it was a damn difficult way for a one-legged man to make a living.

Some months after the accident, he was fitted with an artificial leg. It was heavy and uncomfortable, and in any case, he had adapted to crutches by then. I saw him wear the leg only once, at Grandma Foster's wake. Mostly the leg was stored in the pantry off the kitchen. There it stood at attention, gathering dust and guarding Mason jars full of green beans, beets, peas, corn, and tomatoes. Those old farmhouses didn't have electricity until years later—if ever in the pantry. In the dim light coming from the kitchen a flesh-colored standing leg provided a bit of a shock to anyone who happened upon it unawares.

The blacksmith in Milan welded a four-foot curved steel bar to the left clutch peddle of the John Deere so it could be worked by hand. Ike bought a war surplus Jeep to run around the farm and, when needed, go into town. The Jeep had a hand throttle sticking out of the dashboard, and Ike kept a short stick down beside the driver's seat to work the clutch, but he didn't use it much. Mostly he used his right foot in a sideways manner with a heel on the brake and a toe on the clutch. That way he could work both peddles at the same time—having big feet was a real advantage. The Jeep continued to serve as farm transportation long after he bought an Oldsmobile with a new-fangled automatic transmission. But then, the Oldsmobile was pretty much Reva's car.

MOSTLY THROUGH CLEVERNESS, with an added dash of sheer stubbornness and a lot of hard work, Ike did all the chores you might expect of any Missouri farmer. I can still see him on crutches and stepping smartly across a muddy barnyard with two five-gallon pails of hog slop, each of his big hands doing double duty by gripping both a bucket handle and the crutch handle. The full buckets would balance upright even as their bails angled inward toward the crutch handles. When he got to the trough, Ike would put both crutches together under his left shoulder, balance on his right foot, and pour the feed. I have seen that man shear sheep, shuck standing corn, mend fences, shovel manure, harvest beans, and do a hundred other jobs, keeping pace with any able-bodied man, and all on one leg and two crutches.

I recall that, when the accident happened, the grownups worried that Ike might come out of the hospital depressed, and perhaps he was for a while. There is no way around it, it was a tragedy

Dan, Uncle Ike, Aunt Reva and their son, David

to lose that leg. But he wasn't the type to brood over misfortune, and I never knew him to give any notice of thinking about it. Soon, neither did anyone else. Once his leg was gone, what was he to do about it? He farmed over a thousand acres, a good size spread for northern Missouri. He prospered more than most when grain and cattle prices were high, and he suffered less when they were low. He always had a good head for figuring things out. He had already caught a pretty wife who loved him and gave him a son. The missing leg never stopped him from doing whatever he wanted, and he never cared much for dancing even when he had two legs.

When I look back on it now as an old man, the most amazing thing about knowing Ike when I was a boy was that I never thought of him as special. Didn't every boy have an uncle who pinned the empty left leg of his overalls to his chest so it wouldn't flop free?

12

An Afternoon with Nothing to Do

I REMEMBER my boyhood summer days endlessly drifting by with little apparent purpose or direction. At the time, my overwhelming concern was to fill those days with "something to do"—and to avoid Mom's work details. It never occurred to me that I was, in fact, intensely busy learning how to be in relationship with work, friends, family, self, and the physical world.

———◦———

OVER A BREAKFAST one morning, like many others, Mom laid out a number of chores that needed doing around the house. Then all morning she kept me motivated and on-task with the promise that I would be free to play in the afternoon, a promise that came with a watchful eye in case I should try to slip away early.

Finally, over a lunch of tomato soup, a grilled cheese sandwich and milk, I plotted my promised getaway. It was a delicate business. Although I could always trust Mom to keep the central portion of her promise, she sometimes nibbled at the edges with something like, "Oh, before you go Jimmy, I need you to help with one more, little thing. It won't take a minute."

With Mom's back to me as she worked at the sink, I managed to finish lunch without her noticing. I then quietly rose from the table, pushed my way through the screen door, closing it silently behind me, and mounted my bike before calling, "I did all the stuff you wanted, Mom, I am going now, like you promised."

Her voice didn't reach me until I was nearly across the lawn.

"Jimmy!" she called. I clearly had caught her by surprise and that didn't happen often. Now that I held an out-of-the-house-and-on-my-bike advantage, I willingly stopped at her call.

75

"Yes, Mom," I called allowing a dejected note to color my voice.

"I meant to have you take up the dining room rug and clean it. It is a good day for beating the rug. The clothesline is empty," she called, coming to stand behind the screen door. "It isn't much and wouldn't take long."

"But you promised. You said I could play in the afternoon.... Can't I do it tomorrow?"

"Well...." I had played this right—I could feel her relenting. Then, she gave in entirely with, "Where are you going?"

I hadn't thought about where I was going—except to get away from the house. Still, without hesitation I made up a pretty good answer. "I am going over to John's house. He's built a downhill race car."

With that I was on my bike peddling toward freedom. As a last word in the negotiation, she called after me to be home *in time for supper*—as if I might forget a meal.

ALTHOUGH NOTHING HAD been planned, four of us showed up that afternoon at John's. We were all ten and eleven, we had bikes, and we had somehow escaped our chores. We were free to roam the small, rural town and the surrounding countryside. And we were all faced with the same dilemma: In this perfect playground, on a perfect Missouri summer day, there was absolutely nothing to do.

The other boys were attracted to John's house for the same reason I was: John and his dad had built a downhill racer and John was painting it green. The body was made from eight-foot long, pine 1x12s that had been nailed together at both ends. These boards were then spread apart and braced in the middle to provide sitting space. A solid floor was added and then a top, leaving an opening for a cockpit and a boy. When finished it would be steered with ropes tied to either side of its front axle. But on this day, the car was definitely not finished. It sat on cinder blocks, wheels off, waiting for its paint to dry, at which point John planned to add red racing stripes over the basic green background.

Well, we stood around and looked at the wet green paint. Then we looked at the can of red paint—closed. Then we looked, and then we looked some more. And then, we commented on how fast it would go—when it had its wheels on. And then, we commented on how good it would look with the red stripes—when they had been painted. And then, we opined that the wheels themselves ought to be painted black. Definitely the right color for wheels.

Now, three of the four of us boys standing there had never made a downhill racer, nor had we ever painted one, nor had we ever seen one—except in comic books. We thereby felt well qualified to offer expert opinion about downhill racers. John, being a tolerant sort, allowed us to make the most of our opportunity. Like most boys, he enjoyed the admiration of his peers, even when it came in the form of advice, advice which for a while that afternoon flowed freely: *You better grease them axles good.... Nah, my dad said graphite is faster than anything. You'll need a windshield. If you don't have a windshield the wind will slow it down. You better add brakes, too. You wouldn't want to wreck....* And so on.

With such a free-flowing outlet, it wasn't long before our reservoir of advice ran dry, and with the growing silence there was nothing to distract us from our torment: We were bored and had nothing to do. A downhill racer can hold a boy's attention only for so long, especially if it is laid up on blocks waiting for paint to dry. Finally, someone suggested that we go swimming in one of the local ponds that he knew about. He claimed it was a neat pond and not too far from town.

At first this didn't seem like such a good idea; the afternoon had grown hot, and walking or even riding our bikes for any distance had little appeal—and how far was this pond anyway? The boy who mentioned it was suspiciously vague about the actual distance. Then John suggested that he knew how to drive the old '35 Dodge that was sitting nearby in the yard. We could all go in it.

What a great idea! Not only were we going swimming, but we would be driven there in style. The adventure was heightened by its being "slightly" illegal for any of us to drive on the official roads of Missouri—the oldest of us was still five years away from a license.

With such a wonderful opportunity before us, four brains were soon silently weighing the odds of a trouble-free trip, planning our individual excuses should we be caught, and trying to convince ourselves that we were not doing anything wrong. I am not sure how the others reasoned—necessity being the mother of prolific invention and all that. But two points stood out for me: First, we wouldn't be out on State Route 5, and the rough dirt tracks crisscrossing Sullivan County could hardly be considered *Official Missouri State Roads*, could they? And, second, the most impressive and significant fact to me was that if we got caught, I could argue that I was only a passenger. It would be John who got in trouble, not me. What could be more perfect? Of course, somewhere deep I knew this outstanding second point was as false as the first. But putting the two together distracted my conscience enough for me to embrace the plan enthusiastically.

It did not hurt that, as this was an all-male occasion, there was no need to stop by home for swimming trunks. If I went back home, I might have to explain to Mom about my afternoon plans. It was not that she would have minded my going swimming, but she would have had questions. And she would have discovered that I was not going to the Milan Country Club pool east of town where they had an occasional lifeguard. And she would have asked, "Where is this pond?" And she would have offered the opinion that "John is not old enough to drive, is he?" And so on, and on. Mothers can make a fellow slow, once they get started on his case.

BY THE WAY, DON'T MAKE too much of this mention of a "Country Club." Now, some seventy years later, the term might be a little misleading. It was a club in that it was funded through dues, but anyone could join for a modest fee. And it was in the country, but that was true of the small town itself and everything else for miles around. The Club pool that Mom would have referred to was a concrete hole in the ground with a flat bottom on its deep end. That is, two inches from the edge it was eight feet deep, and no slope. I had used this feature to teach myself to swim two summers previously.

My approach was to hold my nose, jump feet first into the deep end, sink to the bottom and then give a strong push for the surface. Breaking into the air, I would breathe, grab for the side of the pool, climb out, and do it again. Of course, if I had always practiced this routine perfectly, I might never have learned to swim. But from time to time, I would miscalculate, and as I came up for air the pool's edge would be out of reach. In such cases, I had two choices: splashing a few strokes to safety or taking a deep breath and sinking to the bottom for another try. Gradually, my splashing came to resemble swimming.

But that was two summers ago. This summer we were four boys in an old Dodge, rambling south of town over a dirt road. The pond was only about a mile from town, and soon I caught a glimpse of it up ahead. I could tell immediately that it had been a pond for some time. That is to say, trees grew around it, grass grew on the bank, and tall cattails grew in the water at the shallow end. As we came closer, the whole scene had a soft, inviting air about it.

THAT PART OF MISSOURI is dotted with such ponds built with an earthen dam across a shallow ravine. The ponds provide water for the cattle and are always fenced. Instead of allowing cattle to wade directly in the pond, making it muddy, an open watering tank is provided below the dam and outside the fence. A one-inch pipe carried the water from the pond to the tank, drawing off clear water.

The drain pipe in this particular pond played an entertaining role in our afternoon adventure and deserves a brief explanation for those not from the area. Because my dad was an excavator and dug his share of these ponds, I received an early education in dam construction and pipe laying.

The pipe would reach horizontally from the watering trough and low through the earthen dam to the deepest part of the pond. At that point it would be joined with a threaded elbow to a second pipe dotted with drilled holes and about five feet tall. This second pipe, capped at the top, would stand straight up, drawing clear water through its many small holes. When the pond was full, these pipes were hidden by three or four feet of water.

WHEN THE OLD DODGE STOPPED by the pond fence we piled out and were soon stripped of our clothes and splashing in the water. Its coolness was wonderful on such a warm day. We cannonballed from the dam into the deep part of the pond, splashed water in each other's faces, and had a couple of races from bank to bank. After we'd had our fill of the newness of the experience, things grew quieter, and I lay down on a grassy patch on the dam.

During this quiet we were all astonished to see John grinning at us from the middle of the pond and treading water with his *head and neck completely out of the water*. Of course, we all knew how to tread water, but this was an amazing feat. At first, I thought there must be an underwater hill in the middle of the pond. Then the truth came to me: John was standing on the upright drain pipe. He had accidentally kicked the pipe with his toe, and he was only pretending to tread water as he balanced his weight on the end of the pipe. It was an impressive performance.

As the secret got out, we all had to try the trick, repeatedly. The pipe was hard to find in the middle of the pond—there were no markers and one had to judge its position indirectly from the trees on the bank—but that was part of the fun. It was also hard to keep balanced on such a narrow perch, but that too was part of the fun— and our eventual problem. With so many boys taking turns on the pipe, it eventually came loose and, turning on its threads, flopped over on the muddy bottom, eight feet under water.

If we had had another distraction, we might have left that pipe where it was for the farmer to worry about when he noticed his tank was full of muddy water. But we didn't. After some talk about what must have had happened, we took turns swimming to the middle of the pond, diving to the bottom, and trying to find the pipe. Swimming to the middle was easy, and diving to the bottom wasn't hard. However, finding the pipe down there in the murk was tough. It took many dives and considerable luck. After a couple of the boys had tried, and failed, I took my turn. I was determined to succeed.

With help from others on the bank I chose the best place to dive. And after several tries, I touched the pipe with my right hand. The hard part was done, or so I thought. Grabbing the pipe with both hands, and planting my feet firmly on the bottom, I lifted with all my strength. Slowly the pipe swung back to its upright position.

Having been underwater for a while before I found the pipe, and having taken some time to lift the pipe, I was now running out of air. However, when I started to swim to the surface, I noticed something was different. I wasn't moving! The good news was that my hands worked just fine. The bad news was that my feet didn't. The worst news was that my feet were held fast by the mud. It turned out that in my haste to lift the pipe I had buried my legs all the way to my knees—it felt like up to my hips! At first, I tried to lift my left leg free by pushing with the right—that just drove the right leg deeper into the mud and did nothing to free the left. Enough of this, I needed air.

Finally it occurred to me to grab the pipe with my hands and climb it, hand over hand as you would a rope. Soon, I shot to the surface, and just in time. God, it felt good to breathe again. Slowly, I rolled over on my back and floated aimlessly, resting. The blue sky, the white clouds, and the green trees never looked so good as I lolled on the pond's surface recovering my breath and slowly kicking the last of the mud from my feet and legs.

Revived, I showed off by standing on the pipe one last time and then swam to shore. Seeing me renew the trick, the gang plunged in and returned to playing with the pipe, its value having soared by being lost and now found.

Soon the play ended. After all, it was not a brand-new toy, just one that was lost and newly found. And it was never the kind of thing that could hold our attention for long anyway. We slowly dressed, piled back in the Dodge, and with John at the wheel, made our way back to town. I was getting hungry; it was time for supper, which is always served early in that part of the country.

On the way back, I thought about Mom. I knew she would have been cautious about this expedition and might have made me stay at home. In a sense, I had to admit that she would have been *sort of* right to be concerned. What we were doing had been *slightly* risky. However, I reasoned that now it was perfectly safe. There was no longer any reason to worry. I now knew what the dangers were. I had successfully faced them, and I had learned how to guard against them. I took pride in my new-found knowledge—and I reasoned that it was not necessary to tell anyone about how I had obtained it.

AS I HELPED MYSELF to the mashed potatoes that evening, Mom asked, "What did you do this afternoon, Jimmy?"

"Oh, nothing really. I just went over to John's house and played with him a couple of other guys. John and his dad built a new downhill racer."

13

"Smarter Than the Horse"

THERE WAS NOT MUCH daylight left as we made our way over the rough, winding, dirt road. It was warm. All the windows were cranked open to afford as much breeze as possible. From the backseat I held the flat of my hand out the right-side window, letting the wind lift it. I pretended I was a WWII fighter, climbing high and then swooping low. Jane, my younger sister by three years, was in the backseat with me. When the roadside trees got close enough, she crowded over and we both grabbed handfuls of leaves.

It was the 3rd of July, 1951. The family was headed for Aunt Reva and Uncle Ike's farm, east of Milan. Dad was driving the '39 Ford we had bought from Aunt Esta when she married. Mom was in the front seat holding Becky, who was only two. I was ten. Although the farm was less than ten miles from town—three years later a friend and I would walk it as a day-long adventure—the roads were so poor that the trip took the better part of an hour. It would be completely dark by the time we arrived.

As the trip wore on, Jane and I leaned over the front seat to peer past the dashboard glow, helping Dad watch for the "fun" part of the road. Just before the farm the road turned south and then due east across three small ridges. What made this section so much fun was that the road contractors had not bothered to level the road with any "cuts and fills," and when driven even at modest speeds, the road offered a fair imitation of a roller coaster.

Nearing this special section of the road, Jane and I sang as a chorus, "Go fast, Daddy, go fast." Dad, who enjoyed roller coasters as much as we did, got a big grin on his face and gave the Ford extra gas. Away we flew over the ridges with Mom staring straight ahead and saying in a low stern voice, "Slow down, J.B. Slow down!" This treat, just before the farm, meant that Dad and we kids arrived in good spirits, even if Mom was a bit tense.

I HAD BEEN SHOOTING OFF firecrackers since mid-June. In anticipation of going to the farm, I had begged Dad earlier in the day for firecracker money to "stock up." To my surprise, he didn't just give me the money, but drove me to the firecracker stand on the east side of town. That had never happened before! Ever since I had gotten a bike, I was expected to make such trips on my own.

Dad watched while I picked things out. He insisted that I get some sparklers for Jane and some Roman candles for the whole family. I didn't much care for sparklers and Roman candles. They were pretty, but they didn't make much noise. When I asked if I could buy one of the large rolls of firecrackers, Dad had not only agreed, but suggested that I buy *two* rolls. It was a lot of firecrackers, a hundred in each roll. When we were finished, Dad paid nearly four dollars for it all, a truly stupendous amount of money.

I should have been suspicious of his sudden interest in my need for firecrackers, but I was just happy he was buying. The fact is, I was flat broke. Since the weather had turned dry, the grass had stopped growing, and I wasn't earning any lawn mowing money. Times were tough.

AS WE PULLED INTO THE YARD that night, the dog set up his usual barking, letting Ike and Reva know that they had visitors. Instead of opening the door when he stopped the car, Dad turned to me and said, "Gimme that sack." Unsuspecting, I reached down and gathered up my sack of firecrackers and handed it over the seat. I didn't even worry as he reached in and grabbed one of the huge rolls of firecrackers. I figured he was gonna unpack and light one or two to scare the dog. Instead, and before I realized what was happening, he lit the whole roll of a hundred firecrackers and threw it out the car window. At the sudden loss of so many firecrackers, my mouth dropped open in disbelief. *How could he!* Dad had clearly been planning this grand arrival when he went with me to the firecracker stand. He just hadn't told me about it.

Because their fuses were braided together, the night was soon filled with a long bombardment of popping firecrackers. Uncle Ike came out on the porch grinning from ear to ear; Aunt Reva, and my cousin David—Jane's age—soon joined him, their faces lit by the car's headlights and by the bursts of color from the firecrackers. The dog headed for the barn, howling in fright. Dad sat comfortably in the front seat, pleased with his cleverness, while, in the back seat, I fumed about my loss, momentarily forgetting that my sack still contained another full roll of a hundred regular firecrackers, plus Cherry Bombs, M80s, Lady Fingers, sparklers, rockets, and other assorted pyrotechnics.

After the noise died down, and it became safe to walk among the spent fireworks, we piled out of the car. The adults greeted each other with hugs, handshakes, and "how-ya-beens." I wasn't much interested in such greetings and turned to more serious business. Dumping the remaining contents of the sack on the porch floor, David, Jane, and I were soon raucously lighting up the night. Dad had brought cold beers from town that were opened, and all four adults arranged themselves in chairs to watch us kids play as they engaged in grownup talk. Despite Mom's best efforts, Becky burnt her finger on a spent sparkler that hadn't yet had time to cool. An hour later, although there were still plenty of firecrackers, we lit kerosene lamps and headed into the house.

THE MORNING OF THE FOURTH was a beautiful day, bright and clear. After an early breakfast of bacon, eggs, fried potatoes, biscuits and jam, the grownups wanted to loaf around the kitchen drinking coffee. We kids were restless. David and Jane headed outdoors to play, and I asked Uncle Ike if I could ride his horse, Lady.

"Sure, she's out there in the pasture. Just go to the barn and get her halter. It's a-hanging on a nail to the left, just inside the door. When you get the halter on 'er, you can lead her to the barn and saddle her up there. That-a-way you won't have to carry the saddle."

I headed for the barn, found the halter, and then headed back to the pasture near the house. It was going to be a fine day.

With the halter in hand, I unfastened the top of the barbwire gate, stepped through, refastened the gate, and walked toward the horse. Lady was standing quietly, eating grass. At first, she seemed not to notice me. However, when I was about ten feet away, she lifted her head and trotted about forty feet to my left, just as if she had, at that very moment, noticed a better patch of grass. This surprised me, but I figured it was no great problem, and I, too, trotted forty feet to the left. I was thinking, *I'm not a horse, I don't eat grass, maybe this grass is better.* But then, just as I drew near a second time, she ducked her head and headed for another part of the pasture. Again, I trotted over, and again she moved away.

Now, as everybody knows a horse can trot a lot faster than a boy. Even I knew that, even then. So the fourth and fifth times I approached vveerryy sslloowwllyy, trying not to spook her. It made no difference. Just as I thought I was near enough to catch her, she would trot to another part of the pasture.

After a few more steps in this dance, the horse was as fresh as ever. The boy was not. The horse was clearly having a fun time. The boy was hot, tired, frustrated, and angry. The boy headed for the house in a black mood, while the horse quietly returned to eating grass.

AS I CAME THROUGH the kitchen door, the adults were all smiling broadly. The pasture was clearly visible from the kitchen window, and the horse and I had provided an entertaining show as we did the catch-me-if-you-can polka.

Barely able to contain his laugh, Uncle Ike spoke in a sing-songy tone of voice, "What's the matter, Jimmy?"

"Lady won't let me catch her," I groused.

Dad opined, "If ya wann'a ride a horse, you've gotta be smarter than the horse."

After a few more chuckles they took pity on my plight, and Uncle Ike said, "I'll tell ya what you gotta do. Go over to the counter there, get a couple of Reva's carrots, and bring 'em here."

Aunt Reva and Mom had been to the garden and the counter was strewn with vegetables, peeled and ready for lunch. As I reached for the carrots close at hand, Aunt Reva stopped me, "Not those, Jimmy! Feeding that horse from my garden is bad enough. I'm sure not going to peel carrots for it too. You can have some of those others," she said, pointing to the far end of the counter.

Grabbing three or four of the unpeeled carrots I turned to Uncle Ike who said, "Now, go back to the pasture and hold the carrots in front of you in your left hand, like this. And with your right hand, hold the halter behind you—like this. Now, you do it that-a-way, and stand still. *Don't chase.* Wait. Let her come to you. Then, when she's a-eatin' them carrots, gently slip the halter over her head."

With an uplifted heart I headed back to the pasture. This time I did as Ike had told me, and like magic, it worked! It amazed me then and amazes me still today. That horse became so interested in eating carrots I could slip the halter on her with no problem. I guess when it came down to it, she couldn't hold two thoughts in her head at the same time. 'Course, now that I think on it, I've been that way myself sometimes.

With the halter on, Lady was an entirely different animal. I easily led her back through the barbwire gate and over to an old half-barrel. She stood patiently as I climbed up on the barrel and then onto her bare back. We headed to the barn at a slow walk.

IT WASN'T THUNDER—there were only a few puffy clouds in a clear sky—but halfway across the barnyard both that horse and I heard a loud bang. One moment I was sitting, spraddle-legged on Lady's flat, broad back. The next moment, I was sitting on air.

Now, given the different density properties of horse flesh, air and dirt, and given the average weight of a surprised ten-year-old boy, and finally of course, given Newton's law of gravity, which one must always factor in, there came the inevitable third moment that found me sitting on hard-packed, barnyard dirt, stunned by the instantaneous, five-and-a-half-foot vertical drop that my bottom made, and that the rest of me had promptly followed.

When I had recovered enough to look around, the horse was standing quietly about ten feet away, no doubt still savoring the taste of carrots. In the other direction, my sister and my cousin, whom I hadn't noticed until then, were laughing so hard tears ran down their cheeks. My first thoughts were for death followed by torture for two close relatives. Fortunately for them, my hand was stayed. The drama with the horse had continued to interest the adults, and when they saw me fall from such a height with my legs at the horizontal, they worried that something might be broken.

My wrath was diverted to saddling the horse as Dad and Uncle Ike took an active role in my project. My sister and my cousin got a stern lecture about firecrackers and horses. Soon Uncle Ike was holding open the gate to the north pasture, and I was turned free with a horse and a thousand acres to explore. Once again, it was a fine day.

I made it back to the house in time for lunch, satisfied with my ride—though still a little sore from my fall. Soon after lunch we climbed back in the Ford for the trip back to town. It had been a good visit.

A BOY LEARNS all kinds of lessons from his father and his uncles. One thing I learned that Fourth of July was I don't have to give up loving firecrackers and roller coasters, even as an adult. A harder lesson to remember, and apply, was that when I am running after something that is always just out of reach, I should stop chasing. In those moments, it is time to put some thought into figuring out how "to be smarter than the horse."

Jimmy and Lady
(Jimmy is wearing a sailor's cap his dad brought home from the Navy.)

14

"Tain't No Way They'd Be Good fer Ya"

IT WAS THE NEED for bait that did it. My fourth-grade friend, Tom and I had decided that particular hot August afternoon to go fishing. For reasons long forgotten, we came to the notion that Walsh's Grocery Store on the levee was the perfect place to procure alluring, grownup, "fish-can't-pass-it-by" bait.

THOUGH IT WAS HOT, we were not drawn by the air conditioner that Mr. Walsh had just installed the day before—we didn't know about it. We didn't even know that such a machine existed. However, I will confess that had we known the store had air conditioning, we—and perhaps half the town—would have been suddenly gripped by a powerful need for items that could be had only from that store. This may have been the first appearance of air conditioning in Milan. Regardless, only Tom and I, and a couple of farmers, found our way to the store that hot afternoon.

Of course, by 1951 we boys knew that cool air could be manufactured. After WWII, even households in rural towns such as Milan were giving up their oak iceboxes for gleaming white refrigerators. In fact, a year earlier, Mom and Dad had bought a Crosley refrigerator with an ice compartment all the way across the top. I remember being intrigued: Our old, oak icebox on the porch had used large twenty-five pound blocks of ice delivered by the iceman from Milan's icehouse on Second Street. These kept the inside cool as the ice slowly melted, but the Crosby *made its own ice*—two trays at a time. Still, it was one thing to cool milk, soda pop and other food stuff in a refrigerator; it was something else to cool a whole room with people in it—let alone a whole building.

ON THIS PARTICULAR DAY Tom had showed up on his bike just after lunch. Our moms had kept us busy all morning with chores, but now that we were free, we were at loose ends as to what to do with our freedom. We sat on the back porch with our feet dangling over the edge and discussed our situation. Our mood lightened when one of us mentioned fishing. The town had two reservoirs east of town and the thought of their cool, tree-shaded banks had some appeal. But even more alluring was the possibility of breaking our past record and this time actually catching a fish. Even though we had not managed to catch a single fish in our past fishing expeditions, we just knew they were out there waiting for us—big fish, three or four pounders, real fighters.

Now, it might seem a bit strange that such casual talk of fish could inflame the passions of such inept fishermen. But that's the way it always was for the two of us when bass, crappy or catfish was mentioned in our conversations.

Gradually our talk turned from dreaming to planning. We each owned a rod and reel, already strung with line and hook—we had gear. We both owned bikes—we had transportation. What we didn't have, was bait. In the past we had simply dug for worms, but it was August. There hadn't been much rain, and the ground was dry and hard. The prospect of worms napping comfortably in their cool, deep tunnels while two boys sweated overhead trying to reach them was too painful to consider. We drifted into gloomy cogitation.

After a bit, there was a spark of insight. It came to us in a flash. The worms had been our problem all along! We just hadn't seen it. Big fish don't like worms. Worms were what little kids used to catch baby fish. What we needed was bait that grownups used: store-bought bait that big fish hungered for, bait that they would find so delicious and tempting they would eagerly swallow it whole—hook, line, sinker and all. And, not coincidentally, bait that didn't require digging under a hot August sun. Grownups didn't dig for bait; they bought their bait.

Now all we needed was money. We went inside the house to see my banker, and Mom readily gave us a whole dollar without a fuss—much more than I expected. I suppose looking at us standing there, she figured that outfitting a two-boy expedition should be twice as expensive as a one-boy venture. Whatever Mom's thinking, we didn't spend any time pondering Mom's generosity; we now had money and we were on our bikes and gone.

THE HEAT SEEMED TO HAVE made the whole town sleepy. There was no other traffic as we slowly climbed uphill to the Courthouse Square, crossed the square, and coasted down East Third Street to the levee. Approaching the white building with "Walsh's Grocery" painted on its side, we left our bikes and headed for the door. It wasn't much of a grocery store—it was smaller than most convenience stores found in today's gas stations. There was just enough room for a counter, a chest freezer, two coolers, and three short aisles of canned and dry goods.

As we came to the door, drops of cool water fell on our heads, causing us to look up, wondering where it came from. Then as we pulled the door open, we were suddenly distracted from the dripping water by an engulfing flood of cool air. It was such a surprising shock that it took us a minute to realize that we had interrupted a conversation. Mr. Walsh was grinning from ear to ear, shirt sleeves rolled to the elbow and brawny arms spread wide along the counter. He had been talking to two older men, both clearly farmers in bib overalls and heavy work boots. The farmers had their backs to us and turned halfway to see who had come in.

Facing us, Mr. Walsh spoke first, "Howdy, boys. What can I do for you fellers?"

Tom spoke up, "We need fish bait."

And I followed with, "Boy, it sure is cool in here."

"Yeap, just got me an air conditioner," and he nodded to the unit over the door. "Da ya like 'er?"

"Yeah, it feels great," I said.

"Glad ya like 'er. Just got 'er in yesterday. Ahh...what kind'a fish you aimin' to go after?"

Answering at the same time and speaking over one another, Tom said, "Bass," while I said, "Catfish."

At that, one of the farmers eyed us a bit and said, "Why don't ya boys get yaselves some worms? There tain't nothin' better 'n a good worm."

The second farmer added, "Er, maybe some grubs. Them's good too." Half turning back to Mr. Walsh he added, "Did I ever tell ya about that mess a' catfish I pulled outta the Clariton River last spring? I was a'pullin' 'em out as fast as I could throw in the hook. Got me so many I got plumb tuckered out and had ta quit. We ate fish that night till they was a'comin' out our ears."

After nodding noncommittally, Mr. Walsh asked us boys, "How come ya don't wanna use worms?" and we explained about the dry ground. Understanding, he paused before saying, "Well, if you don't wanna use worms.... I ain't got much in the way of bait, but I guess fish will eat most anything. Why don't you boys look around back there and see what you can find? I got some baloney you could hang on your hook. Then there's always cheese... And I heerd tell peanut butter's good too. Though I ain't never tried it myself."

Happy for a ready-made excuse to remain in the cool air, we began to drift among the aisles. We took our time, slowly evaluating each item for its potential fish appeal—peas, baking soda, lima beans, canned corn, and so on. Tom hesitated at the canned corn, but I shook my head and we moved on.

As we wandered, Mr. Walsh turned his attention back to the two men and his favorite topic of the day. Clearly proud of his new acquisition, he said, "Well, as I was a'tellin' ya. They came and put 'er in yesterday afternoon. We fired her up, and in no time at all, it got cool in here. When I closed up last night, I turned 'er up and just let 'er rip all night long. This morning the place was so cold I had to turn 'er off and find a jacket to wear till things warmed up some."

There was a pause at this point as Mr. Walsh stood beaming at his audience, waiting for a reaction. Not looking directly at him, the first farmer studied the outside scenery through the window as if he was thinking on whether to plant beans or corn next spring on his bottom land. The second one said, "Seems to me she'd use a powerful lot of 'lectricity."

"Yeah. Well, I got the biggest one they had. It's 9000 BTUs. They say it don't use no more than a couple of fans.... 'Course, I reckon a body could make do with a smaller one at home."

After another pause. The first farmer asked, "BTU.... That tain't like horsepower, is it?"

"Yeap, it's the same thing. It's just like a car," Mr. Walsh responded.

Again, there was a pause. Then the second one said, "Ya say, ya got 'er down in Chillicothe?"

This meager show of interest was all the encouragement Mr. Walsh needed to launch into why air conditioning was going to be good for his business and how he had first experienced air conditioning in a Kansas City movie house before the war.

As Mr. Walsh finished, the farmers began to offer their opinions. "Well, it might be like ya say... good fer business and all, but seems to me, it'd give a body the chills... Tain't nothing worse than summertime chills."

The second one added, "Tain't no way they'd be good fer ya. All that cold'll make it harder on the body when ya go outside. It seems ta me it'd be a powerful shock. The body ain't got no time to prepare."

Undaunted, Mr. Walsh continued smiling. When it was his turn again, he told how he had bargained with the Chillicothe salesman to get a right smart deal. Being natural born "horse traders"—as were all the men from Sullivan County—this was a topic the farmers could appreciate. It was with some interest that they listened to how Mr. Walsh had worked the deal by pretending not to be the least bit interested in buying an air conditioner. Instead, he had acted as if he had entered the shop only because he was interested in a fan. As Mr. Walsh finished, the first farmer brought the discussion back to the previous topic by allowing as how he could agree, "Ya mightn'a got a yerself a right smart deal, but I'd not have one, not even if they gave it to me free."

At this, Tom whispered in my ear, "I sure would."

I quietly replied, "So would I."

Looking down, I saw Tom was holding a package of frozen shrimp. Now shrimp was an exotic food that neither of us boys had ever tasted, and that turned out to be a powerful appeal. It took only a moment of consideration before we convinced ourselves that the local, landlocked fish would go crazy over a taste from the sea. We could hear those big fish calling. It was time to go.

Once outside with our purchase, we rode our bikes side-by-side through the heat. I said, "It don't make no sense. If those two fellers don't like air conditioning, why'd they not leave? There weren't nobody a'making 'em stay there."

Tom replied, "Yeah, it don't look like they're a'plannin' on buyin' anything."

THE REST OF THE AFTERNOON we played at the water's edge, feeding the shrimp on our hooks to small fish as they took it a nibble at a time. That evening as I came in the back door, hot from the afternoon, Mom asked if we had caught any fish. I replied, "Nah, it's too hot fer 'em, they weren't biting."

Later, over supper I mentioned that Mr. Walsh had an air conditioner in his store, and it felt great. Mom said she thought it was the first one in Milan. As we talked, it came out that she and Dad knew all about air conditioners from the time they had spent in Kansas City and Chicago. After a bit more discussion, Mom put the topic to rest, "No, we can't afford such a luxury. No matter how good they feel, we won't be buying one for the house."

Casually Dad asked about the fishing. I told him we hadn't caught a thing and described how little fish nibbled at our bait until it was all gone. He was not surprised.

Then Mom thought to ask, "What'd you finally use for bait?"

When I said, "Shrimp," Mom choked on a bit of food and began coughing. Dad just got a big grin on his face and chuckled.

Finally, recovering some, Mom said, "That's mighty high-class bait. What on earth possessed you to buy shrimp?"

I replied, "We couldn't find nothin' else."

As was typical of her, Mom corrected me with, "We couldn't find *anything* else." To which I dutifully repeated, "We couldn't find anything else."

15

"Jimmy" Becomes "Dan"

FIFTH GRADE had started with the familiar pattern that had begun every other school year. In the previous grades we had had different teachers, but as a class we had been together and done this before—we had the routine down pat. This fifth time Mrs. Thompson assigned us to our seats and introduced herself, though we knew all about her, and she about us. Milan was a small town.

The fall months were uneventful. Mrs. Thompson wasn't a bad teacher, but what can I say? She was a teacher. She assigned work, and we did it. It was all rather routine. However, coming back from the winter Christmas break was definitely not routine. All thirty of us were shocked by the unfamiliar face before us.

The woman standing at the front of the class introduced herself and explained that Mrs. Thompson had moved and that she, Miss Reeves—whom we had never laid eyes on (she was from out-of-town)—would be our teacher for the remainder of the fifth grade. Since we did not know her, nor she us, she wrote her name on the board and said that she would pass around a paper. We were to write down what she should call us.

I had been born "James Dan Knifong," and as was the custom, I was usually called "Jimmy" or sometimes "Jimmy Dan." Only when Mom was angry with me, did she, and no one else, ever call me "James Dan." For example, she might say when I came home from school, "Jimmy, there are some cookies on the counter, if you're hungry." By contrast it would be, "James Dan, don't you ever again touch a cake that I've baked without asking. I made that cake for your Aunt Reva and Uncle Ike. You know they're coming for dinner tonight and now the frosting's all a mess. What on earth were you thinking?" Such utterances were not really questions, and I knew better than to attempt a reply.

Now, until Miss Reeves sent around that paper asking what she should call us, I had never thought much about my name. It was not like I hated it, or loved it, nor had I wished I could be called something else—except maybe "Roy" or "Gene" so when we played cowboys and Indians, I could claim a leading role and shoot the bad guys. It was just that there were sixteen boys in a class of thirty or so, and it felt like the name "Jimmy" created too much confusion. In previous years, whenever the teacher would call on "Jimmy," I would start to respond, even if she were calling on another "Jimmy." There were no other "Dan"s in the class. Wouldn't it be less confusing if the teacher were to call me "Dan"? My best friend at the time was named (what else?) "James Cincinnati Pilsworth." I suppose that if I had had "Cincinnati" as a middle name, I might have paused and thought twice about what I did, but when the paper came to me, I impulsively wrote "Dan."

Being from out of town and therefore not knowing any better, Miss Reeves started calling me "Dan" and slowly the rest of the class did too. The following year my sixth-grade teacher was Mr. Sayers, a long-time Milan resident. As such, he surely would have known

Sixth grade: Dan in the second row from Mr. Sayers, third seat back

to call me "Jimmy," but he didn't. Perhaps he too, thought Milan had enough "Jimmy"'s in sixth grade. Or maybe it took only a few months for "Dan" to take hold.

That's not how it worked in my family. My sisters switched to "Dan" fairly quickly, but my parents called me "Jimmy" for years afterward—through high school and college and beyond. And I watched as my aunts and uncles paused and struggled with the name "Dan" until, one by one, they died.

NOW THAT I'M INTO my eighties, "Jimmy" is way in the past, but "James" is making a comeback. Social Security, Medicare, and therefore most of my doctors all insist on using my formal first name.

I've thought about how my life might have been different if Miss Reeves hadn't taken over from Mrs. Thompson that winter. Logic tells me it wouldn't have made any difference. After all—what's in a name? But then I recall there was a President called "Jimmy" not too long ago. Maybe if I had just kept the name....

16

"Let It Out Slowly.... Well, Faster Than That"

————— *March 1952* —————

I GREW QUICKLY as a kid, and by the age of eleven I was 5' 6". Dad was no doubt pleased with my development in a general sort of way. I suppose every father likes to see his son grow tall and healthy. However, Dad saw a special significance in my new size that had little to do with my standing tall. He saw in me a body that was big enough to hold its head above a steering wheel and to hold its foot on the throttle. And, most importantly, there was now enough of me between head and feet that I could manage both tasks at the same time.

It might seem a bit strange, now we have entered the twenty-first century, that a parent would look at their child's healthy growth and think first of that child's suitability for driving, especially at age eleven. Today, most of us live in cities and suburbs where even quiet residential areas have more, and faster traffic, than the rural Missouri roads did in the '50s. Today's parents would more likely think of their child's suitability for basketball, soccer or some other sport, and most would be horrified at the thought of teaching an eleven-year-old to drive. Considerations such as insurance, liability, traffic, the danger of high-speed highways and the like would flash to mind, never mind that it is illegal for eleven-year-olds to drive.

Dad, however, had grown up in a different time and place. In Dad's youth rural Missouri roads were more rutted, bumpy wagon trails than the smooth paved streets we think of today.

Though such considerations were not totally unknown during the '50s they were of little importance to the farming community around Milan. There was no traffic to speak of. The country roads were rough and difficult to navigate when dry and worse when wet. And only on Missouri Routes 5 and 6, which meet on the edge of town, could a car travel much over thirty miles an hour—and even on those routes one could only speed briefly on the occasional straight-aways. In that time and place, learning to drive was *not* about high-speed cruising, multilane traffic, signaling a left turn at a stop light, and such. Instead, learning to drive was much more about mastering the fine art of choking a Ford engine to get it to start, releasing the clutch slowly and smoothly, and not sliding into the ditch when the road was soft from rain or getting stuck up to the axle in a deep pothole. And after the road dried, mastering how to straddle deep, wandering mud ruts that had become concrete-hard.

AFTER THE WAR, Dad had started a one-man excavating business, which meant that he was always running off on the weekends and evenings to "see a man about a job." On one of these evenings, while there was still plenty of light, I rode with him in his new Ford pickup to go and see about digging a farmer's pond.

After a good bit of bouncing over back roads, we came to a farm house where we were greeted in typical fashion by a pack of curious dogs, all barking loudly to signal our arrival. The racket alerted the farmer that he had visitors, and pausing his evening chores he soon appeared from a gray, weathered barn. After greeting us, and telling the dogs to quiet down, he and Dad were soon walking out over the hillside, sweeping their arms in wide arcs as they discussed when, where, how large, how deep, and how expensive to make the new pond.

I had heard it all before, and adult talk held little interest for me. I stayed in the farmyard playing with the dogs. Then, after a bit, I investigated various farm implements that were standing idle. These implements, originally designed to be pulled behind horses, were now pulled by a tractor. Each performed a short-lived but necessary once-a-year task during planting, cultivating, or harvesting season.

The rest of the year the equipment stood abandoned, grass growing straight and tall among the rusting bars, frames, blades, and iron-spoked wheels.

I did not have long to wait. Dusk was falling and soon the men came strolling back. They stood a moment and shook hands. We were about to leave. Unbidden, I moved to the Ford.

The road back ran along the top of a ridge through countryside that was quickly growing completely black. (It would be a few years before the federal government would prod the utilities to bring electricity to the farms.) Occasionally, at some of the high points, we could see the lights of Milan in the distance. The road was empty of traffic. The farmers, having finished their evening chores and supper, were heading to bed. They would rise before sunup.

AFTER ROLLING ALONG through the blackness of the night for a bit, Dad stopped the Ford dead in the middle of the road without saying a word. Curious, I looked over at him and saw him grinning from ear to ear in the faint dashboard light.

He asked, "Ya wanna drive?"

Sure, I wanted to drive, but my surprise only allowed me to say, "I don't know how."

"Well, ya gotta learn some time." Then, not waiting for a reply, he turned off the engine, got out and walked around, opened the door on my side, and said, "Get over there. Ya cain't drive it from this side."

I slid across the bench seat to the driver's side. As I put my hands on the wheel, I hesitated. I couldn't believe this was really happening.

After watching me just sit there behind the wheel doing nothing, Dad observed, "Ah... ya gotta start 'er up before she'll go."

With this prompt, I flipped the key to "On" with my right hand, and pressed my left thumb on the chrome starter button, just as I had seen Dad do hundreds of times.

Well, maybe not quite like Dad. When I hit the starter, the truck moved forward a bit, trying to start, but only coughing before it died. We had perhaps gained a foot or two on our trip home.

Surprised and trying to help, Dad had been saying, "Clutch. Hit the clutch. Ya gotta hit the clutch to start it."

I wasn't intentionally ignoring him; I was just too overwhelmed by the task to absorb what he was saying. Pausing to let the meaning of his words sink in, I asked, "Which one's the clutch?"

"The one on the left. The other'n's the brake. You know the gas pedal, don't ya?"

I automatically replied, "Uh-huh," but my head was still thinking about the clutch. I was having a surprisingly hard time recalling which shoe held my left foot. When it finally came to me, I mashed the clutch to the floor and held it there.

The pause gave Dad a moment to rethink his lesson plan. He said, "I didn't show ya the gears, did I…. Here." He reached over and waved the gear shift around in what seemed to be a random fashion, while saying, "Down here's first. Second's up here. This's third. Reverse is up here—close to ya, not away from ya, like second…. Ya got that?" Without waiting for a reply, he moved it one more time and said, "Let's start in first."

Not understanding a bit of what he had said or any of the gestures he had made with the gear shift, I continued to hold the clutch to the floor as I reached for the starter. This time the engine turned over rapidly, but it didn't catch.

Dad was saying, "Gas, ya gotta give 'er gas."

I released the starter button, and while still holding the clutch to the floorboard, I tried to attend to what he was saying. Then, I noticed my right foot was resting on the floorboard in a decidedly un-driver-like position. Intent on correcting the matter, I mashed the throttle to the floor and made ready to try again.

Dad was getting a good chuckle out of my actions, but he was also learning to watch me a bit closer. As I reached for the starter button, he said, "Whoa, wait a minute. Not so much. Just give 'er a little gas."

I brought the throttle about halfway off the floor and held it there. Reaching over he pulled the choke about an inch out from the dash and added, "Let's choke 'er a bit, too."

This time the Ford started readily—though with the engine racing rather faster than it should—a minor detail that went unnoticed until, at Dad's direction, I pushed the choke in and let up on the gas. The engine slowed to a comfortable idle. After checking things over, Dad decided we were ready and said, "Well, let out the clutch and let's go."

I did. But we didn't, at least not very far. Lifting my foot quickly from the clutch caused the pickup to lurch forward, stop abruptly, and die. We had gained perhaps another foot or two, maybe a bit more.

Amused, Dad tried once more to be helpful, "Try it again. Only this time, let the clutch out slowly and give 'er a little gas."

After fumbling a bit, I managed to get the Ford running and once more ready for travel. But before I did anything more, Dad repeated, "This time, let 'er out slowly."

And slowly I did. Cautious of the bucking that I had caused the last time, I was extremely slow in my movements. Dad must have felt he was watching the hands on a clock move. Perhaps he was thinking that the clock wasn't moving at all. Finally, he said, "Well, faster than that."

In response, I quickly brought my foot off the clutch. Again, the Ford lurched forward and died as it had before. This time we had gained maybe five feet.

Thoroughly amused, Dad said, "Try 'er again, only don't let it out too slow. And don't let it out too fast either. And give 'er a little gas." (I had forgotten about the gas part.)

This time, I didn't forget. The Ford shot forward and kept on going down the middle of the road. Finally, I was driving, albeit in low gear and at the giddy speed of five miles per hour.

But to me the speed seemed plenty fast as I concentrated on steering between the meandering ruts cut during the last rain and now hard as concrete. As I drove along, I gradually began to relax. I even practiced speeding up and slowing down a bit by modulating the gas as we drove around turns and up, over and down the hills.

As Dad saw that I was getting the hang of things and was not too likely to put us in the ditch, it was time to go a little faster. He said, "I'd like to get home before tomorrow's breakfast. Put 'er in second." When I hesitated, he told me to push on the clutch and as I did so he reached over and shifted into second. I again released the clutch too quickly. The Ford surged forward, but it didn't die, and we were soon traveling at the thrilling speed of fifteen miles per hour.

IT WAS OVER TOO SOON. As we topped the last hill and neared town, Dad had me stop to change places. On the remainder of the trip, I studied his movements closely; and I began asking questions, lots of questions: *What does the choke do? How does the clutch work? What are the gears for?* and so on until we reached home.

Dad was a very able and knowledgeable mechanic, and he answered willingly enough, but his attempts to explain brought forth only random thoughts as he considered each topic: "Yeah...ya gotta choke Fords. They won't start without chokin,' even when they're warmed up...." "Well, when you press on the clutch, it releases the engine so you can change gears...." "The low gears give you power, and the high gears give you speed...Then, ya gotta have reverse if ya wanna back up."

I listened carefully to Dad's answers as we rolled along, the night air blowing in through the open side windows. Though I made an earnest attempt to absorb what I could, I understood little of what he said.

We were entering Milan now; we hadn't yet had our supper, and I noticed I was hungry. As Dad parked the car on Painter Street beside the house, I could see Mom through the open kitchen door setting the table. The smell of something awfully good was wafting out into the night. It had been an exciting evening, but now it was time to eat!

—— *Afterword* ——

ALTHOUGH DAD UNDERSTOOD it thoroughly, it was only much later that my Uncle Bud, who was a much better teacher, explained the mystery of the clutch to me. As it turns out, an electric motor will produce power from a standstill, but a gas engine will produce power to drive a car only if running in a certain range of RPMs (revolutions per minute). When engaged, a clutch mechanically separates the gas engine from the wheels so the engine will turn freely while the electric motor gets it started. Once started, the gas motor must be kept running to turn the wheels and drive the car.

Imagine two flat, spinning steel disks the size of dinner plates facing one another very closely but not touching: The one attached to the engine is polished smooth. The other one, attached to the wheels, is faced with a kind of brake shoe compound—think of it as shoe leather. When the foot is off the clutch, strong springs press the two disks tightly together so the disks turn as one, and the engine and wheels rotate together. When the clutch pedal is pressed in, the two disks separate and the electric motor can turn the gas engine sufficiently fast—while the wheels remain stationary—for it to start.

As an experienced stick-shift driver knows intuitively, once the gas engine is running, the secret to a smooth start is to bring the two plates together quickly to the point where they just begin to rub, but don't lock up. As the gas engine plate spins, the friction against the other plate (connected to the wheels) slowly causes the vehicle to move faster and faster until the two plates are in sync and turn as a single mechanical system. At that point the driver's foot comes completely off the clutch and the pedal jumps to its highest position, locking the two plates together. Thus, operating a clutch pedal requires a fast-slow-fast action that I didn't understand and that Dad—though he understood—never knew how to explain.

17

The Only Thing in Sight

—— *April 1952* ——

SITTING ON THE CORNER of Fourth and Painter, our house faced Fourth Street, which was "sort of" paved with asphalt. Painter was more of an alleyway than a street and was "sort of" paved with gravel, which during the winter was augmented with cinders from our coal-burning furnace. Behind the house and lined up on Painter was a storage shed, and then further down stood a barn. Some might wonder at our having a barn in the middle of town barely four blocks from the Courthouse Square, but Milan is in Missouri farm country, and during the '40s and '50s no one thought much about it.

I was in the sixth grade that spring. Coming home from school, I noticed a green John Deere tractor parked near the house on Painter. Perhaps the tractor belonged to one of my uncles who had it in town for repairs, I can't recall. It certainly aroused little interest. Like the barn, occasional farm tractors were a normal part of the town's scenery. I entered the kitchen through the side door, dropped my books on a chair, set a glass on the table, and reached for milk in the refrigerator. I could hear Mom busy upstairs.

As I finished pouring the milk, I shouted, "Do we have any cookies?"

"Look in the tin on top of the refrigerator." Then a moment later, "You can have two of them.... I don't want you ruining your appetite before supper.... There's milk in the refrigerator.... I'll be down in a minute; I'm about done."

These last words reached me as I finished stuffing the first oatmeal cookie in my mouth and laid two more cookies on the table neatly beside the milk. Then, since that first cookie had tasted so good, but was now gone, I stuffed another in my mouth before returning the tin to its place. Finally, I sat down to my two-cookie-and-a-glass-of-milk snack.

IN 1950, HAVING FINALLY completed the changeover from war-time to civilian production, Ford Motor Company was flooding the market with new models. Dad had bought one of these for his excavating business, a good-looking blue pickup. The back of the pickup quickly attracted a permanent load of five-gallon diesel cans, chains, tools, wooden blocks, tractor parts, and various other sundries. Exposed to the elements, this miscellany gathered a covering of dirt mixed with oil and grease—three of the basic ingredients of Dad's trade. The cab, carrying its own share of dust and dirt, provided space for a driver and sometimes a passenger amid a clutter of items that couldn't tolerate rain. And yet, despite its less-than-pristine cargo, this Ford was considered a handsome sight. Many of the pickups and cars around Milan at that time were models built before the war, and they were showing their age.

Coming home that night, Dad had stopped the Ford in front of the barn. There he had unloaded some heavy items—I have forgotten what—into the barn. When done, he had not bothered to back the pickup up to its usual place closer to the house, but had left it beside the barn and walked uphill to the house for supper.

It was turning dark outside as the five of us started to eat. Like many a growing boy I tended to inhale food rather than eat it. I was soon finished, and hoping to duck the dishwashing chores that were sure to follow, I started to rise and leave the table when Dad looked over and said, "The pickup's down by the barn. Why don't ya go back it up 'long side the house fer me."

I had not had time to fully take in the meaning of Dad's words, when Mom exploded, "J.B.! He can't drive that pickup! He doesn't know how!"

Fascinated by both the argument and the prospect of driving, I froze halfway out of my chair.

"Well…he's gotta learn some time," Dad said.

"But first someone has to teach him. He can't just go do it."

"I let 'em drive a while back when we were in the country. He done good, once he got 'er going."

"But you were with him…. What if he tears something up? That pickup is nearly new."

"Hell, it's a truck, he cain't hurt it none," Dad replied.

"Well, he might hit something."

"What's he gonna hit? There ain't nothin' out there for him ta run into."

Though Mom was still fuming, her silence seemed to settle the matter in Dad's favor. I reached for my coat. While putting it on and moving to the door, I kept a watchful eye on Mom, but she only glowered at Dad. What little apprehension I might have had about my first solo drive was pushed aside by the excitement of the argument and my eagerness for adventure. But as I closed the door, I heard Mom say, "Old man, if he tears something up, you're gonna pay for it."

IT WAS COMPLETELY DARK as I climbed into the cab and pulled the knob for the headlights. The key was already in the ignition where it always was. Dad, like nearly all others in town, felt that if once removed, a key might get lost. Why take the chance?

I flipped the ignition on, pulled the choke out about an inch, pushed the clutch to the floor, and hit the starter button. The Ford turned over but didn't catch. Then I remembered to give it a little gas and tried again. This time it roared to life, startling me a bit. I was alone. This was for real, and I wasn't entirely sure of what would come next.

With the engine running I just sat there trying to calm down. Then I remembered to turn off the choke. This dropped the engine to a quiet, slow idle, which soothed my nerves some.

Dad's earlier lesson had covered four subjects:

I.   "Starting"
II.   "Clutching"
III. "Gearing"
IV.   "Straight Ahead Steering."

Of the four, I had mastered ordinary "Starting" and had gained a little experience with "Straight Ahead Steering." But I knew I had only the most rudimentary grasp of the more difficult subjects: "Clutching" and "Gearing." What I didn't know that night was that I also faced two additional subjects that Dad had not bothered to cover:

V.   "Steering-in-Reverse"
VI.   "Stopping"

With only a vague notion of how to get the Ford into reverse gear—actually into any gear—I decided to experiment. Showing uncommon wisdom and restraint (for me), I planted my right foot hard on the brake and determined to keep it there. I then moved the gear shift to some position that I thought might be reverse and tried releasing the clutch. Of course, I killed the engine, but not before I felt the truck try to move. I did this repeatedly, trying different gear positions and restarting the engine each time. Mostly the truck would try to lurch forward as I landed in first, second, or third gear. Occasionally, I hit neutral and nothing would happen, but after several tries, the truck tried to move backward before it died. I had found reverse!

RESTARTING THE ENGINE—I was getting really good at this part—I threw my arm over the back seat and looked into the blackness behind me. Without backup lights, I could just make out where the road was. I had seen Dad do this hundreds of times. It was easy. Determined not to let the engine die, I fed it a little extra gas and released the clutch. The truck lurched backward, but did not die, and I felt the briefest flush of success. Then things became very busy.

Because of the extra gas I had used to overcome my poor clutching skills, the truck fairly flew up the narrow alleyway. Being a novice driver, I knew nothing of the effects of front wheel "caster," the main advantage of which is that, *when moving forward,* the vehicle almost steers itself. The main disadvantage is that, *when moving rapidly backward,* the vehicle constantly tries to veer off course, which is exactly what happened. I managed to stay on the street, but the pickup lurched from side to side as my grip on the steering wheel barely held.*

In less than a minute it was over. There was a quiet, though very solid "thump," and the engine stalled. All was still—all that is except my heart, which was racing at breakneck speed. The truck was sitting beside the house as it should be, but so was the John Deere. I had completely forgotten about the tractor and had not even seen it during my rearward dash through the darkness.

Slowly, I climbed from the cab to study the situation. The left rear fender, now with a large dent in it, was pressed firmly against a large rear tractor tire. I had managed to hit the only thing in sight!

With a heavy heart, I climbed back in the cab, released the clutch, and without starting the engine, allowed the Ford to roll forward a few feet. I set the brake, turned off the lights. I then moved to look a second time at the fender—hoping against hope that the dent had disappeared. It hadn't. With a heavy heart I trudged to the house.

THOUGH MY SISTERS WERE now gone from the table, Mom and Dad were where I had left them. Quiet as the "thump" had been, I am sure they knew before I opened the door. If not, they certainly knew when they caught sight of my long face.

"I hit the tractor. There's a dent in the fender."

---

*For readers interested in why the front-wheel caster on the pickup caused me so much trouble, see Appendix C, "About the Automotive Front-Wheel Caster," p. 242.

Mom, who had only glanced at me when I entered, continued to stare at Dad. For his part, Dad looked away and held his face in his familiar all-purpose grin. Then as he rose and headed for the door, chuckling he said, "I'll go look at it."

Mom, still staring at his back as he passed through the door and without turning to me, said, "Get your coat off and go to your room. Get ready for bed. You've got school tomorrow."

It was pretty early for bed, but I had comic books in my room and was happy enough not to be around when Dad and Mom rejoined their struggle. That night I felt bad about the damage I had caused and figured, incorrectly as it turned out, that my driving career would be on pause for a long, long while.

AS NEITHER PARENT BLAMED me, nothing was ever said directly to me about the event, and I soon lost my sense of guilt. Though later, after the repair, I did overhear Mom relate the incident to her younger sister. It was with more than a little satisfaction, she told Reva, "It cost J.B. Forty dollars to get that fender fixed." Now, I happen to know—though I would prefer not to discuss exactly how I know—that today, a similar dented fender might cost a bit more than $40, perhaps even much as $978.59.

A 1950 Ford pickup

18

Trying to Baptize a Soul — Twice

AS SPRING CHILL succumbed to summer heat, the Reverend Jones made a visit to our Sunday school class. He flattered those of us who had recently turned eleven by speaking of the importance of no longer thinking like children, now that we were becoming adults. Then he turned to the importance of being "baptized in the name of Jesus Christ our Savior."

I did believe, sort of, that Jesus was my savior, everybody seemed to say so. Though, as I think back on it, I would have been hard pressed to say what I was being saved from. I might have answered Hell, but my death was unreal to me. Like most youngsters, I lived in the here and now, which felt like it would last forever. The afterlife wasn't even a consideration.

Today, I realize I was not yet beginning to think for myself, but at the time I enjoyed the attention that came with growing up. Being baptized felt like a normal rite of passage—hadn't all adults been baptized? I was becoming an adult. When I talked with Mom, I learned the Reverend had already spoken to her, and she agreed— it was time for me to be baptized. We were all set.

The next Sunday morning, when the Reverend ended his sermon with his usual "call to all sinners," four other youngsters and I stood and walked to the front of the church. I was mildly bothered by the contrast between our choreographed "coming forward" and the certainty of the fires of hell promised in the sermon if we remained seated. I was more troubled by his concluding "call to all sinners."

Baptist preachers seem to always end their sermons with some variation of the plea: "If there are any poor, lost sinners out there who have seen the light and want to take the Lord Jesus as their personal savior and be washed in the blood of the lamb—you know who you are—stand; rise up; and come forward, that we may pray for you in this glorious hour of your transformation." My discomfiture as an eleven-year-old came from the fact that I didn't *feel* much like that "poor lost sinner" the Reverend kept going on about. His exhortation just didn't fit well-groomed, eleven-year-olds dressed in our Sunday best. Besides, I thought of us as "good kids" who attended Sunday school almost every Sunday. We might have swiped a candy bar at the drug store or pulled our sisters' hair, but I didn't feel we had had time yet to commit the kind of sin that needed the Lord's intervention.

Regardless of how I felt, the Reverend's theology didn't allow free passes for any but the youngest of children. Being eleven I could understand the idea that we were all born with "original sin," and the only way to Heaven was for each of us to acknowledge our inherent sinfulness and accept Jesus into our heart as our personal Savior.

SO IT WAS THAT I WAS second in a line of five, after Ida Mae. We assembled and waited for our turn appear before the congregation in a storage room to the right of the pulpit and directly behind a large tank of water We would return to that same room after the deed was done.

The tank's sole purpose was for baptizing wayward sinners. It was oak-paneled on the outside to match the rest of the church, but on the inside, it was lined with zinc sheet metal and soldered corner joints to make it water tight and rust-proof. Usually it stood empty, but today it was full of water.

When Ida Mae returned, dripping wet, it was my turn. As I stepped out of the storage room to the top of the stairs in a flowing white gown, the Reverend stood waiting in the middle of the water up to his waist. His gown billowed out as it floated just below the water's surface. I tried not to think about my red swimming trunks beneath my white gown, but it was difficult not to think of being so oddly dressed. Was this a solemn occasion or play-time? Even more odd, as I stepped down into the water and came close, I could see that the Reverend was wearing rubber, chest-high fisherman's waders beneath his gown! Since he'd already been saved, he probably figured there was no reason for both of us to get wet.

The Reverend said some words that I don't now recall, but ended with, "I baptize thee in the name of the Lord Jesus Christ." As his left hand cradled the back of my head, his right hand came over my mouth and pinched my nose. He leaned me back under the water and then immediately pulled me upright. It was over in a flash. Before I could think, I was moving up the stairs and beyond them to the storage room where a dry towel and warm, dry clothes waited. Although the Reverend had spoken of a joyous feeling at being "saved," I didn't feel joyous that day or any of the days that followed. Mostly, I felt soaking wet and a little foolish as I wondered what it was all about.

DURING THAT SUMMER Reverend Jones retired and was replaced by Reverend Jackson who took a special interest in me. As I came increasingly under Reverend Jackson's influence, I slowly became seriously religious. Although I never did feel joyous at being saved myself, I began to feel a grim responsibility to save the world.

It was a year later, again in late spring, when the Reverend Jackson mentioned the possibility of being baptized a second time. We were alone, driving the rough dirt roads to see a parishioner whom the Reverend suspected of "backsliding." The parishioner hadn't been seen in church for a while, and Baptists are death on "backsliding."

During the ride, I was talking about how my thinking about God and Jesus was changing, and how I was coming to understand more about God's plan for the world. Then the Reverend said, "Maybe you didn't truly believe like you do now. Maybe you were just going through the motions."

This was certainly true, and I honestly admitted, "Yes, that's what it was like." We talked some more about this and that, and then the Reverend said, "Perhaps you should be baptized again, since the first time wasn't real." I didn't much care for the idea—once seemed enough, and I said so. But he stressed that I had a duty to come down front and declare my newly-enlightened faith. I would be serving as witness for others to God's glory. What if someone else saw me stand and was thereby encouraged "to see the light and be saved?" When put that way (that I would be doing a service for God), I relented. The following Sunday when he made his usual call to sinners, in spite of feeling more than a bit foolish, I stood and walked down the aisle.

The Reverend was prepared. Once I started walking, he took charge of the show. He explained to the congregation, on my behalf, that I had been too young that first time. I hadn't really "seen the light and been saved." But now I was older. This time was different. This time, I truly believed. A baptism—to be held in a few weeks—would honor what was now a "true" conversion.

HE DIDN'T KNOW IT YET, but the Reverend made a serious tactical error by not talking with Mom first. Milan was, and still is, a small town, and the news reached home before I did. Mom greeted me in a dangerous mood. "What's this nonsense about needing to be baptized? You have already been baptized once."

She and I spent much of that Sunday afternoon discussing the very foolishness of the idea. Of course, Mom did most of the "discussing." I remember much of it coming out as exasperated mutterings. Often, I could barely hear enough to catch what she was saying, but the upshot was clear enough—I was not going to be baptized a second time. The new Reverend got another black mark on Mom's list—recently he had been accumulating them at a rapid rate. "...Lacks the good common sense God gave him as a baby," she kept repeating. In the end, she got her way; the idea of a second baptism was never mentioned again, which was fine by me.

YEARS LATER, WELL AFTER the family had moved away from Milan, and I had moved a long way from the Baptist church, I finally worked out what I think was motivating the Reverend back then. Of course, he would have said he was "worried about my soul," but if pressed he would have also admitted that baptizing the body had little effect on the soul. Even in the Reverend's theology, baptism was basically a symbolic act. As I speculate today, the Reverend likely had a less noble motive, though I doubt he was sufficiently self-aware to realize it.

During the time I spent with him, one important truth became clear: Reverend Jackson was focused on selling the Gospel. He poured all his passion into trying to sell Christ to non-believers, and sales had been painfully slow when he proposed that I be baptized a second time. Rural Missouri was, and still is, a saturated market for Christ. By baptizing me he surely was thinking he would gain credit in his private accounting as a "fisherman of men for Christ."

IT IS ONLY NOW, late in life, that I have come to understand the lasting effect of the Reverend's manipulation of my childhood gullibility. It is no doubt a principal reason—there may well be others—I defend myself so strongly against the influence of authority and status. I listen, but if I cannot work out a thing in my own mind, I do not believe it. And I have too often bluntly said so, while overlooking the possibility that, by plainly speaking the truth as I see it, I sometimes offend others and appear to be dismissive of their opinions. It may be the adult's attempt to atone for the child who failed to say, "But the emperor has no clothes."

19

Dining on Squirrel

THERE WAS A TIME and place not so long ago when responsible parents let their children spend whole afternoons seeking adventure in the countryside. But times have changed, and I feel obligated to warn the reader: The following is about four young boys searching for adventure on their own in the woods, dismembering a squirrel and playing with knives, guns, water, and fire. No one suffered damage except the squirrel.

THAT LATE SUMMER AFTERNOON four of us—Billy, Tom, George and I—happened to gather at the bottom of the hill on Fourth Street where there is a small creek. The creek began a couple of blocks north between First and Second, and ran under Fourth before continuing south, quickly disappearing into the woods as it left Milan and headed for the Missouri River. Further down, the creek may have had a name, but up so near to its beginning, we boys just referred to it as "the creek at the bottom of Fourth Street."

Facing a whole afternoon of utter boredom, we decided it would be a great adventure to follow the creek and learn where it went. So the five of us set off—I forgot to mention that Billy's dog, Rascal, was with us.

We had gone just far enough to feel well beyond Fourth Street and civilization when we saw a tree had fallen across the creek. This sight prompted an immediate urge to be on the other side and, hence, prompted some discussion about Rascal: Should we carry him across or let him "swim for it"? He was Billy's dog, and Billy decided to let him swim. So the four of us crossed while holding on to the now upright branches of the fallen tree. Rascal chose a shallow spot about ten yards upstream and waded across, pausing to get a drink and hardly getting his paws wet. In fact, in most places the creek was very shallow.

After the crossing we felt ourselves very much in wild, unexplored territory—though if we had climbed out of the creek bottom, we would surely have seen roads, plowed fields and perhaps a farm house or two. As we rambled along, Rascal ran ahead, enjoying the adventure as much as we boys.

We hadn't gone far when we heard Rascal barking frantically. As we drew near, we saw he had treed a squirrel.

Now, a dog treeing a squirrel is hardly remarkable. The Missouri countryside had dogs and squirrels aplenty, and, though I have yet to see a dog *actually catch* a squirrel, the high failure rate never seems to be much of a deterrent to any dog I have known. Dogs are forever chasing squirrels and barking fiercely when they fail to catch their prey.

Thinking of ourselves as first explorers in uncharted territory, we marveled at the squirrel as if we had never seen one before. Pausing under the tree we looked up at the squirrel and studied the situation. For its part, the squirrel looked down at us, no doubt curious and perhaps amused at the sight of a frustrated, yapping dog and four rather small human beings.

In keeping with the spirit of the expedition, Tom speculated aloud that, if we had a bow and arrow, we could shoot and eat the squirrel. This was a capital idea and led to a discussion about the possibility of cutting down a sapling and fashioning a bow and arrow. We all carried Barlow pocket knives that would have done a credible job on any of the nearby saplings. But after some discussion, we decided that shaping a bow and arrow would be for naught. We had no feathers, and we all knew that an arrow, like a bird, could not fly without feathers. That thought doomed this particular track of thinking, which only led to another.

If we had only thought to bring our BB guns, we could have shot the squirrel. But then we agreed that a BB gun could do no lasting harm to a squirrel. However, this talk about how things might have been different prompted George, who at fourteen was the oldest in the group, to volunteer to walk back and bring his .22 from home. We all agreed this was a capital idea, and George set off directly.

Now, we knew that we'd have to honor the woodsman's code and eat whatever game we shot. But none of us had ever cooked squirrel, or cooked much of anything else for that matter. Being young boys, the closest we had ever come to preparing our own vittles was to pour milk over Cheerios at breakfast. I was perhaps an exception. Once, I had actually mixed flour, sugar and butter together to bake cookies, but that was under Mom's supervision, and with her guidance. Undeterred by our lack of experience, or perhaps undeterred *because* of our lack of experience, we all quickly agreed that it couldn't be that hard.

We needed a fire, and we wisely chose a sandbar that extended into the creek. Using my heel I kicked out a shallow hole to serve as a firepit while Tom gathered dry leaves and twigs. This done, we chose two "Y" shaped branches and pushed them upright in the sand. They would support a straight stick that would serve as a spit. Billy, who had been known to sneak cigarettes from his dad, had a book of matches which served to start the fire. By the time George returned with his .22, we were ready.

All this time the squirrel had been most cooperative. Oh, he had scampered about from limb to limb while watching us plot his demise, but he had not leapt from tree to tree and disappeared into another part of the woods, nor had he climbed higher, either of which he might have easily done. In fact, he had hardly left the low branch where we first saw him.

George did the shooting; after all, it was his gun. Because the squirrel was less than ten feet away, George had to try only once before the squirrel dropped to our feet—bullseye right through the head. Each of us was keenly interested in getting a close-up view of the dead squirrel, but Rascal was a little too keen, and Billy had to grab him by the collar and pull him away. Figuring that the dog would be nothing but trouble during this next part. Billy took Rascal for a long walk further down the creek.

The fact that all four of us were "town boys" rather than "country boys" wasn't much of a distinction in this part of the state. At minimum, three-quarters of our cousins, aunts, uncles and friends lived on farms—farms that grew animals for the dinner table. If we hadn't done the work on our own, we had all helped with the slaughter and dressing of animals.

It was without hesitation that we made short work of that squirrel. We hung the skin over a tree branch—someone might want to make a squirrel skin hat—and we dug a hole in the sand to bury the entrails. In no time, we had the carcass on a stick turning slowly over a fire. A fire that was now burning quite nicely, and, shortly, Billy returned with Rascal.

Now, the next part was particularly hard on the four of us. Waiting for the squirrel to cook was excruciating! It took all the patience we could muster. Finally, after each of us had taken his place at turning the spit, and after repeatedly asking, "Ya think it's done yet?" we decided that it was surely cooked enough. Each of us cut off a leg as our portion and retired to nearby logs to eat our dinner.

All it took was that first bite to utterly vanquish my spirit of adventure and exploration. I can't recall ever, before or since, biting into anything that was so dry, tough, stringy and tasteless. Never have I more appreciated salt, seasoning, and Mom's good cooking as much as I did with that first bite of squirrel leg. Out of the corner of my eye, I saw Billy slyly slip his portion to Rascal. I furtively dropped mine to the ground behind me. I didn't see what Tom and

George did with their portions, but nobody went back for seconds, though there was still meat on the carcass.

Hardly a word was spoken among the four of us as we kicked sand over what was left of the fire and quietly headed back the way we had come. Though we were not exactly depressed, our high spirit of adventure and exploration had completely vanished. We left the skin on its tree branch, forgotten.

I had overheard Mom talking on the phone that morning, as she said that she was going to cook meatloaf and potatoes for dinner. It was probably in the oven right now. Never has the anticipation of such ordinary fare tugged at a young boy's stomach so fiercely. On our way back, all five of us quickened our pace a bit.

I NEVER AGAIN TRIED TO EAT SQUIRREL. However, a few winters later, after the family had moved to Illinois, we were back in Milan visiting friends and my Aunt Reva and Uncle Ike. While there, my cousin David and I went hunting for rabbits. In a single day on my Uncle Ike's snow-covered farm, we bagged twenty-three wild rabbits. After we dressed them, Aunt Reva cooked and served them with a savory sauce. They were delicious!

I have heard it often said often "farm boys make the best soldiers." It has always made sense to me. Not only are boys who grow up on farms used to living close to the land and working in dirt, many are also familiar with killing living creatures as a way of life. In that part of Missouri many a youngster has had the experience of becoming fond of a particular new-born calf, pig, goat, duck or other farm animal. The youngster often gives it a name, say "Betsy," and treats it like a pet. Then after months of personally watching over, nurturing and caring for the animal, there comes the hard day when Betsy is served for dinner.

So many of us now live in cities that it is easy to overlook the fact that the sanitary, plastic-wrapped meat we buy at the grocery was once a living creature much like ourselves. Although it was not the custom of my childhood, nor is it my custom today, I can understand why some, who are keenly aware of this reality, choose to be vegetarians.

20

Learning to Hunt Quail

IT WAS JUST BEFORE DAWN and I was sweating as I struggled to reach the buckles on my rubber overshoes. At twelve, I was supple enough that the task should have been easy, but Mom had insisted that I dress warmly and that meant starting with two pairs of thick socks, a full-bodied "union suit" of underwear, and finishing with boots, a winter coat, gloves, a warm hat with built-in earmuffs, and a wool scarf, not to mention the layers in between. I wasn't wrapped quite as tightly as a mummy, but it sure felt like it.

When I finally stepped from the warm kitchen, the cold December air was refreshing, but I knew the feeling wouldn't last long. It was not yet light, and the morning had a bone-chilling dampness to it. The waterlogged, six-inch snow that had fallen during the night melted under my boots as I crossed the yard.

Dad was coming from the barn with Queenie, his "$100 dog" as Mom called her, referring to the price Dad had negotiated with a local Missouri farmer. The dog sensed we were going hunting, and she pranced and circled Dad as he moved toward the pickup. That dog did love to hunt, and she was good at it.

***

I NEED TO TAKE just a minute here to set the matter straight. Most dogs in Milan, Missouri, were free if one was willing to provide the vittles. It did happen on rare occasions that someone might pay $5 or $10, but only if the dog was special in some way. Though she was a mutt of uncertain pedigree, Queenie, with her short white hair and patches of brown, looked and acted like the real thing. And Dad had not exactly paid $100 for her, a princely sum in those days. (Think $1500 in today's dollars.) The dollar amount was just

Mom's way of complaining about Dad's wintertime hobby. $100 was high enough to impress the neighbors and friends as a serious expense, and yet it was low enough that Dad would not challenge the claim.

The real cost of the dog was never determined. Dad was an excavator and had taken the dog in trade for a small earth moving job he had done for a farmer. The reason for the trade depended on who was telling the story: The farmer said he could not pay until next fall's harvest, at least ten months in the future. Mom bought this version. Dad claimed the farmer would never pay, and the dog was the best he could make of a bad debt. And so, the issue remained open, providing an entertaining sideshow that played well at private gatherings of friends and relatives.

⟫•⟪

DAD YELLED FOR ME to bring the broom he had left on the porch, and I swept the snow off the truck. Dad tied Queenie in the back; and we climbed into the cold cab. I held Dad's Remington between my knees, carefully pointing straight upward as I had been taught. It was not so much that an unloaded gun was regarded as dangerous, but it was considered downright rude to let a gun wander in the direction of another person, loaded or empty. I was considered too young to have a real gun. My role in the hunt was to help flush the game.

Dad started his skillful routine for a cold start of the pickup. He knew just how much choke to apply and how many times to pump the accelerator. Still, the pickup was a Ford and had to be started twice before we were off. It took only a minute to cross the small country town to Pete's house.

Pete was a tall, young, happy fellow who ran a small lunch counter with his wife. I didn't think about it at the time, but he must have promised her he'd be back in time to help with the lunch crowd, which is why we were leaving so early. As we pulled up in front of Pete's place, he and his dog, Red, were waiting for us. Red, so named for his reddish-brown coat, was some kind of large, long-haired dog. He, too, was a mutt, but he somewhat resembled an Irish Setter—and he was young.

As Dad and I waited in the cab, Pete handed me his double-barreled Browning and went to the back to lower the tailgate and let Red jump up with Queenie. All this took more time than expected. The two dogs had never met and, quite aside from the usual formal sniffing ritual that dogs go through by way of politely shaking hands, there was an immediate personality clash. Red was a good-natured, exuberant youngster with oatmeal for brains. He wanted to play and be friends with the world and everything in it: people and other dogs for sure, but also such things as fence posts, guns, and truck tires. Queenie was quiet, mature, reserved, and professional. She was all business, especially on a hunt. And she was not at all sure she wanted to share this hunt with a boisterous, ill-mannered pup. After much shouting from Pete and some low growls from Queenie, who backed up her displeasure with a few snaps, a truce was established: Red took the back half of the open cargo area while Queenie settled in the front near the cab.

IT WAS JUST TURNING light as we left town, though the gray sky was to be with us all day. The wet asphalt roadway cut a sharp, black path through a countryside whose blemishes were covered with snow and thereby made kind of pretty. Soon Dad slowed and turned off the hard road onto an easterly gravel road (really more of a dirt road as there was precious little gravel on it). The pickup settled into tracking the two muddy ruts plowed by previous traffic.

Not long after the turnoff, the road led us to the top of a ridge and started us down the other side. From our elevated position we could see the road led over a small creek at the bottom and headed straight up to the top of another ridge. As we moved along, Dad pointed out an open field on the far hillside where we were to hunt.

The sloping field was bounded by the creek at the bottom and a crossing road at the top. The sloping sides were marked by the road we were traveling and an opposing stand of trees.

After taking the wooden bridge over the creek, we climbed the far ridge, joined the crossroad where we turned left and drove past the field we were to hunt and the woods beyond to the Hartmeyer place. Since Ollie Hartmeyer owned the land, it was appropriate to pay a courtesy call before he heard gunfire and felt obligated to investigate. Of course, Dad had made arrangements with Ollie earlier in the week, but still, we took a minute to let him know what we were doing.

The stop took but a minute, and soon we were turned around, back at the high side of the field and stopping the pickup on the side of the road. We let the dogs down from the back. Dad put his foot on the middle strand of the barbwire fence, pushing it down while lifting the top strand. The dogs jumped through the opening, and Pete and I followed. I then held the wires for Dad, and we arranged ourselves in a straight line and loaded the shotguns as we prepared to move down the hill, sweeping the field. I was in the middle with Dad on my right, near the trees, and Pete on my left near the road. Queenie and Red were in front, already sniffing the ground.

THINGS DIDN'T GET OFF to a very good start. After only a few paces, Queenie smelt something and froze on point. As Dad tried to move closer to what he thought were quail, a rabbit sprang from hiding and bounded across the field. Queenie wanted to chase it but Dad called to her to stop and gave her a scolding. It wouldn't happen again, she understood. We were hunting quail, not rabbit.

We reformed our line and hadn't gone but five yards when Red scared up another rabbit and went bounding after it. Pete shouted for the dog to stop, but there was no hope for it; the dog was having the time of his life as the rabbit darted this way and that across the field. Exasperated, Pete raised his gun and placed a well-aimed shot closer to the dog than the rabbit. Kicking up dirty snow in front of Red's nose, the shot brought the dog to an abrupt halt and refocused his attention.

As it happened, the shot also scared up a small covey of quail, most of which flew across the field, allowing Dad to get one. A single bird from the covey, perhaps confusing the dog as the danger, flew directly toward Pete. Pete raised his gun and as the bird passed overhead, he fired. Fortunately, he missed—if he had hit the bird at such close range, it would have disintegrated into pieces. However, as Pete raised his gun higher and higher to track the bird, he became unbalanced and the gun's recoil pushed him backward. He fell flat in the snow. Red, thinking this was a game like they played at home on the couch, bounded over and landed on top of Pete as he was trying to rise.

This halted the hunt. Dad, Queenie, and I held our places while Pete struggled to get the dog off his chest and rise. It was with much shouting and cursing that Pete tried to come to a new understanding with Red about the serious business of quail hunting: About *rabbits*—they were to be ignored. *Quail*—they were what Red was supposed to smell and find, and then, *holding a point*, wait until Pete could get within range. At one juncture Pete declared to the dog that even he could smell the difference between rabbit and quail!

Being a little overly excited, Pete imparted this information to Red in loud angry bursts as he tried to ward off the dog and rise from the ground. Even with considerable arm waving by way of illustration, and a fair bit of cursing for emphasis, it was clear that Red didn't understand what led to this outburst. Oh, he was contrite enough. He knew he had done something wrong, but he didn't seem to know what it was.

After Pete had regained his feet, Dad called Red to him and let him smell the bird he had shot. This seemed to help, and we again started marching the line forward. Still contrite, Red paid closer attention to Pete's shouted commands, but he was clearly confused about what they meant. He continued to point rabbits, but he stopped chasing them when Pete called to him.

By contrast, Queenie was showing herself to be the experienced professional she was. She had set a crisscross pattern, gracefully trotting back and forth in front of Dad, never getting too far out ahead. Although she did once point a rabbit, she did not chase it, and when she pointed a covey, she held that point long enough for Dad, and even Pete, to move within firing range. Unfortunately, it once happened that Queenie's long point made Red curious and gave him time to join her. Of course, his extra presence flushed the birds early, much to Pete's displeasure.

As we marched across the field, we flushed up three or four more coveys and several single birds. Gradually as the hunt progressed, the "newness" of the experience that had fed Red's excitement wore off. He began to pay attention to Queenie, who seemed to be doing everything right. Dad and Pete bagged nearly a dozen birds between them, mostly after Red had burned off his youthful energy and settled down.

We still had a bit to go before reaching the creek at the end of the field, when Dad turned to me and said, "Why don't ya go get the pickup and bring it around? We'll meet you at the bridge."

"Sure," I said and turned to head back up the way we had come. As I trudged uphill toward the pickup I heard a few more shots, but no more shouting. Red was learning his job.

The first time I tried to start the truck, I let out the clutch but forgot to give it gas. But with a lurch, it started down the hill in first gear, and I was soon at the bottom of the hill near the bridge. I waited for Dad, Pete, and the dogs to finish the hunt; then we all arranged ourselves in the pickup for the trip back to town. On the way back Dad and Pete talked about the hunt. They had gotten several more birds after I left them, and they were in good spirits, though Pete kept complaining about Red.

He, Pete, kept saying that he would have to spend some serious time trying to train that dog. But in my mind, Queenie's professional demeanor and skill had highlighted each of Red's faults, making him appear worse than he really was. He only needed more experience—and, perhaps some age would help as well.

It was approaching 11:00 a.m. as we dropped Pete and Red at their house. We then headed home to feed Queenie and have our own lunch. And after lunch, we cleaned the birds.

THE FOLLOWING SUNDAY, Pete and his wife came over for a dinner of baked quail. The men retold the story of the hunt, including Red's chasing the rabbit and Pete's mishap. And when Pete praised Queenie, Mom made the most of her opportunity to complain about that "$100 dog." Mom had cooked quail before, and it was delicious, as long as one was careful about biting down hard on the occasional buckshot; but for me the highlight of the meal was her apple pie, which I had been smelling all afternoon.

21

Witnessin' for the Lord

PART I
Witnessing

IT WAS A COLD, DAMP MARCH morning—overcast to boot. There were only six of us standing in a ragtag line, different heights and different grade levels from fifth grade to a high school junior. I was in sixth grade that year. We were barely willing, but we were finally ready, as we arranged ourselves on the cinder alleyway beside the school. We boys wore blue jeans; the girls wore simple, plain dresses, though nothing much showed beneath our winter coats, scarves and stocking caps. Our schoolbooks, temporarily forgotten, lay beside us on patches of ground that were clear of snow. That morning, we were there for more serious business.

Sullivan County Consolidated Schools served both the small town of Milan (pop. 1987) as well as much of the surrounding countryside. The building itself, built during the '30s, was three stories of red brick set atop a modest hill with a large expanse of sloping lawn running down to the street. The high school occupied the top floor, grades one through eight were on the first and second floors. We knew by name each of the kids who stepped off the bus that morning; some were good friends, but there were no glances of friendly greeting. Heads down, they headed straight for the side door.

As the buses arrived, we looked at each other and began to sing. After a rousing stanza of "Onward, Christian Soldiers" to shore up our courage, we took turns reading Bible verses. "For God so loved the world, He gave His only begotten Son...." Then, tall, leggy Jane Gistby, the high school junior, the oldest in the group, and consummate "good girl," gave a testimonial to the power of

Jesus in her life: "The other day in the Rexall drugstore the devil tempted me to steal a Butterfinger candy bar. It would have been *so* easy. But I felt Jesus come into my heart, and I put it back...." Then we prayed: "God, help those who have lost their way, help them to see the light and be saved..." We prayed loudly, so others could hear us. We were there to save their poor wayward souls, and we wanted to make sure they knew it.

After the testifying and praying, and more than ready to be done with it all, we closed with a thin, weak version of "The Old Rugged Cross." Difficult though it was, I tried to hold to the earnest passion pressed on us Sunday evening by the Reverend James Jackson when he spoke of our duty to "witness for the Lord."

PART II
Testimonials & Marshalling the Troops

THE PREVIOUS SUNDAY night—after morning Sunday school, after morning church, after evening church school, after evening church—after all that Sunday worshiping, the kids had a get-together in the parsonage until ten o'clock. (The Baptists like to get full use of their buildings.) Fifteen of us crowded into the Reverend's too-small, overheated living room on that chilly Sunday night. We each took turns testifying about how the devil had tempted us during the week, and how we had relied on Jesus to help us overcome the temptation.

Now, for those who might not know about Baptist testimonials, they are sort of like Catholic confessionals, but without the privacy part in the middle and the forgiveness part at the end. During my time in the Reverend Jackson's parlor, I had become a master at testimonials. The heart of the trick is to choose your sin carefully. It must bad enough to reveal you as normal, but not so bad as to attract gossip and get you ostracized by the congregation.

For example, among us kids it was okay, perhaps even noble, to stand and say, "The devil came into my heart this week when

I got angry with my little sister. She broke my airplane. I'd been a-buildin' that model for three weeks, but I shouldn've set to yellin' at 'er like I did. She's only six."

However, by the age of twelve I knew it was definitely *not* okay to say, "I lusted in my heart when I saw Susan Winfield's magnificent heaving breasts durin' last Wednesday's choir practice."

Now, as everybody knows, lust is a major preoccupation for right close to one hundred per cent of the adolescent male population—and for a good number of us older males as well. However, although lust is a mighty temptation and as common as grass, that doesn't make it an okay testimonial on much of any occasion.

I was lucky to learn this testifyin' business so early in life. Just how lucky became apparent when a fellow Baptist, Jimmy Carter, even as a grown man about to enter the White House, revealed he hadn't figured it out. Lusting in his heart and then talking about it to *Playboy* magazine brought him a peck-full of trouble.

WELL, NONE OF US MENTIONED lust that Sunday evening. Instead, we listened to the Reverend as he spoke quietly and passionately about how people in that very town were headed to hell because "they had not taken Jesus as their personal Savior and been baptized." This part was not new; we had heard it many times before. And we had heard the next part, too: It was our duty to save as many lost souls as we could before it was too late, and they went straight to hell. Oh yes, we were well tutored in God's overall plan.

What the Reverend slipped in that night that was new, and what made every one of us start to sweat—it wasn't just the closeness of the crowded room—were the *particulars* of our duty. I tasted salt forming on my upper lip as the Reverend got particular about us praying, singing hymns, and quoting and reading the Bible aloud on the cinder path the following Wednesday, at eight in the morning as the other kids arrived on the school buses. Now, it doesn't get much more particular than that. When he added that we'd be a-goin' to do it every Wednesday morning till the end of the school year, my body began to sway like tall prairie grass. It was going to be a long stretch of Wednesdays.

The Reverend never explained why he chose Wednesdays as the day for us to "take a stand for Christ," and we never asked. I just figured that coming as it did, smack dab in the middle of the week, Wednesday was an otherwise slow day for religion. Whatever the reason, it was the Reverend's conviction that we could convert the lost souls of our classmates by making a public stand of our love for Jesus. Of course, such a stand also would have the effect of showing that we thought others didn't, but should, have that same love for Jesus. Being the good Baptist that he was, the Reverend never gave a moment's thought to the possibility that blaming people might make them defensive and drive them away rather than bring them into his church.

Some of the weaker spirits in the group—or maybe they were just the more clever, smarter ones—found reasons why they could not join such an early morning "save-a-soul-for-Christ" demonstration. Jim Livingstone mentioned that he lived way out in the country and rode the bus. "It don't get here till just before school's a-startin' and it's mostly late." Mary Becker and Susan Meyers declared that their mothers wouldn't let them out of the house so early, *especially* on Wednesdays. Jim Smith remembered that he was coming down with a cold and shouldn't be outside so much with the cold weather.

After many excuses were made and accepted, there was still a small band of us who agreed to gather, Bibles in hand, at 7:55 a.m. on the porch of the same house we were in that evening. We would then go as a group up the hill to be near the school's side door where the buses let out. Since I had not been able to think of a plausible excuse that Sunday night (not for want of trying), and while I was with those other kids, agreeing to the Reverend's plan seemed like the only way out of a high-pressure situation. Although many were ducking his plan, nobody was really objecting to it outright. He was the adult in the room, and he was a Reverend. During the fifties, even children had an obligation to *do the right thing*. I especially had trouble resisting the Reverend. Mom had not raised me to be a shirker, and this was being presented as serious business—more serious than life and death itself. Did I actually want my classmates to wind up in *eternal* hell? I did not!

PART III
Mom & the Reverend

AS IS TYPICAL, it did not stay Sunday all week long. Wednesday morning I awoke wishing that I had been one of those country kids who rode the bus, or that I had a cold coming on, or pneumonia, or arthritis, or a broken leg, or whatever it took to stay home that one day. But I'd been raised to believe that *a promise made is a promise kept.* So I grabbed my zip-up Bible, the one with my name in gold letters on the front given to me by my Aunt Esta. I slipped it in among my school books and papers, and, while my sisters were still eating breakfast, I headed for the door. Mom noticed that I was leaving early, but she didn't know about the Bible, and she certainly didn't know about the plan for the morning or my role in it.

It's not that my mother wasn't a "good Christian woman." At least, that's what she always claimed. It's just that she watched me pretty closely, and she worried about Reverend Jackson "going off the deep end," and me following right behind. In her eyes a *little* religion was a good thing—a lot was not. She had been the one who'd insisted—Dad didn't care—that I start going to Sunday school when I was in the second grade. "A well brought up gentleman should have a little religion," was the way she put it. What bothered her about Reverend Jackson was the all-consuming intensity of his love for Jesus. That, and her belief that he didn't have "the-good-common-sense-God-gave-him-as-a-baby." She was afraid that his foolishness might rub off on me, and above all things, Ma Knifong was dead set against raising fools.

IN HIS MID-THIRTIES, the Reverend Jackson was a tall, slender, pale-faced man who never seemed to get enough sun. He had recently been called to lead the First Baptist Church of Milan. The previous minister, Reverend William Jones, couldn't have been more different. He'd been a short, heavy-set, easy-going fellow, who had grown old and retired. The young Reverend, fervent and ambitious, preached a powerful hellfire and brimstone sermon. And, from what I could tell, hellfire and brimstone went over well with the congregation—as long as sin was attacked as a general evil and the Reverend didn't get too close to home with the particulars.

As an adult, I recall the Reverend freely attacking the "godless Catholics" as a general matter of principle, but then I don't remember many Catholics in town. Or maybe they were just more quiet about their beliefs. He even got particular and faulted them for drinking wine during communion—we righteous Baptists drank Welch's grape juice. In fact, wine drinking was a rare-to-non-existent habit among the locals. In that part of Missouri, the alcoholic drink of choice was beer, and on this topic he treaded lightly. He rarely preached against an occasional beer, nor did he ever mention tobacco, though chewing and/or smoking were nearly universal among the males in his congregation, and more than once he confided to me privately that he saw both tobacco and beer as the "devil's tools." "Don't ever touch 'em," he advised.

Preaching about "helping lost souls see the light and find their way" was always popular and safe. Since each member of the congregation was satisfied that they themselves were saved, it had the benefit of focusing on the sins of others, which always went over well. The Reverend spent a good deal of time on the topic. In fact, Reverend Jackson was so focused on soul saving that I suppose if God had given him an annual *Job Performance Evaluation Form* to complete, the Reverend would have had eyes only for the one box that read: "During the last year, how many souls did you baptize for Jesus?"

He was well aware that other pastors, when summarizing their annual achievements, would pad their evaluations. He once explained to me that some even counted efforts such as comforting the sick, giving to the poor, and so forth. Not the Reverend Jackson! If others wanted to run their ministries by providing service, so be it. The Reverend concentrated on sales. I suppose he figured that once a body had been saved, that body could get more comfort from the Lord than from the Reverend—which, now that I think on it, might well have been the case.

PART IV
Wednesday Morning

THE EARLY WALK to school that Wednesday was the good part of the morning; and the meeting at the Reverend's house directly in front of the school was okay. He was in good spirits to see more than one or two of us show up. He spoke briefly about the importance of what we were about to do, and started us toward our appointed site. Halfway up I glanced back and saw him as we had left him—standing

We stood on the hill where the car is parked and where the buses let out.
There is a side entrance just out of sight.

138

on his front porch in his long black coat watching us trudge up the hill. It struck me that he looked the part of a general who might be sending his troops to battle—while staying safely back from the fray.

I gained some comfort from the meager group, but as we crested the top of the hill, our task slipped out of the realm of the abstract and into vivid reality. I began to get sick to my stomach. The ordeal I'd been dreading was at hand, and we had to go through with it; we had to witness for the Lord.

There followed twenty-five minutes of hymn singing, praying, and Bible-reading *agony*. My stomach churned, my palms were sweaty, my head ached and my knees wobbled. The cold made me want to pee so badly, I thought I'd wet my pants right there in front of everyone. For sheer pain, the event ranked up there with having my teeth drilled on with an old-fashioned pedal-operated drill and without Novocain—except the drilling happened on a Saturday morning, in the privacy of a dentist's office, and I was allowed to cry.

At 8:25, it was suddenly over. The six of us, stiff from standing so long in the cold, gathered up our things and headed inside for warmth and the chance to blend with other regular students. Incredibly, mercifully, no one ever said a word to me about the event—not the kids, not the teachers, not on that day nor any other. It might have been they worried that, given half a chance, I'd start preaching at them about their sins. I, too, never mentioned it. Instead, I went straight to my seat, hid my Bible deep inside my desk, opened a school book and started to read. I had had enough embarrassment to last a lifetime. Even to a seriously religious boy in 1953 Bible-belt country, having a Bible in my desk *felt* wrong. It just didn't belong among the English, math, history, science and social studies books.

PART V
Speculation on the Quiet Aftermath

WELL, WE DIDN'T do that again. I don't know whether the Reverend feared he'd never get us kids to agree to a second performance, or whether he just realized that in the economics of soul saving, there was not going to be much return on that investment.

As a kid I didn't wonder why. I just kept my head down and prayed that nothing concerning the event would ever surface. As an adult, I've come to wonder at the quiet, but abrupt, ending to our effort to save souls—even the Reverend never mentioned it.

Although I will never know, I have pondered on how it could have ended so abruptly and so quietly. The Reverend had clearly said he planned for the witnessing to continue until the end of school. I *think* —but I don't know—that some adult must have complained to the Reverend, and I *think* I know who it might have been.

JACK OGLESBY, Superintendent for Sullivan County Consolidated Schools, was a short, wiry man who had an office on the second floor of the school. He surely watched our Wednesday morning performance, as did most of the teachers and staff. I did not know him well, but from what little I remember about him, I doubt he liked what he saw. He must have regarded our demonstration as less about saving souls and more about interference by the Baptist minister in public education—Mr. Oglesby's domain.

The phone call from a man used to being obeyed would have been brief, frank, and direct: "Reverend Jackson, I don't think it's a good idea.... Yes, I understand that you see this as in praise of God, but others may well see it as in praise of your church.... Well, we may have to agree to disagree on that point.... Just understand this: I won't tolerate it happening again, either on or anywhere near school property. Is that clear?"

PART VI
The Futility of It All

THINKING BACK ON IT, when the Reverend moved to Milan and chose to measure his success by how many Sullivan County souls he could save for Christ, he set a goal that was tragically impossible for him to achieve. Though many locals did not see-eye-to-eye with the Reverend on some of the finer points, each of the nearly two thousand souls in that town and each of the nine thousand souls in the surrounding countryside had already declared themselves Christian and hence considered themselves saved—there just wasn't anybody left for Reverend Jackson to save. You can't save a soul twice, and the body gets agitated if you try.

As a kid, I just wanted to go to school and fit in with the other kids. I figured that if I had to save souls, I wanted to do it in a place far from where I lived. I reasoned that saving souls in Africa would be a much better experience. For one thing, they hadn't heard of Christ which should make it easier—being virgin territory and all.

Of course, there was more to it than that, or I would never have stood on that hill. At the time, the logic seemed simple and compelling. The preacher preached, and I believed: Hell is the greatest disaster; Heaven is the greatest salvation; there's the Lord's work to do; it's our duty to do it; and nothing else matters. That was what was right; and Ma raised me to do the right thing—at least when I was being watched.

MY FAMILY MOVED away from Milan in '55. The years passed without the Reverend's influence, I grew older, and my thinking came to take in more of the outside world. Gradually, I came to appreciate how the Reverend's simple formulation of our Christian duty glossed over some finer points that might have encouraged me to be more tolerant of others' beliefs. For example, how come the Baptists have such better insight into God's plan than do all the rest of the Christians? From what I have known of them, Baptists were not smarter or holier than other Christians, just louder in their self-centered declaration that they are going to Heaven and others are not. For a second example: If God has infinite love and compassion for mankind, how come the Baptists believe he punishes good-hearted, thoughtful people just because they don't agree to declare their faith publicly and be baptized with a good dunking? Why would God care?

PART VII
Sancho's Role

BACK IN 1953 neither Reverend Jackson nor I spent much time pondering such difficult questions. We just got on with the Lord's work. When I was out of school that summer, I often rode with the Reverend as he roamed over Sullivan County "a-house-callin'," looking for souls to save. It never occurred to me, and certainly not to the Reverend, that we were trying to convert farmers who already regarded themselves as saved, whether they attended the Baptist church or not. If he'd been asked, I suppose he would have reasoned that most of the citizens in Sullivan County were lost souls who often hid the darkness in their hearts by joining some other church, such as the Methodists. (The Methodists, among others, were suspected of admitting such people to their congregation—no questions asked.)

Although I rode beside him, I was not a very good "Sancho Panza" for the Reverend. Aside from providing companionship, the ever-practical Sancho tried to soften Don Quixote's more bruising encounters with reality, as when he tried to convince the Don that the "giants" the knight had chosen as jousting opponents were only inanimate windmills. Being so young, I provided no such check on the Reverend's detachment from reality. Instead, just as my mother feared, I was ready to follow the Reverend wherever his folly led.

142

AS I GREW INTO ADULTHOOD, my views on saving souls tempered considerably, but I have often wondered what became of the Reverend Jackson and his quixotic soul-saving mission in the rural Missouri town where I was born. I'd like to sit down with him and chat about how he now remembers those times and what he did after I left town. Did he eventually come to see his mission as the hopeless folly that I now believe it to have been? Did he become an African missionary, spreading the Word to those who had not heard, or did he continue trying to save the souls of those who didn't attend the Baptist Church but who, nevertheless, already considered themselves Christian and hence already saved?

22

"Slow down, Jimmy. Slow down!"

IT WAS SUMMERTIME. I had relaxed into a daily routine that no longer included sitting for hours in Mr. Sayers' sixth grade classroom. I had also relaxed into not hurrying to breakfast. It was hard to be enthusiastic about getting up when Mom always seemed to fill the morning with house-cleaning chores.

On this particular morning when I came into the kitchen, Jane and Becky, my two younger sisters, were already at the table and nearly finished. As usual Mom was working at the kitchen sink. I dumped Cheerios from the big yellow box, spooned sugar over them, poured milk into the bowl and sat down to eat.

"Hurry up and eat your breakfast. We're gonna go berry picking this morning, and I want to get to it before the sun gets too high," Mom announced.

Mostly out of habit, and with no real hope of success, I objected, "Awwhhh....Do I hafta go?"

"Yes, you do. I'm not leaving you here by yourself, and that's the end of it."

Then after a bit she added, "You'll be just as happy as the rest of us to eat those berries, so, you can be just as happy as the rest of us to pick them.... Besides if we find enough of 'em, I plan to make a couple of pies. Now finish your breakfast, I need you to help get things ready."

I conceded to myself that pie was a decent reward for a morning spent picking berries. Besides, exploring creek banks, fence rows and abandoned farms was sometimes interesting. And, while picking, I could eat as many of the wild strawberries, blackberries, raspberries and gooseberries as I liked. Though I didn't really care much for gooseberries—too tart. Still, they made a good pie.

All in all, it definitely looked like a better way to spend a morning than doing the house-cleaning chores I usually had to deal with and which I hated.

I was surprised when, after a pause, Mom continued, "Besides, *if*—and that's a mighty big '*if*'—you behave yourself, and *if* the roads are not too bad, and *if* there isn't any traffic—now mind you this isn't a promise—I thought *maybe* you might practice driving the Chrysler. Not the whole way, and you've got to do exactly as I say, but *maybe* you could drive for part of the way."

Wow! My whole outlook changed in a heartbeat. I could now see berry-picking as my favorite way to spend a morning.

This was a stunning offer from Mom. Just a few months earlier, she and Dad had fought over his minimum-supervision, hands-off approach to teaching me how to drive. Unfortunately, Mom had been right in that I needed supervision, but at the time Dad had won the argument. At least, he had been winning until it cost him a dented fender. When that happened, I figured my driving career was over, at least for the foreseeable future. I guess Mom, who had once been a school teacher, figured that she knew more than Dad about teaching.

With the prospect of driving so close at hand, I developed a real enthusiasm for helping with the preparations. I even washed the dishes while Mom made sandwiches for our lunch. Then, as she got my sisters ready to go, I went to the basement and to the barn, rounding up an assortment of buckets, cans and pans for the berries. After they were assembled on the back porch and all was ready, I helped load the car.

WITH MOM AT THE WHEEL, my sisters in the back, and me in the front passenger seat, we headed across town. Soon we were in the country on a dirt road that climbed a ridge and then ran along its top past the Foster farm where my Uncle Bud lived. Mom had been born on that farm (and so had I). She had known this hilly

Missouri countryside all her life, and she had a pretty good notion of which creek banks and abandoned lanes were likely to have a good crop of wild berries.

Once beyond the farm, but still on top of the ridge and out of sight of anyone who might notice, Mom stopped the car. Eager, I opened the door and was nearly out of the car before Mom had shut off the engine.

"Whoa, slow down."

I stopped and turned, and waited for instructions, though I could hardly sit still.

"Now if you are going to drive, you have to calm down. This isn't a race track.... And, you have to do exactly as I say."

I knew what was expected of me. I nodded agreement and turned to look her full in the face as I said, "Uh-huh." But of course, I didn't really calm down.

"Okay, now...."

I interrupted her with, "I already know how to start the car."

"Well, may be, but there is whole lot more to driving than just starting.... This car is not like the pickup."

I gave her my full attention as I tried to look calm and serious.

Finally, Mom said, "Okay, get out and come around to this side, and do exactly as I say."

This time I moved slowly around the car and climbed in behind the steering wheel, trying my best to assume a sober, adult demeanor. Mom slid over to the passenger side of the seat.

"Now, there is the key. First, you turn it on. And then you turn the key even further, and it will start. It doesn't have a separate starter button like the pickup. But first you have to push in on the clutch. Also, here is the gear shift. It is different from the pickup. It has only two forward gears—not three. You have low up here where second should be, and you have high down here, but you don't have to move it when driving. Just put it here and leave it. You only have to let up on the gas a bit and it will shift itself. Don't touch the stick."

Mom may have been a better teacher than Dad—she was certainly more watchful and controlling—but her explanations that morning were limited—probably because she lacked a complete knowledge of the mechanics involved. As a result, her explanation had the same effect as Dad's—I understood little of what was said. Also, like Dad, Mom's tutorial had completely skipped over a couple of topics which would turn out to be important.

THOSE OLD CHRYSLERS HAD a unique and somewhat strange clutch and gear arrangement. Just before WWII, Oldsmobile had been the first—and only—car company to offer an automatic transmission. After the war, the other car companies hurried to develop their own automatic transmissions, and in its haste, Chrysler had cobbled together a hybrid arrangement. Chrysler had dubbed it "Fluid Drive," but it was often referred to as "Slush-o-matic." It lasted only a year or two.

To a driver unfamiliar with the arrangement, the car looked like it had a standard clutch/stick shift: There was a shift lever on the steering column and a clutch pedal on the floor next to the brake. Indeed, the car's clutch and transmission were rather ordinary, except for two features.

First, there was a fluid coupling between the clutch and the transmission—not a mechanical one. One might think of two identical fans set close and facing one another; if one is turned on, the blowing air will cause the blades of the other to spin as well—albeit not as fast. This made it much easier to accomplish a smooth start. Second, to be able to claim it was an "automatic shift," the Chrysler transmission was designed so that it would disengage when the rear wheels were not receiving power from the engine. This allowed the transmission to shift using a speed-sensing solenoid and oil pressure to move the gears whenever the driver let up on the gas.

The effect of this second feature was that, when the car was traveling downhill, the engine could not be used to slow down the car. Instead, when the driver let up on the gas, the car would continue its free coasting until the brakes were applied. I believe that most, if not all, modern automatic transmissions work this way—that is, unless the driver forces the transmission into low gear, the car will coast freely until brakes are applied. When driving the pickup with Dad, I had used the gas pedal to control my speed, both when the road was level and when traveling up and down the hills. I had come to think of using brakes only for stopping.

Skipping over the effects of the odd technical features of that 1950 Chrysler turned out to be a mistake—they would have been helpful to know in what followed. Instead, she took some time stressing my need to do what she said, to not go too fast, to get over to the righthand side of the road if we met another car, and to not do anything foolish. For my part, I listened as attentively as any school boy ever had.

IT WAS GETTING HOT as we sat in the car parked in the full sun. My sisters had been fussing and started to whine. Finally, Mom said, "Okay, start the engine, but go slow." I pushed the clutch in, turned the key and started the engine. No problem. I had mastered the unit on "Starting."

Expecting the worst, I gripped the wheel tightly as I released the clutch and remembered to feed the engine a little gas. To my amazement, the car began smoothly moving down the road. This was great! There was absolutely no violent jerking as there had been in the pickup.

I dutifully guided the car along the winding, dirt road at a very modest ten miles an hour. At first, Mom sat bolt upright gripping the door handle and watching me and the road intently, concerned that I might head for the ditch. But after a while, she sat back, released the door handle and just focused on the road ahead. Only then did I allow the speed to creep over ten miles an hour.

When Mom told me to "Let up on the gas," I did so, and the car shifted into high gear.

AS I DROVE THE CHRYSLER sedately along the level top of the ridge, I was pleased with myself. I had mastered "Starting" under Dad's tutelage in the pickup, and it looked like I had now mastered, or perhaps more accurately skirted around, the hard subjects of "Clutching" and "Gearing." True, I would need practice on "Steering Backward" and perhaps some other subjects as well, but "Steering Forward" was a subject I had down pat. And I thought I had mastered "Speeding Up" and "Slowing Down"—you merely gave it more or less gas. In my mind, I would need practice, but I now could claim to my buddies that I knew how to drive. Such were my thoughts as I guided the Chrysler sedately along that country road.

Unfortunately the road didn't remain on top of that ridge forever. As I was to learn, the road eventually made its way down the sloping side of the hill to bottom land. Once at the bottom, it made a full right turn, then a sharp left turn to line up on a wooden plank bridge over a small creek. The short bridge was a little higher than the road on either side and just wide enough for a single car. Once over the creek, the road crossed the flat bottom land and eventually climbed another ridge.

I wasn't aware of all this meandering before the fact, but it really wouldn't have made much difference. As we left the high ground and started our decent, all was smooth and well under control. However, as we continued downward, gravity exerted its influence, and the car began to pick up speed.

At first Mom said, "Take your foot off the gas and slow down." Obediently I eased my foot from the throttle just as I was told. Not so obediently, the car continued to gain speed. Soon things were happening very rapidly. Seeing the sharp turn ahead, Mom's next words were a high-shout, "Jimmy, slow down. Right now!"

My attention was fully concentrated on the increasing speed and the need to keep the car on the road. It was hard to listen to Mom as she repeatedly shouted, "Slow down, Jimmy!"

Finally, I shouted back, "I have my foot off the gas," and as the car leaned into the first curve, I held my right foot aloft near the dashboard so she could see it was no longer on the throttle.

We seemed to take that first turn on two wheels as the car leaned to the left. Then in the next turn, the car quickly leaned to the right which caused my foot to come down. Somehow, I lined up for the bridge, and we shot over the creek in a heartbeat.

Finally, beyond the creek and on level bottom land, gravity no longer caused the car to speed. When its momentum was spent, the car gradually slowed to a crawl.

Trying to sound calm, Mom only said, "Stop the car. That's enough for today." As it turned out, what she really meant was, *That's enough for me, forever.*

We sat for a while, both of us waiting for our hearts to slow back down to normal. My sisters, oblivious to what had happened, asked if we were there yet. Finally, Mom asked, "Why didn't you slow down?"

"I did what you told me to do. I took my foot off the gas, but the car didn't slow up."

"Why didn't you use the brake?"

"Uhhh…. I didn't think of it. I thought you only used the brake when you wanted to stop."

"Yes, you use the brake to stop, but you should also use it to slow down when you are going too fast. I thought you were going to put us in that creek back there."

"Sorry. I didn't know."

———⊰•⊱———

FOR DESSERT THAT NIGHT we all enjoyed blackberry pie. My driving experience was never mentioned. It was clear Mom had decided to cede my education in this area to Dad, regardless of any concerns she might have about his methods. It was also clear that she wanted to make this concession as quietly as possible. After all, she was only giving up in this one small area of my upbringing. She was still intent on keeping a close eye on other aspects of my development for some time to come.

23

Fire at the Chevy Dealership

MILAN'S RED BRICK FIRE BARN stood near the northwest corner of the Courthouse Square. It was really nothing but an overlarge, single-car garage with a siren on the roof. But for me, on that Missouri afternoon in 1953, the location was most fortunate. The fifty cents I had earned mowing Mrs. Dorsey's lawn was burning a hole in my pocket, and I had wandered uptown to spend some of it on a root beer float, 25 cents—and a Superman comic book, 10 cents. I still had money left over.

What made the position of the fire barn so convenient was that it was barely a half-block from the drugstore soda fountain. Stepping out on the square, I was feeling satisfied with a cool root beer on the inside and the warm sun on the outside. I was looking forward to reading my comic book and, after that, thinking some on what to do with the rest of the lazy afternoon. As it turned out, planning "what to do" with the afternoon was not a problem.

WHEN THE SIREN BEGAN WAILING, my unread comic book went in my hip pocket and I started running. Mr. Sharpway and I were the first to arrive at the fire barn. I helped him swing open the double doors and hold them with concrete blocks so that they wouldn't close. I then stood back and observed the developing commotion. I was old enough to understand what needed doing, but, other than helping with the doors, I was too young to join in such a serious adult enterprise. So I stood to the side and watched.

Mr. Sharpway grabbed a fireman's hat and climbed up to the open cab of the red Mack fire truck and turned the key. By the look on his face, he was somewhat amazed when the truck actually started. Mostly it sat neglected—I think the last time it had been run was during the Fourth of July parade the previous year. A huge

152

plume of white smoke filled the barn and framed the truck as Mr. Sharpway eased it out into the afternoon sun. Letting the engine drop to a rough idle, he set the handbrake and began checking gear while waiting for others to arrive.

FIRE TRUCKS HOLD A NATURAL fascination for boys of all ages. They are big, red, powerful, noisy, and loaded with gadgets, levers, knobs, and dials that do neat things; and when in use, they call a lot of attention to themselves and their operators. No wonder boys want to grow up to be firemen.

Although Milan's single fire truck—the only one in Sullivan County—was an old, rather simple affair, it was no less wonderful to my twelve-year-old eyes. It had an open cab for the driver and two firemen. Along its sides and back ran platforms for men to ride while standing. The truck also had a wonderful, polished brass bell with a clapper tied to a cord. The bell was mounted high and directly behind the front seat so that the driver could pull on the cord over his shoulder as they drove along. Besides hats, the truck stocked boots, trousers, axes, ladders, hoses, and various other wondrous pieces of equipment.

Other than the missing brass bell mounted high behind the front seat, this firetruck is exactly as I remember the one from 1953.

ON THAT WARM AFTERNOON, donning a hat was deemed sufficient by the volunteers to identify themselves as firemen; few bothered with the boots and heavy canvas trousers.

The men came running from the shops on the square and others roared up in their cars. In turn, all shouted exactly the same question, "Where's the fire?" The news was relayed repeatedly to all within earshot, "The Chevy dealership is burning."

One of the last to arrive was Mr. Mayville, who lived across the street from us. He had been in Poole's Hardware buying gate hinges. As soon as he grabbed one of the fire hats and jumped on the back, the truck was ready to roll.

As the driver now had a crew of six, he had released the handbrake and was about to take off. Those who came later could make their own way down to the levee, just as half the townspeople—men, women and children—would soon do anyway. Standing there, slightly apart from the turmoil, I was able to apply my own common sense and youthful logic to the situation. I reasoned that it was going to be a long bike ride down to the levee. And, it being a warm day, I would arrive exhausted and hot. Wouldn't it be better to ride? There was plenty of room.

THE MOMENT THE TRUCK LURCHED forward, and quite unnoticed, I stepped up onto the rear platform beside Mr. Mayville. Just as I grabbed the handrail, we were off, barreling around the courthouse and heading down Third Street, red lights flashing and bell clanging. It was a grand way to travel! As the ride progressed, the men got used to their hats and recovered some from their initial excitement. They began to take stock of their surroundings, looking to see if the onboard equipment was in place and secure and, when that was done, waving to people they passed.

At first, Mr. Mayville was busy buckling his chin strap on his hat, but when he finally glanced to his right and saw me, he was surprised. I had had time to plan for this encounter and was prepared. He was not.

"What're you doing here?" he demanded.

"Goin' to the fire," I replied.

"Well, you can't be on here. Get off."

"I can't. We're a-goin' too fast."

Fortunately, my reply had the virtue of being true. I looked up at him innocently, trying not to show the self-satisfaction I was feeling inside. Mr. Mayville turned to other matters with a backward comment, "Well, get off as soon as we stop."

With that issue resolved, I relaxed and began to enjoy the ride. Dogs came out of their yards to chase the truck. As we sped down Third Street, we passed the house where my classmate Bill Pfeifer lived. He and some others were playing in the yard. They looked up with amazement at the sound and the fury. It was a look that turned to envy when they spied me on the back of the truck. I smiled and waved. This was turning out to be a pretty good afternoon.

AS WE APPROACHED THE LEVEE, we turned north onto Pearl Street and neared the dealership. I, and I am sure the rest of the crew, had anticipated mighty flames reaching high into the afternoon sky, but that's not what we saw. As the truck came to a halt in the graveled parking lot, the men stepped slowly from the truck—their excitement replaced with puzzlement. All we could see was a typical one-story white block building with a flat roof and a few people milling about. Was it a false alarm?

Turning to the spectators, Mr. Sharpway asked of no one in particular, "Where's the fire?"

Pointing to the back of the building someone said, "In back."

Most of the firemen headed in that direction, and I followed. Rounding the corner, we saw three men peering into a window. As it turned out, they were staring into the paint room, which was filled completely with dense smoke. They could see nothing, a fact that just served to heighten their curiosity. At least they had found smoke, and "where there's smoke...."

The firemen were confused about what to do next. One of them, Mr. Hickman, started pulling a ladder off the truck, while others tried to figure out what to do about water.

THE ISSUE WITH WATER was that the truck carried only three hundred gallons and a couple of small fire extinguishers of five gallons each. Basically, the truck was a pump on wheels. It was designed to carry only firemen and equipment. To be effective, the truck had to pump water from some source, such as a well, a pond, or a fire hydrant. Unfortunately, the dealership was on the edge of town, and the town being Milan, there wasn't a fire hydrant in sight.

When firemen asked about a well, one of the spectators allowed as how, "They tain't got no well."

But that couldn't be right. "They have an indoor toilet, didn't they? Where did the water come from?"

This prompted a general discussion about the relative merits of a typical, hand-dug, shallow well versus a "deep well." Deep wells were wells that had been drilled into the ground a hundred feet or more. They supplied more reliable water, but had only a three-quarter-inch pipe—far too small for the massive pump on the truck. The dealership had drilled a deep well.

Someone pointed to Locust Creek about a thousand feet away, which ran through a field on the other side of Pearl Street. But, as they all lamented, the truck had only a hundred feet of hose. Someone else mentioned that the creek was mostly dried up this time of year anyway.

The volunteer firemen stood around and discussed this water problem among themselves and with the spectators. It was a hard moment. A fireman had to have a hose spraying a powerful stream of water. Without water they were just spectators like the rest of the crowd, a crowd that was now growing rather large, at least for Milan.

NONE OF THIS WAS REALLY noticed by Mr. Hickman, who had managed to dismount one of the extension ladders and lean it against the building by himself. He, alone among the volunteers, had donned the fireman's full regalia of heavy trousers and boots. With his fireman's hat slightly askew and with an ax in hand, he climbed the ladder to the roof. When he got up there and stepped out on the roof his face dropped in disappointment: He couldn't see a thing—well, that's not quite right. He could see an ordinary expanse of a serviceable flat, black, tar roof. And, looking beyond that to the east, he could also see, more clearly than we on the ground could see, a field planted in beans, Locust Creek and the wooded hill beyond—a rather pretty sight. To the west, he could also see the town as it climbed the near hillside. On top of the hill, he could see a church spire and the standpipe that supplied the town with water—again, pleasant scenery, but not to the purpose at hand.

Bewildered as to what to do, he wandered around on the roof for a while, peering over the edge. He looked down at the crowd on the ground while we looked back up at him. Seeing he was the center of attention, he waved. The crowd waved back.

Meanwhile behind the building, Mr. Sharpway was growing frustrated that he couldn't see through the thick gray smoke that filled the paint room. Finally, frustration got the better of him, and, using his ax handle, he broke one of the small panes of glass in the steel casement window. His idea was that if he let some of the smoke out, maybe he could see what was going on inside.

In a way, it worked. That is, some of the smoke did come out. But in another way, it didn't really work all that well. The smoke remaining in the room was still so thick he could see nothing of the fire—if there was a fire. But there *had* to be a fire to produce the smoke, didn't there?

On the roof, Mr. Hickman noticed the rising gray smoke, and when he looked over the side and saw the men peering in the window below, he figured that this must be where the fire was. At last, he saw his duty clearly. With a full overhand swing, he buried the head of the ax in the roof directly over the paint room. He then paused to take in the crowd's reaction. We in the crowd all obliged him by watching with proper, attentive interest. I must admit that as a boy it was dramatic to see a man on a roof swing an ax. The act had an air of delicious destructiveness I had rarely seen indulged by the sober adults of Sullivan County.

Assured of our attention, Mr. Hickman swung again, and again, until he had opened a good-sized hole in the roof. At this point, instead of the gray smoke we had seen through the paint room window, black smoke came pouring from the hole. Mr. Hickman then paused, and grinning from ear to ear, he turned and looked at the crowd. Being a fireman had its better moments, even without water.

AS I WATCHED THE ACTIONS of the men on the ground and Mr. Hickman on the roof, my excitement changed to horror. Letting air in at the bottom—and smoke out at the top—would cause the paint room to behave just like our home furnace. When I filled our furnace with coal and then opened both the damper and the flue, the fire would really take off, but I said nothing. As a child, one of the lessons I had learned early on was that grown men don't want to hear a boy's opinion about nothing, no time—especially when his thinking so obviously corrected their own.

Well, with a hole for the air down low and a hole for the smoke up high, the plume of smoke was soon showing a mix of leaping flames. It was these flames that gradually pulled Mr. Hickman's attention away from his audience. He understood the danger—at least he understood it when it scorched his backsides. Moving to the edge, he wisely abandoned the roof and removed the ladder from the side of the building. No one else would be going up there for a while.

Slowly at first, and then with a will, the fire began to rage. With flames shooting through the hole and presenting a clear target, the firemen now knew their duty. This is what they had come for. They sprayed their meager three hundred gallons of water on the flames. It was completely used up within a few short minutes and all to no effect. There was too little water, and the roof, doing what roofs do best, caught most of what little water there was and drained it to the eave troughs, which channeled it to the ground at our feet. The system worked perfectly to shelter the fire inside.

SOON, THE WHOLE BUILDING was being consumed by the bonfire which we had expected to see when we first arrived. Once the fire was going well, there was nothing the firemen could do without water. It had to burn itself out. The entire structure, excepting the masonry, was reduced to ashes in the space of two hours.

One by one the firemen, who had been filled with such hopeful purpose and sense of duty so shortly before, returned their hats to the truck. They began blending into the crowd. In turn, each became just another spectator opining on how the new-fangled deep wells were OK, but old fashioned, hand-dug ones were really better, especially in case of a fire.

After the building had burned, and after the ladder and hose had been remounted and secured on the truck, there was nothing more to do. With their excitement spent, the firemen got rides with friends among the spectators and left early. Mr. Sharpway was alone as he started the truck and turned it back to the fire barn.

With no one to notice, I again hooked a ride on the back. It was a slow, quiet trip across town, and with no clanging bell, I had time and space to ponder the strange adult world I was soon to enter.

—— *Afterword* ——

AS A BOY, I was only aware of what the firemen should *not* have done, that is, encourage the fire to roar to its full potential. As an adult, I realize that without much water, no matter what the firemen did, the building was probably doomed. There is only an outside chance that, if they had left the roof intact, not allowing the fire to breathe, and instead had sprayed their three hundred gallons of water through the broken window pane into the smoke-filled room, they might have drowned the fire before it grew unmanageable. It would have required a bit of luck to quench the fire before it left the paint room. They could not see the fire's exact location, and they had only the three hundred gallons. But then, the paint room was only the size of a large closet. They might have gotten lucky.

24

"Not in Front of the Children"

KIDS LEARN FROM their parents in all sorts of ways. Some of them are verbal directives: *Jimmy, don't touch that stove. You'll burn yourself,* etc. But a great deal of what we learn is nonverbal. I am convinced that I would never have started smoking if both of my parents had not been smokers. And, without instruction, I picked up from Dad the subtleties of my voice and articulation. People would phone the house and start talking business with me until I interrupted with, "I think you want to talk with my dad." To which they would reply, "You sound just like him. I thought you were J.B."

Although American society has become more tolerant over the last sixty-plus years, during the '50s the country was uptight about sex. Most people regarded homosexuality and sex before marriage as sins, and many people pretended neither existed, which only meant the behavior went underground. Married couples in the movies were shown only as sleeping in twin beds, no one publicly admitted to being homosexual, sex education in the schools was unheard of, even the idea of there being transgender people didn't exist, and so on and on.

Although they clearly loved one another, I never saw my parents hugging, kissing, or showing any other physical signs of affection. And like many Midwestern families of the time, in my family nobody mentioned sex. But of course, being a curious youngster, I once asked my mother about it. She immediately became flustered and asked me, "You know babies come from a woman's body, don't you?" I did know this much, and said so (though at the time of the conversation I didn't know how they got there in the first place). My problem was broader than that: I sensed there was much more to know, but I didn't know what to ask. This—that there was much more—was confirmed, in part, by Mom's becoming so flustered

161

by my question. In the end, she referred me to a home medical book that had a short section on sex and reproduction. I read and reread the section with avid interest. But it was rather prudish and brief, and stuck mostly to the biological mechanics of reproduction. Again, I sensed there was more to learn, but I didn't know where to begin. I couldn't even form the questions to ask. It was such a taboo subject among adults.

A few years later, I was getting a glass of milk from the refrigerator near the hallway to the dining room. Across the room Mom was washing dishes at the kitchen sink. Dad came in the back door, walked over near her, and with a mischievous grin grabbed her buttock with his left hand—I don't think he had noticed my presence. Mom, startled by his action, but clearly pleased at his sign of affection, let out a squeal and exclaimed, "Oh, Jay, not in front of the children." It didn't go unnoticed by me that her only objection was his lack of discretion. She didn't say, "Stop." She had only said, "Not in front of the children."

Mom and Dad in West Chicago kitchen,
behaving themselves

WELL, I AM NO LONGER a young boy, but am now an old man. Over the years I have known my share of women, and I have heard both men and women comment, and complain, about their sex life—often inappropriately. Also, film and literature have become much more adventuresome in exploring this topic—again, often inappropriately, but also, sometimes with great insight and sensitivity.

I now realize both Mom and Dad might have behaved very differently in private with one another depending on what kind of relationship each had with their own body, and what kind of relationship they had with each other. But as a child I had only this one example of how adult men and women behave when alone. Fortunately, it was a good one. I learned from that small event that my parents clearly had an active sex life, that it was filled with mischievous playfulness and was a pleasure for them both. It was an important lesson that has served me well over the years.

25

A Young Man's Spiritual Journey

If God did not exist, it would be necessary to invent Him.
— Voltaire

THE FIRST BAPTIST CHURCH of Milan, Missouri, still stands as it did when I was a boy. Located near the center of the small farming community, it is a red brick building on the corner of Fourth and Market, just a block south of the Courthouse Square. I remember it as the mainstream church in a town where everybody I knew at least paid lip service to one version or another of fundamentalist Christianity. As a boy, I was unaware of any Quakers, Episcopalians, Unitarians, Presbyterians, Catholics, Lutherans, Jews, Buddhists, Muslims, or Hindus in town, though I am sure there were some Catholics and probably a few Jews and Lutherans. I never heard anyone speak favorably of a non-fundamentalist faith. I did know of people who were silent about their religious beliefs. My Uncle Ike and my Dad were two, as were my mother and many other adults in town. But silence is a weak form of dissent and the possibility that this silence might have a deeper meaning never occurred to me.

By the time I was thirteen, I was what Eric Hoffer, the long-shoreman/philosopher from San Francisco, called a "true believer." I had sort of believed ever since being dunked in the large tank of water in front of the Baptist congregation a couple of years before. However, my belief gradually became more intense as the Reverend Jackson set about grooming me to become a preacher spreading God's word to the world. It is only as an adult that I have come to understand that the Reverend had these plans for my future. Back then, I didn't wonder at his behavior; I just enjoyed his adult attention.

IT HAS NOW BEEN CLOSE on seventy years, and I can no longer recall the details of the setting, but the question I asked—and the Reverend's response—are as clear in my mind today as they were the day they were spoken. I was just becoming aware that there were people in the world who did not believe in Jesus Christ as "*the Son of God who died for our sins that we may have everlasting life.*" I didn't know of any such people who lived in Milan, and I thought most non-believers must live in China, India, Africa or some other far-away place. I particularly imagined them living in an African jungle so dense and so remote that our missionaries hadn't yet reached them. And that's how I framed my question, "What happens when someone dies who has never had the chance to hear about Christ? For instance, someone who lives in a remote part of Africa where our missionaries haven't yet spread *The Word?* Do they get to go to Heaven?"

The First Baptist Church of Milan. Its new wing was built after I left in 1955, and the entrance under the steeple facing the corner has been closed.

The Reverend sensed the sincerity of my question. I was not trying to challenge him, but had been worrying about a genuine conundrum that troubled me. I had heard that babies and young children who die before they can understand about God get a "free pass" to Heaven, so to speak. But I was asking about adults. Could they, too, make it to Heaven if they had never had a chance to hear about Christ?

It was clear the Reverend had also thought about this question. His earnest reply came readily, "They can't go to Heaven if they have not known Christ. It has to be they go to Hell. Think about it. If it were otherwise, our missionaries would be sending people to Hell by spreading *The Good Word!*"

It was obvious from the look on my face that I didn't follow his reasoning. He went on, "Imagine it otherwise. Imagine a tribe in Africa who has had no contact with missionaries, and imagine, as you suggest, all of them are going to Heaven. Then imagine that one day a missionary comes along and preaches *The Good Word.* Some, let's say half, accept Christ as their Savior and are baptized. Clearly, that half would go to Heaven. But then think of the other half, those who hear *The Word* and reject it. That half, who would have been going to Heaven, are now going to Hell. It cannot be. Our missionaries would, in effect, be assured of sending a certain number of people to Hell who otherwise would be going to Heaven."

I was overwhelmed by his presentation of such a cruel, capricious God. The circular, self-serving nature of the Reverend's argument did not strike me until much later. At the time, I was struggling just to accept the contradiction that God, whom the Reverend had often described as full of infinite love and forgiveness, could condemn innocent people to eternal damnation—people who never had a chance!

The Reverend was so certain in his pronouncement, I did not argue the point. He must know God's nature better than a mere boy. Still, it troubled me that he described God as being so mean and cruel. Intuitively, I felt something about his reasoning wasn't quite right, and I remember thinking at the time, *Even I, whom I know full well to have a limited capacity for love and forgiveness, could not be so cruel.*

⎯⎯⎯◦•◦⎯⎯⎯

I WAS FOURTEEN in the spring of '55, when Dad moved his excavating business to the suburban town of West Chicago, Illinois. After school let out in the summer, Mom and we kids followed. It was there that I entered high school as a freshman. For me, the move was perfectly timed. It gave me space, well away from the Reverend's influence, to deal with this vexing dilemma of faith (and others that would soon come to mind). I didn't know exactly what I believed, but I was having difficulty accepting such a mean-spirited God as the Reverend had presented.

Arriving in West Chicago, I found that the town did not have a Baptist church. Without its condemning, judgmental presence, I felt free to explore my own thoughts about God. Besides lacking Baptists, West Chicago had two life-changing influences that had been missing in Milan. First, there was a town library filled with books on every subject. I started reading books I never even imagined existed, particularly on religion and philosophy. And second, there was a neighbor, Tom, just a year older than I, who had an inquiring mind, and we became friends.

To my complete surprise one day, Tom revealed that he was an atheist. He was the first one I had ever met, and, promptly, I saw it as my Baptist duty to convert him. I made little progress, and instead, his mere existence presented me with a serious challenge to my own faith: How could an intelligent, well-meaning fellow like him be condemned to hell simply for not believing there was a God?

After Tom revealed that he didn't believe in God, we argued for hours about whether Heaven, Hell, and God existed. The

167

summer following my freshman high school year I got a job at the local Dog-n-Suds, a fast-food place. I would get off work at 11 p.m., and Tom and I would take long night-time walks through the town's empty streets, each trying to convince the other of his point of view. In the absence of the Reverend, I sought support in the library as I grappled with the seemingly endless challenges posited by my friend.

It was in the town library—Milan did not have a library until after I was gone—that I came to realize that the world was a much larger, more varied place than I had imagined. For example, I learned that the religious problem that had so vexed me was not limited to the wilds of Africa. There were millions of people, even whole civilizations, who did not worship Christ. To be sure, some had not yet been visited by a Baptist missionary, but some had lived before Christ was born, and others had their own god(s) and simply chose not to believe the story about Christ being the son of God.

When I came across Plato, I fell in love with the Greeks. It was such a relief to learn of a society where a man could be a fool and do stupid, even mean, cruel things, but where there was no concept of sin. I came to use Plato as a shield against my Baptist teaching

West Chicago Public Library

as I struggled to find my own understanding of God. Only years later did I notice that, in my youthful naïveté, I had readily glossed over some serious distortions in Greek thinking and society. For example, they equated beauty with goodness, that is, a beautiful person was automatically a good person; there were more slaves in "democratic" Athens than there were citizens; only men could vote; and they had a large pantheon of gods. All was not well with the Greeks. But none of that enter my thinking as I read Plato and argued with Tom.

In addition to Hoffer, Plato, and others, I read Dante, figuring he surely had as good a chance of understanding God's will as the Reverend. To my surprise, in *The Inferno*, Dante addressed a closely related version of my vexing question to the Reverend by describing different levels of Hell, each for a different type of sin. Although Dante did not mention African natives, he did write about the ancient Greek and Roman poets and philosophers who lived before Christ. Because he thought of them as basically worthy people who had had no chance to even know about Christ, he placed Plato, Aristotle, Virgil, etc., in the uppermost ring of Hell—their only punishment was not being allowed into Heaven.

For the Reverend it was a binary choice: We either followed the path to Hell, which was a singular fire-and-brimstone place, or to Heaven with its eternal bliss. He never spoke of there being different levels of Hell, and I never thought to ask him about those who lived before Jesus. It would have made my question more challenging.

IN MY SEARCH to understand what I believed, I examined and slowly abandoned each of the tenets of my Baptist faith. My coming to believe that there was no God, Baptist or otherwise, was difficult and took some time. At first, I was frightened by the idea of a Baptist God who demanded that I believe in His existence or be punished with an eternity in Hell. But then three things came together for me:

» *First*, I could not believe God would punish someone who was pure of heart and earnestly seeking the truth.

» *Second*, a belief in God was something I couldn't fake: That is, I couldn't choose to believe something that I doubted was true. Pretending to myself, as well as to others, was not good enough. If God existed, He would know what was in my heart, and deep in my heart, regardless of what I wanted—I didn't believe.

» *Third*, if there was no God, it could not be a sin to believe He doesn't exist. In fact, "sin" must not exist. Sure, a person could do bad things that hurt others. A person could commit reprehensible acts in the eyes of man, but if God did not exist, no act could be considered a transgression of God's law.

STILL, THE BAPTIST TEACHINGS about God's wrath were strong, and I was reluctant to take such a scary step into the unknown. It took some time, but in my senior year, after Tom left town for college, I was alone with my thoughts. It finally came in a rush and I stopped trying to believe that there was a God of any description. I gave up on the whole idea of religion, and finally, over time, I gave up on the idea of a spiritual existence of a soul separate from the body.

Had we ever met later as adults, I would have been a serious disappointment to the Reverend Jackson, and he certainly would have pronounced me damned for the "Godless" belief I reluctantly, but now firmly embrace. From his point of view, all of God's words were written in the *Good Book*. I should not have turned to other sources, but should have studied the Bible, and believed its every word.

26

A Good Christian Woman

I WAS SURPRISED RECENTLY by a national survey of religious beliefs. You know the type, *67% of Americans say they are Christian, 2% Muslim,* etc. This survey was different. It hinted at the diversity I had long known existed, but I had never seen explored by a poll. The survey found that among Christian Protestants, 19% are not absolutely certain there is a God. There were even more doubters among the Catholics. I quietly chuckled to myself as I read the findings and recalled an afternoon sixty-five years ago in my mother's kitchen.

Try as I might I can't recall any earlier or later time when Mom so explicitly spelled out her religious beliefs as she did that afternoon. Still, she was my mom, and I had a vague knowledge of her beliefs long before that day. She had been raised and lived the first half of her life in Bible Belt country as a member of the First Baptist Church of Milan. She was born a Foster, and in that part of rural Missouri, everyone knew the Fosters to be sober, honest, salt-of-the-earth, God-fearing people. And so, she mostly was, even after she married a Knifong, a family that expended somewhat less effort pursuing such noble attributes.

— ✸ —

THIS PARTICULAR SATURDAY afternoon in West Chicago, a town we had moved to as I started high school, I had come home from my first year at college. Lunch was over and cleared away, and Mom was casually thinking about what to fix for supper. As she turned over possibilities, she realized she was short on a few staples. She asked if I would make a run uptown to Tom's grocery; she also

171

suggested I get some apples for a pie. The offer of pie still turns my head, and I happily set off on my errand.

Returning sometime later with the groceries, I entered through the side door and heard Mom's voice from the kitchen. In a hurt, indignant tone she was saying, "I don't know what she thought I was going to do with that sweater. I'm a good Christian woman."

I hesitated just beyond the kitchen doorway as I removed my shoes. What was this all about? Although I had heard her say it often, I knew that some of her beliefs were decidedly non-Christian. Like many young people, I had spent time trying to sort out religious beliefs in my own mind, and that spring I had been deep into religion and philosophy courses. College had provided both the encouragement and a setting to ferret out contradictions in my beliefs and those of others—an activity I had started in high school and taken to with youthful exuberance in college. Of course, away from a college campus, arguing about such matters is not always endearing to others, especially those others who were unaware, and often unconcerned, that their beliefs might hold such contradictions.

Continuing to listen from the hallway, I soon learned that Mom was describing an unpleasantness she had suffered in Carson, Pirie, Scott & Co., a large suburban department store. Joyce Ann from two doors up had dropped by to borrow a recipe, and she had stayed for coffee—and to offer a sympathetic ear.

As it turns out, Mom had chosen to buy a sweater and some other items for my sisters who were still living at home. When she brought the items to the department counter to pay, there were no clerks. After waiting longer than she thought was right, she had gathered up the items, and headed for a distant counter where she could see clerks busily processing purchases.

As she made her way, a clerk came from a back room, and seeing Mom leaving her department, came after her and remarked sternly, "You'll have to pay for those clothes, madam."

Affronted by the comment and turning to see the clerk for the first time, Mom responded, "Indeed, I do, but since the clerks in this department seem to value their backroom break more than their customers, I decided to go to the men's department where the clerks still care about serving their customers."

Throughout the rest of the purchase, the atmosphere between Mom and the clerk had remained subzero chilly. Now, several days later and at home in her own kitchen, Mom was still indignant, and angry—and enjoying Joyce Ann's comforting understanding.

AFTER GETTING THE GIST of the story from the hallway, I finished removing my shoes, entered the kitchen and greeted Mom and Joyce Ann. We exchanged pleasantries, and Mom made a few more indignant remarks about the clerk, but Joyce Ann had finished her coffee and used my arrival as a cue to leave.

I put the apples and other groceries on the counter, and as the door shut behind Joyce Ann, I turned to Mom and said, "Why did you tell Joyce Ann you are a Christian? You're not a Christian."

"What do you mean? Of course, I am," she huffed, still thinking of the department store, but refocusing her indignation on me.

Not wanting to directly contradict her, I asked, "Was Mary a virgin when Jesus was born?"

Mom's anger with the clerk still held her attention, and she was puzzled by this unexpected question. Still, she hesitated only a moment. Then, taking me seriously she said, "Of course she wasn't. You know how babies are made."

"Well, do you believe that Jesus is the Son of God?"

"You've never heard me say that!" Then she added, "But what does that have to do with anything? He was a good man. He had a lot of good ideas."

Again, still trying not to challenge her directly, I asked, "When Jesus died, did he remain dead or did he rise up and live again?"

"Don't be foolish, when you die, you die.... Maybe they made a mistake and only thought he was dead. He might have been in a coma or something. ... That was a long time ago, how should I know?"

I then asked, "Do you believe you will go to Heaven or Hell when you die?"

"Those are just ideas. Hell is right here on earth. That's what I think."

Mom had forgotten about the incident with the clerk and was finally fully focused on my questions. I next asked, "Do you believe God is going to punish us for our sins and reward us for our virtues?"

"No, God doesn't bother with that."

"What happens to you when you die?" I asked.

"What do you mean, 'What happens?' I just said when you die, you die. That's it."

"What about your soul, does it live after you?"

"Oh, that.... Well, sure, your soul lives after you in others as long as they remember you."

"And when they die?" I persisted.

"Well, when there's nobody to remember you, then I guess, that's it."

Finally, knowing what her answer would be, I asked, "Mom, do you believe there's a God?"

"No, of course there isn't. That's just as plain as the nose on your face."

"Well, why do people believe there is a God?"

"Oh, I don't know, Jimmy.... I guess a lot of people are lonely and afraid." Then, after a bit she added in a brighter, yet more determined tone, "They say it helps, but I don't see it. If I am going to die, I am going to die. It won't matter a twit what I believe."

Then she added, "Just because you've now been to college doesn't mean you can come in here and pester me with all these foolish questions. You know how I feel. I've never kept it a secret from you or anyone else."

That was a signal that she wanted to finish with this nonsense and get on with her afternoon. Unable to help myself, I had to ask one last question. "Mom, these are the basic tenets of Christianity. You don't believe any of them. How can you say you're a Christian?"

That did it. I had raised her ire afresh and she responded with, "That's just ridiculous. I've been a good Christian woman all my life. I don't care what you or anybody else has to say about it." Her tone let me know that she would not tolerate further foolishness. But just to make sure, she took charge of both me and the situation.

"Look, I can't get started on that pie before someone peels those apples. Then before we can eat that pie, we have to eat supper, so someone has to put an extra leaf in the table. Then, when you get that done, you can see to the silverware and plates in the hutch. They won't just fly to the table by themselves, not without help they won't. It is high time someone got busy and made himself useful around here."

She had assigned me chores, and from long years of training, I understood I had better get to work. There was also a delicate matter that I'd been thinking on since the trip to the store. If I made nice with Mom, I could possibly get her to spread butter, cinnamon and sugar on the extra pie dough and make cinnamon rolls. These I could have well before supper, fresh and warm from the oven and with ice-cold milk.

Moving to the counter I rummaged through a drawer and found a paring knife. "How many of these apples should I peel? All of them?"

⟶•⟵

IT HAS BEEN A WHILE since that afternoon. Mom has passed. I have married—twice—grown old, and I have grandchildren and great grandchildren. And I have long since disavowed all the theological tenets of the Christian faith that I had grilled my mother on so many years ago. Still, in how I actually try to live my life, I strive to remain my mother's "Good Christian Boy." I believe in the redeeming force of loving your neighbors—no exceptions, of being honest with others, of being kind—even to those who do not return kindness, and in general, not being prideful, deceitful or cruel—all values espoused by Jesus in his teaching, and by example in the life he lived. As an old man, I have long thought that the pollsters' reports of America as a "Christian Nation" are woefully misleading—they simply don't reflect the complexity of belief and practice that exists. Unfortunately, their methods ensure that they will never fathom the depth of this complexity.

Mom

27

A Short Detour

STILL FRESH OUT OF COLLEGE in the summer of 1965, I had just finished my first year of teaching. It had been good to have a steady income, but my salary was too meager to see me through the summer. So, needing to find work, I picked up a summer job driving a six-wheeler dump truck for Siebert, a suburban trucking company. We were rebuilding Illinois Route 38 west of Geneva. Another company, Alfredo out of Chicago, also had trucks on the job. Between Siebert and Alfredo there were about fifteen of us hauling dry mix from an equipment yard just west of the town.

I was assigned #18, an old, green International with a ten-yard box that was positioned so the two rear axles carried most of the weight. The front wheels carried only enough of the payload to keep the truck stable and prevent it from tipping over backward (though once or twice I managed to lift the front wheels well off the ground when I quickly raised the box too high). This arrangement of the wheels worked pretty well on dry pavement, but in a dirt field, those dual rear axles tended to have a mind of their own. There were times when driving a loaded dump truck in some soft field for Dad's excavation work, I would turn the wheel fully to the right only to have the truck obstinately plow straight ahead.

Gravel, sand, and dry cement were stored at the equipment yard where they were mixed together in a huge, steel tank that stood upright. The bottom of the tank formed a funnel with a trap door, and the whole affair was elevated fifteen feet or so off the ground on legs so we drivers could pull our trucks under the mixer, receive our loads and then drive the ten miles to the job site. Of course, those "ten miles" became shorter and shorter as the finished road slowly moved toward Geneva and the yard. Once at the site we would dump our dry load in a machine that would add water, stir the mixture and spread the wet concrete ten inches thick on a carefully-graded gravel base. This operation was very precise, and the State of Illinois had an engineer on the job constantly taking measurements and quality-control samples.

Before I started in June, road graders and other heavy equipment had leveled the rises and filled the valleys that are common in that part of the rolling countryside. The old road had faithfully tracked up and down each undulation. The new road we were building ran smoothly, straight through the hill cuts and above the filled-in depressions. In the spring, before the road construction had gotten underway, local farmers had planted their cornfields beside the old road. The corn now grew right up to the cuts and fills made by the new, wider road.

At first, we were permitted to run our trucks down the center of the smooth, wide expanse of the gravel base that was to become the new road, but it wasn't long before ruts and ridges appeared. This meant that the base had to be re-graded to restore its original precision. In order to maintain the roadbed's pristine shape, it wasn't long before we truckers were restricted to the shoulders.

Not the original #18, but a dead ringer for it, rust and all.

These shoulders were not as critical as the main road bed itself and would, in any case, require further gravel filling and grading to bring them level with the finished concrete. Because of the position of the machine at the site that received and spread our load, we drove English style. That is, on the left (south side) shoulder going west, and on the left (north side) shoulder returning east.

I HAD BEEN DRIVING dump trucks in dirt fields for Dad since I was fifteen. I considered this assignment of driving on a good gravel road rather posh. The Alfredo drivers, used to paved Chicago streets, complained bitterly about the rough conditions.

Driving on the shoulders worked fine until the day it didn't.

I had picked up my load as usual and headed out to the job site. The corn was standing head high and proud as I guided old #18 along the left shoulder of the highway-to-be. In the distance I saw the dust kicked up by one of Alfredo's red trucks and prepared to wave as he drew nearer.

Most people don't realize how lonely and boring driving a dump truck can be. A driver is almost always stuck with dull, short runs back and forth over the same stretch of road. Since this road passed through the countryside, I seldom saw another living creature until I reached the work site.

I was passing over a filled-in valley when I felt the left rear of the truck begin to sink. The rear wheels had gradually come too close to the soft edge. In a car or an empty truck, a driver could have successfully turned to the right and climbed back onto the solid roadway, but with the heavy load on those rear axles, such a move would surely have caused the truck to roll over down the embankment sideways, spilling its load as it went. Instinctively I turned the opposite direction—sharply to the left and pointing the front of the truck straight down that loose dirt embankment toward the tall corn. The truck responded well to this strange command, which is only to say it didn't roll over.

In the brief seconds I had as I flew down that steep, 45º embankment, it flashed through my mind: *Don't slow up!* I had had enough experience driving in soft dirt to know that if I stopped or slowed when I reached the bottom, I would be stuck there until a tow truck was called to pull me free—a truly embarrassing situation. Keeping the accelerator floored, I roared through the standing corn, frantically shifting gears with that one thought in mind—*don't get stuck.* I could barely see over the corn stalks well enough to aim the truck for the notch where the hill matched the level road before climbing above it. I bounced across an unseen shallow stream, and when I hit the notch, there was a rough transition as the truck lurched to one side and then the other, but this time the weight over those rear axles worked to my advantage; it kept me upright and moving straight ahead. In a flash I was back on the shoulder of the road, rolling along as if I had never taken that detour. The only evidence that anything had happened was the wide trail of flattened corn.

THE EQUIPMENT YARD where we parked the trucks had a large water trough so truckers could wash off the dust before heading for home. That evening as I was washing up in the cool water, an Alfredo driver joined me.

"I saw one of Siebert's trucks go off the road today. Do you know who it was?" he asked.

Washing vigorously, but without looking up, I replied, "Na. Anyone hurt?" Then I asked, "Didn't get his number, did ya?"

—— *Afterword* ——

SOME WEEKS LATER, slowing as I brought my load to the job site, I saw an Alfredo truck on its side, leaning against an embankment which kept it from rolling over further. Resting at a 45º angle, its left wheels in the ditch and right wheels high in the air, its box still held most of its load. Someone else had gotten too close to the soft edge—though at low speed and in a "cut" rather than a "fill." When he rolled, the hill caught the truck, and it didn't quite roll all the way over. An audience of nine workers watched as the poor fellow, unhurt, climbed out the passenger's side door, face red with embarrassment.

28
My People

IN 1970, WITH THE COMING of mild weather, I walked to the University of Illinois campus through a beautiful tree-lined neighborhood. It was an early April morning and everything was spring-fresh and green. Later, after working for several hours on my graduate assistantship duties, I headed to the main library to spend the afternoon on my dissertation. Impromptu antiwar demonstrations had been appearing on campus, and it was such a beautiful day, I thought I might grab a sandwich from the cafeteria and eat lunch outside while listening at the fringes of a demonstration.

A struggle for the country's soul had been building on several fronts during the 1960s. Perhaps because of my age and circumstances, the dissension I was most keenly aware of was between generations over the Vietnam War. Many older adults were nostalgic for the '50s and early '60s, which they remembered as an idyllic respite of peace and prosperity following the disruptions of the Great Depression and WWII. Those who had lived through such perilous times didn't know what to make of the civil unrest that had been growing as Blacks and women spoke up for equality and as the college students protested what was viewed at the time by some as a rather small, inconsequential war in Vietnam. That spring the student protests were about to grow to their full force.

Although my sentiments were with the students, I was very much in between generations. At twenty-nine, I had already acquired the responsibilities of a family man: I had a wife, two sons, a dog and payments on a Plymouth station wagon. What I didn't have was much in the way of a steady income to support them. I had left high school teaching after two years, in part because of its meager salary which I tried to supplement with summertime work. We had been living in a trailer park during most of the '60s, and now I seriously needed to finish my degree, get a job, buy a house and start supporting my family with earned income rather than with long-term debt, and a low-paying, half-time graduate assistantship.

Though ashamed to admit it now, I was so self-absorbed in my own struggle that I generally overlooked the inequity of the racism and sexism that still runs deep in our society. And because of my age, I could have ignored the tragedy of the war and the draft as well.

During the Vietnam War the government was drafting only nineteen- to twenty-six-year-olds. Being twenty-nine I was never included in the lottery, but my age was close enough that I thought about what I might do if the draft were extended to include me. I was brought up to do the right thing regardless of how hard it was, and I recall thinking at the time that, like my father, I would go.

Looking back on it, I realize it would have been a tragedy for me (as I am sure it was for so many others), and it would have been a mistake for the Army. Certainly, by the time I would have been in Vietnam, if not long before, I would have been completely discouraged, disgusted and dismayed by the hypocrisy and futility of it all. I would have constantly questioned the purpose of what we were about, and I would have constantly sought ways to follow my own thinking rather than automatically obeying commands. I would not have been a good soldier.

⸺◆⸺

SMALL, PORTABLE BULLHORNS had recently become available that allowed the young speakers to attract large crowds for protest demonstrations. Although it was unintentional, the speakers also attracted "black-suits." It was unnerving to see J. Edgar Hoover's G-men, leaning from upper-story windows and taking pictures of the scene below to document the demonstrators for later identification.

Still, critical issues were at stake, I was sympathetic to the antiwar movement, and I was drawn to be a part of it, if only on the fringe.

Walking along Green Street that morning—the main thoroughfare through campus—I saw students crowding between Engineering Hall and the Metallurgy and Mining Buildings. Tension was in the air. Something was happening, but those of us on the outer edges couldn't see a thing. I knew the narrow alley led to the University fire station, but I couldn't imagine why a fire station would attract a crowd. Glancing upward, I saw office workers leaning out of open windows overlooking the alleyway. It was the perfect place to see what was happening.

Entering the Engineering Hall, I climbed the center staircase and hurried to an open door at the end of the hall. From the doorway, I could see across a room filled with desks, typewriters and file cabinets. The clerks had their backs toward me as they watched the events below. No one noticed as I joined them, just as if I, too, belonged in that office.

IN FRONT OF THE FIRE STATION below, I saw two firemen taking down a large white flag emblazoned with a peace symbol. Someone had run it up in place of the Stars and Stripes. Four campus policemen stood facing the crowd. While the firemen were removing the peace flag, the crowd was shouting, "Hell, no, we won't go," a popular chant at the time.

Although tensions were high, I had no sense of impending violence. It helped that the police, the firemen and the students all belonged to the University. The University president had been asking students to remain calm. And as I had read between the lines of the campus newspaper, it appeared he had ordered the University police to protect property and prevent riots, but otherwise allow demonstrations. No doubt he was hoping to keep the University out of the national news.

Just as the peace flag was removed, thirty state troopers came trotting in single file from a narrow sidewalk that led from the back of the fire station. Their sudden appearance was a surprising escalation of the situation. The troopers were ominous in their olive-green uniforms, black Sam Browne belts, holstered automatics, high-top boots, white helmets, two-foot-long nightsticks and disciplined movements. They took a single-file position in front of the campus police and faced the crowd. It was clear that the troopers were now in charge.

When I looked at the troopers, I saw older men in their late thirties and mid-forties. To me they looked more like my father and uncles than the young students they were facing. They all seemed old enough to remember the struggle of the Great Depression during their youth. Many surely served in WW II. For most of their lives, they had seen hard times. When the '50s brought much welcomed peace and prosperity, these men were finally able to buy houses for their families, take vacations, own new cars and *send their children to college*. This last achievement was well beyond what most had dreamt possible in their youth. I had heard people from that generation speak disparagingly about college students, referring to them as spoiled, disrespectful ingrates, who wanted to destroy an America that had required so much of their effort and sacrifice to build and defend.

When I looked at the crowd of students, I saw my younger brothers, sisters and cousins. Their generation rejected a life spent struggling for more and ever bigger houses, cars and television sets. It seemed to them like unbridled materialistic greed to always be buying bigger "things." They despised GM's tail-finned behemoths and chose to drive smaller VW Beetles built in a country their elders had fought to defeat. The students had not known a time when food, clothing, college and jobs weren't available to all those with talent, ambition and a willingness to work. They took it as matter of course that they should prepare themselves for work in an office.

Born in the '50s, the students could not imagine the desperation felt by an unemployed man with little education and few skills, who was desperate to support his family with work of any kind, at any pay—a fate so many had experienced only two decades previously. Nor could they understand the existential threat that the country had faced during WWII, a threat that had drawn people together with a shared, single-minded purpose.

IT TOOK SOME TIME for the firemen to raise the American flag. The troopers in their helmets stood in the hot sun, glaring at the crowd. The crowd repeated its chants for the newcomers. Then, with the Stars and Stripes raised to the top and tied off, a loud feedback squeal came from the captain of the trooper's bullhorn. Clearing his throat, he announced that the alleyway was a fire lane, that the crowd was creating an unauthorized fire hazard, and that the students had to clear the lane or they would be arrested.

The more aggressive students in front jeered, stood their ground and did not move. After a while, the captain repeated his order and announced that his patrolmen would clear the lane—with force if necessary. As a whole, the crowd was confused. Those in back could not see or hear what was happening in the front and did not move. Those closest to the front tried to back away some, but there was no place to go.

A few students, hoping for a confrontation that would get them on the evening news, shouted catcalls of "oink" and "fascist pigs." But most were not so provocative. I doubt that any in the crowd had given a moment's thought to the fire trucks and their function. They had simply gathered for a non-violent peace-flag-raising.

Finally, the captain gave the order, and his troopers began marching forward, shoulder to shoulder, swinging their nightsticks in wide, menacing arcs. At this, even the most aggressive in the front tried to move back and maintain a distance from the clubs.

But the space between the two buildings was narrow, and the immobile rear of the crowd hindered those most in danger from the clubs. Inevitably it happened that one of the young men at the front stumbled, coming within reach of a baton. After a first stunning blow, those nearby troopers on either side surged around the fallen student, flailing with their clubs until the victim lay unconscious. The beating, clearly an expression of personal anger, went far beyond what was necessary, lasting well after the student lay unconscious and still. Finally, the line reformed and continued its forward progress.

I was shocked. I wanted to cry out. I wanted it to stop, but there was nothing I could do except witness the violence. I just stared.

As the troopers reached the end of the lane, an ambulance arrived, passed easily through the crowd, and then through the police line. Medics emerged to attend to the seven or eight students lying in odd postures on the pavement, unconscious and bleeding.

I LEFT THE BUILDING, crossed Green Street with a break in traffic, and walked toward the cafeteria, sobered and numbed by what I had just seen. I moved along the sidewalk with my head down, oblivious to my surroundings.

Suddenly I was stopped by a white, refrigerated truck blocking my path. "Frank Miller Meats" was printed across its side panel in large arching letters. Under the letters was a picture of two Holsteins peacefully munching grass and staring down at me. The truck had been trying to back up to a loading dock twenty yards away, but students were crowding around the back of the truck and chanting.

As I started to cross in front of the truck, I glanced at the driver to be sure he saw me and that it was safe. What I saw was a face about my age, frozen with fear. The driver's eyes were unfocused as they stared straight ahead into the distance. It was anything but safe. I crossed anyway.

Having spent many summers driving dump trucks, I fully understood the driver's fear. The truck's mirrors allowed the driver only a view straight back and along the sides of his truck, leaving an eight-foot-wide blind spot directly behind the truck. The situation was even more precarious because the students filling the blind spot seemed oblivious to their danger.

Just as I crossed to the driver's side of the truck, a bullhorn squawked to life. A city squad car was parked on the far side of Green Street and had apparently been watching the truck for some time. An authoritative voice boomed loudly, "Driver, you have the right-of-way. Ignore those students. They have no right to be there. Put your truck in gear and back on up to the dock."

Shocked by the policeman's order, I stepped to the driver's door, pulled myself up on the running board and bellowed through the open side window, "Get this truck out of here. If you back over someone, they'll throw your ass in jail. That cop'll claim he wasn't even here."

Though I was yelling loudly only inches from the driver's ear, it had no effect! Like a deer caught in the headlights of a car, he continued to stare straight ahead, transfixed.

I tried again, "You're not getting paid for combat duty. If your boss wants this meat delivered so bad, let him do it. If you kill somebody, you'll be fired."

That did it. Determination and purpose replaced fear. His eyes became focused and alert. The engine roared. His right hand reached for the gearshift, and I jumped clear as the truck pulled forward, smoothly joining the eastbound traffic.

Thinking they had won a victory, the students cheered his departure. A moment later, the squad car also pulled onto Green Street and disappeared in the westbound traffic, as if it had never been there. I blended into the crowd, made my way to the cafeteria and then on to the library. I accomplished little that afternoon.

———▸•◂———

JUST A WEEK OR TWO LATER, in Ohio, National Guardsmen shot and killed four students on the Kent State University campus. When I watched the news that evening, I was devastated as I relived what I had seen on our campus. These were my people and we were killing each other.

Years later, I had some occasion to be at Kent State—I don't recall the reason, but I made a point to visit the area where the shooting had occurred. I can still recall the peaceful beauty of the green hillside and the scattered trees, and I remember how grateful I was that, at least on the Illinois campus, we hadn't killed anyone.

29

What's in a Name?

WILLIAM SHAKESPEARE was at his romantic best when he had Juliet ask of Romeo's surname, *Montague.* "What's in a name?" Shakespeare then had her answer with the memorable line, "...That which we call a rose by any other name would smell as sweet."

In general, I appreciate Shakespeare's observations on the human condition, but I think he got it wrong about surnames. It may simply be that he got caught up in the romance of his story and forgot his childhood experience. We know little to nothing about Shakespeare's youth, but his mates surely played with his name, making up phrases such as, "Beware of he who '*will shake* his *spear* at you,' "spear the shaking William," and other such taunts. Because Shakespeare wrote the play sometime before 1595, it's certain that he was not thinking of the oddball surnames we Americans came up with when we became a nation of immigrants.

"KNIFONG" IS ONE SUCH strange immigrant name. My family pronounces it as "knife-fong," but those who are unfortunate enough to see it first in its written form before hearing it spoken, rarely know how to pronounce the strange combination of letters. Store clerks, colleagues, auto repairmen, and countless others have struggled with it. I've been called to the front of a waiting room with pronunciations that suggest the speaker has given up and just blurted out something, hoping for a response. From a lifetime of hearing "k'-niff-ing," "king-fong," "k'-niff-fong," "niff-ing," etc., I have become sufficiently familiar with the variations that I answer to any of them.

Once as a callous, and somewhat impertinent young man, I had a college history professor try to survey a large class of a hundred students to learn their majors. He would call a name and the student would answer with his or her major. The professor got the English names right, but the class would interrupt with laughter when he mangled the Polish names like Jaskowski. After the class had settled down, the student would then offer the correct pronunciation and go on to state their major. When it came my turn, he called out "Niffing." I corrected him, saying that my name was "Knifong" and my major was mathematics. This brought forth such laughter from the class that the poor professor didn't hear my major, got a bit flustered and then repeated his original mispronunciation asking, "Well, Mr. 'Niffing' what's your major?" The opportunity was too good to let pass. I replied, "The name is 'Knifong.' The major is math. M.A.T.H." I spelled it out slowly and loudly as if he might have difficulty with the "math" part as well. My prank created a roar that brought the house down. Fortunately for my sake, he didn't take offense at my rudeness and laughed with the rest of us. I don't recall my grade in that class, but it was an "A" or "B."

I SPENT MOST OF MY CHILDHOOD in the small, rural, town of my birth, Milan, Missouri. I can't recall any special notice given to my name nor do I recall people having trouble pronouncing it. I suppose that part of Missouri had seen enough "Knifongs" that the name, if not as familiar as "Smith" or "Jones," was at least familiar enough to be considered normal. However, when I got a bit of distance from the state, people began to have difficulty.

I was fourteen when my family moved to West Chicago, Illinois, and I entered high school. Teenagers can go to incredible lengths to play with names. Thus, my classmates reasoned that "if the knife was long, perhaps the spoon would be medium," and therefore I became "Forkshort." The nickname was such a stretch, I let it die when I left for college. Until now, sixty years later, I have never shared it with anyone.

BECAUSE IT SOUNDS VAGUELY oriental, perhaps Chinese, high school students are not the only ones to find humor in the name. When I was just a toddler, a funny thing happened because of the name. At the time, I was too young to understand what was happening among adults; however, the story was told, and retold, until it became a family legend. But first, I must describe my mother and father.

All her adult life Mom was physically fit and slender. She had a prominent "Roman" nose and angular features. Dad looked more like six feet of genuine "good-old-boy-from-Alabama"—red neck and all. At the time, both of my parents spoke with a noticeable "hillbilly" accent, reflecting the Missouri farm country where they had been born. It was/is strikingly different than the accent spoken in Illinois.

As it happened, Dad had taken a job in the Chicago area and, before Mom and I arrived, he found us a second-floor apartment in a large, three-story house in suburban Maywood. When the owner, Mrs. Hughes, saw and heard the name "Knifong" she said, "That sounds like a Chinese name. Are you Chinese?" Thinking the question funny, and with a wide grin on his face, Dad replied in a single word, "Yeah."

It was summertime and large oaks shaded the front porch where Mrs. Hughes and her renters would often sit for a morning chat. After a few days passed, Mom and I arrived from Missouri. Late the next morning, Mom decided to take me in a stroller to the local grocery store. As she stepped out on the front porch she said, "Hello," to Mrs. Hughes and the others settled in their usual places. They responded with the typical, "Good morning." But something wasn't quite right about the exchange. They seemed to over-articulate their words, and Mom felt they were staring at her as she made her way across the porch.

Her first thought was that something was amiss with her clothing. Once on the sidewalk and away from the house, she paused to check herself out. Finding nothing wrong with her appearance, she thought, *What peculiar people,* and, putting it out of her mind, she proceeded on to the store.

However, as she returned and approached the house, she was again confronted by staring eyes that seemed to study her head-to-toe with intense curiosity. Finally, while crossing the porch and before entering the front door, Mrs. Hughes ventured, "You know, you don't look Chinese." Caught by surprise, Mom replied with some indignation, "That's because I'm not Chinese. Whatever gave you that idea?"

Mrs. Hughes with Jimmy when he was three years old.

A somewhat embarrassed and flustered Mrs. Hughes respond-ed, "Well that's what your husband said, and the name 'Knifong' is somewhat unusual. It sounds, just a bit like ... you know ... like, maybe it's Chinese."

Unlike Dad, Mom found nothing humorous about the situation. Returning from work that evening, Dad found the apartment to be hostile territory. "Why on earth did you tell Mrs. Hughes we were Chinese?" No answer he offered was good enough.

IN 1973 I WAS JUST a few years younger than Dad was when he rented from Mrs. Hughes. During that summer, I got a call from West Virginia University inviting me to a job interview. A date was set, I flew to Pittsburgh and then, rather than eating in the Pittsburgh airport while waiting for my scheduled connecting flight, I got an earlier flight into Morgantown. (Before the long lines at TSA, one could often "jump ahead" on connecting flights.)

At the Morgantown airport I asked about a good restaurant, took a cab into town and had a delicious trout dinner at The Flame. After dinner, I took a cab to a private home address and arrived on time for a preplanned get-to-know-you cocktail party. The next day I met with various potential colleagues, the dean, etc. It was all very pleasant. I was hired and I moved to Morgantown to start the fall semester.

It wasn't until the following spring, when colleagues had come to know me a bit, that I learned the story-behind-the-story of my arrival. It turned out that, without telling me their plans, the host of the evening party had intended to meet me at the airport. At the time of my scheduled arrival, he and his wife had gone to the airport looking for a Chinese man. Much to their consternation I was not there. Adding to their confusion, when they asked around, they learned that no one had seen an Oriental-looking man in the small airport in weeks—it was/is a very small airport. At the party that evening, the host had served egg rolls with a nod to what they had thought was my heritage!

UNTIL RECENTLY I HAD ASSUMED that people who were quick to believe the name "Knifong" was Chinese were simply reflecting the ugly "white American" prejudice toward the Chinese. Although nothing has happened that leads me to believe that such prejudice has much diminished, a recent event somewhat broadened my understanding of my name.

By 2019 the "Nigerian Prince" Internet scam, which seeks to learn one's bank account information for nefarious purposes, had gained some notoriety. So I was prepared, though still surprised, to receive an email out-of-the-blue from a Mr. Li Chen, who claimed to be an account manager with China Trust Bank. (Hint: Google it. No such bank exists.)

In his email Mr. Chen explained that he had had a long-time customer who had recently died, leaving tens of millions in his account. Mr. Chen was writing to me because I "bear the same last name as the deceased...which would allow Mr. Chen to readily transfer the funds directly to my bank account." All he needed from me was certain account information and authorizations.

I did not take Mr. Chen up on his offer to make me a millionaire several times over. It seems that the name "Knifong" appears Chinese even to the Chinese!

SO... WHEN SHAKESPEARE has Juliet ask, "What's in a name?" I think, "A fair bit," if we are talking about surnames and not confining ourselves to roses. Even in Shakespeare's play, Romeo Montague and Juliet Capulet, and three other characters die because of their surnames. Although Mr. Chen was prompted to attempt bank fraud because of my name, I have yet to hear of anyone who has died because their last name was "Knifong."

Afterword

WHEN STRANGERS FIRST MEET ME, they are often curious about the origin of my family name. Sometimes they ask "Where'd you get a name like 'Knifong'?" Depending on the situation, I sometimes respond with the deadpan answer, "From my father. Where'd you get your name?" Of course, such a response doesn't really answer the question. For those who are truly curious about the who, what, when, where and why, I have written out what I know of the history of the name since 1505. (See Appendix B) It may be more than you care to know.

30

Meeting Jean

I MET JEAN because I met Margaret. I met Margaret because I went to a singles dance on July 4th, 1980.

I was helping myself to raw carrots from the hors d'oeuvre table when I noticed two equally attractive ladies standing alone, one on my left, the other on my right. When the music started, I turned to my left. I don't know why. Those who believe in "fate" tell me I was led to the right choice. Always the skeptic, I reply, "We'll never know, the one on my right might have been rich." In any case, it was Margaret I whirled around the dance floor. And it was Margaret whom I tried to impress with some smooth repartee, which wasn't all that smooth because of those carrots. Apparently, however, it was smooth enough. We fell in love with that first dance.

Now, if you're honest with yourself, you have to admit that new love can make you a little addlepated. You just don't think quite as clearly as you otherwise might. So it was later that year at Christmastime that Margaret, thinking I was something of a catch, insisted on dragging me to Pueblo, Colorado, to show me off to her family.

Thinking back on it today, meeting Margaret's mother, Jean, puts me in mind of Old Moe, the well-mannered, much-loved house cat of my childhood. One day she brought home a dead mouse, proudly dropping it on the clean rug at my mother's feet. She then looked up expecting praise and perhaps a pat on the head or a scratch behind the ears. To no one's surprise but the cat's, Mom was not pleased.

It was not that Jean regarded me with quite the disgust one might have for a dead mouse on a spotless carpet, but she did greet me with more than a little skepticism. Her reaction was the most natural thing in the world—after all, Jean was Margaret's mother, and she wanted the best for her daughter. And, regardless of what Margaret might have thought at the time—remember she was noticeably addled—Jean wasn't at all sure that I represented the best Margaret could do. (In hindsight, Jean may have been on to something there.)

Well, Jean was who she was: open, welcoming, warm, polite and suspicious. And, being an astrologist, she consulted her horror-scope. Not surprisingly, she found much horror, which she promptly shared with Margaret and me. She told us she clearly understood the attraction: The moon of Mars was tugging on Jupiter, which was aligned with Saturn and Uranus, and that meant something about Venus. I didn't understand a single detail, though the prediction was clear: wide-spread disaster! There would be storms, earthquakes, fire and ice, and milk would sour in the refrigerator.

As lovers do when faced with dire warnings, we completely ignored her. Happily, the next forty-five years didn't turn out the way she predicted, except for the milk part; without kids in the house, we just don't use it fast enough. And though maybe not quite so addled as we were in 1980, Margaret and I are as much in love today as we were when we met—if not more so.

CONTRARY TO THE MORE COMMON mother-in-law/son-in-law relationship, Jean and I became fast friends. We were eager to spend time with each other when she visited College Park or when I visited Pueblo. She privately complained to me when Ed, her husband, went to a nursing home: It felt like a divorce; she missed being touched. We laughed together at the ways of the Catholic Church and we traded stories of growing up in small town America—she in central Iowa, I in northern Missouri.

Years ago, not long before she died, Jean and I were alone together, sitting on her porch in Pueblo, taking in the afternoon air, when she confided a secret. She told me she'd gone back the week before and rechecked her horoscope, and, as it turns out, she had discovered an arithmetic error. She wanted me to know that it seemed there was a chance, just a chance, mind you, that things might work out for Margaret and me after all.

Jean and Margaret

31
Esta

SOME YEARS AFTER Margaret and I both had earned our pilot's licenses, we purchased a Cherokee 180 and used it to take flying vacations across country. On one of these trips, we made a rare visit to Milan, Missouri, the town where I was born and lived until I was fourteen. We stopped first to see my Uncle Junior. After giving him a ride over Milan and back on the ground, we chatted awhile about how he was getting along, and I asked, "How's Esta doing?"

"Oh, about the same, getting old like the rest of us.... Still keeps a 'doll house' there on Fourth Street," he replied with a wry grin.

Indeed, she did. She had always kept her house, her person and, before he died, her husband, neat and tidy. She was the eldest of a son and three daughters born to Daniel and Byrd Foster. She was the valedictorian of her high school class, and before she married, she was a career woman. After she married, she "kept house."

Dan and Uncle Junior

ALTHOUGH SHE KNEW ME from my birth, my earliest recollection of Aunt Esta was when she was serving as a Sullivan County social worker in the courthouse on the town square. One afternoon she had to attend to some duty or other in a far corner of the county. She asked me to ride along in her black '39 Ford to "keep her company."

I had recently heard that people in other countries didn't use our words to name things. They used different words. As we rode along, I asked her if she knew any foreign words. She replied that, well, yes, she did. She had studied Latin in high school. I asked her to say some Latin words so I could hear how they sounded. After a pause, she said, "Amor."

Of course, I then asked, "What does 'amor' mean?"

"Love," she said, glancing briefly my way with a wistful, half-embarrassed look before turning back to the winding dirt road. To a late thirty-something woman who had never been married, or even proposed to, I suppose "amor" was very much on her mind. At that time the people of rural Missouri viewed any woman not married by her early twenties as an "old maid," doomed to a shadow-life of unfulfilled promise and loneliness. However, as a boy of four, I was sorely disappointed in her girlish choice of an example. It would not do. I asked her for some more important words like "dog" and "cat," which she told me were "canis" and "feles." Now this was better stuff. These were words a fellow could actually use in everyday conversation.

BEFORE DAD WENT OFF to war, he rented the five bedroom "Baker house" for $18 a month. Just four blocks from the Courthouse Square, and yet near the edge of town, it wasn't a grand affair. We called it the "Baker house" because it was Mr. Baker who owned it. The name helped keep things straight as we moved through several rental houses around that time. While Dad floated around in a Liberty Ship, Grandma Foster and Aunt Esta moved in with us in

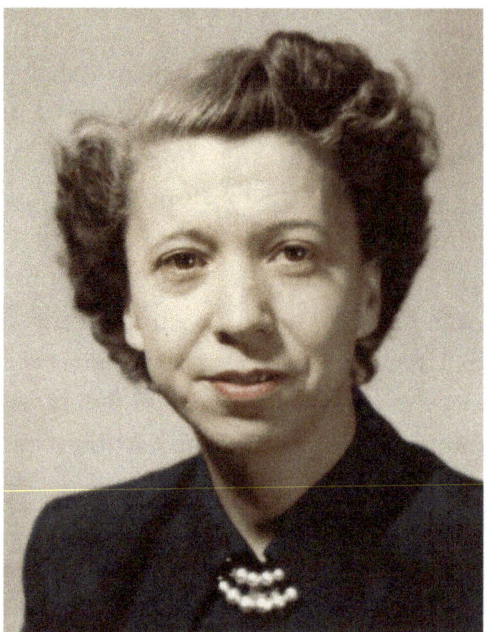

Esta, 1949

the Baker house. They stayed for the duration of the war and for some time even after Dad's return.

I can still remember when Franklin, a tall, handsome fellow who had been in the war, came calling for Esta's hand in marriage. She was forty-two, but the romance could not have put the house in more of a stir than if they had been teenagers, a stir that seemed way overblown to me as a young boy. When Franklin was due for an afternoon visit, the place had to be cleaned a second time (we cleaned every morning), Mom would try to have something in the oven so the house would "smell good," and Esta would dress in something special—and take a long time in the bathroom.

When he arrived, Franklin would sit awkwardly in the living room, flushed with embarrassment, wanting to make a good impression and yet unsure how he ought to behave. He would stiffly try to make small talk with Mom, or even with me if I happened to pass through the living room. I liked him well enough, but our conversations never went very far. I knew he had been a Marine, and I wanted to hear about storming beaches and hand-to-hand combat in the South Pacific—experiences he was struggling to forget. His only relief was when Dad was home. They would go outside and stand by the car, smoking and talking quietly until Esta was finally ready.

Perhaps every true romance must have a drama of some sort. The drama that summer arose from Franklin's having been previously married before the war. The marriage had been brief and hadn't worked out. But it had left him a "divorced" man. Esta didn't know what to do. Would it be proper for her to marry such a fellow? The Baptists didn't ban second marriages, but for her it was a social issue, not a religious one. What would the rest of the town think? Was this something that a proper, well-brought-up daughter of Byrd and Daniel Foster should do? Would there be whispered gossip about her being a "loose woman?" In the end, she mustered her courage and took the plunge. After all, Franklin was a mature, sensible, reliable, kind, and gentle person. She was coming to care for him deeply, she had no other prospects, and she wasn't getting any younger.

The marriage was a happy one, and she needn't have worried about Milan gossip. The whole country became a looser place after the war. Franklin had a job as the point person opening new lumberyards for Sutherland Lumber. The company prospered as the after-the-war housing market boomed. Franklin and Esta spent the rest of their lives—at least until retirement—traveling the country and living in a string of cities. In each new place, Esta would keep house for Franklin, even though it was usually only an apartment. After he got the new lumberyard started, they would move on. The people they met never knew or cared about Franklin's first marriage. Franklin and Esta were what they appeared to be—and what Esta had always wanted them to be—a respectable married couple.

It was a good life and the frequent moves were not a problem. Well, almost not a problem. Over the years they had to travel quite a bit through the Rocky Mountains, and Esta did not like heights. Though she understood why it could not be, she often lamented that the AAA would not provide them with a route through the mountains that kept the car "on the inside lane the whole way," that is, close to the mountain wall and away from the precipitous dropoff. Of course, she enjoyed panoramic vistas as much as anyone. It was just that she preferred viewing them from the valley floor rather than some perch halfway up a mountainside. Flying in our Cherokee was out of the question.

By getting married, Esta had finally fulfilled the expectations for a woman of her time. She had had a working career until she married, and then she kept house for her husband. If children didn't come, well, sometimes things worked out that way. I didn't realize it at the time, but my cousins, my sisters, and I served as her surrogate children. All I knew was that she, and Grandma before she died, were sort of extensions of Mom. They loved me and they watched over me. And they told me what to do.

Mom used to say to her younger sister Reva, who had a son, that without children, Esta had had an "easy life." This seemed to imply that by having children, Mom and Reva had had a hard life—and that there was virtue in life being difficult. Mom also used to complain to Reva that Esta was "bossy." Perhaps, being the eldest, Esta was bossy with her sisters, but I now think such comments were prompted by typical sibling rivalry. I never knew Esta to be anything but thoughtful, kind, and gentle. And, although I never heard her speak of it, now, as an adult, I can understand that wanting children and not having them isn't an easy thing.

After Franklin retired, he and Esta returned to Milan and bought a house on Fourth Street, right across Painter from the Baker house. Esta was living there the day she had her fatal stroke. It was this house that Junior was referring to when he mentioned her "dollhouse." Franklin had been dead for some time. There was nobody to disrupt things about the house or the garden except Esta, the occasional visitor, and weeds.

I can remember helping with the dishes after lunch on the day Margaret and I visited. Esta was washing, and I was drying and putting things away. At first, I didn't notice it. She was very quiet about her movements—almost furtive. But I gradually became aware that after I would put an item away, she would follow behind and move it to a slightly different position in the drawer or on the shelf. Every plate, every knife, every glass had its own special place—exactly so. When I finally caught on to what was happening, I chided her, "We're not becoming just a little obsessive, are we?"

She chuckled quietly and admitted with a smile and in a soft tone, "Well, yes, perhaps I have become a little addled. I'd always known that there are people who might think the things I do were a bit peculiar." Then, she held up a spatula she was washing. "Now you see, Jimmy. This handle is broken, but it fits in the palm of my hand just so; and I like it better than a new one. If I have to have each cup and plate in its place, it don't make no never mind. I don't have much else to do, and I have always done things that-a-way."

Aunt Esta and Dan at lunch

THE JUNE DAY was warm, but not yet hot. She was eighty-nine and by herself in the garden out back. It was a small garden, only about ten by twenty feet. She now grew only enough to bring freshness to her summer meals. She had long abandoned putting up vegetables for winter and she hadn't planted corn for years. You had to plant at least four rows of the stuff before it would produce ears, and she was never able to eat or even give away so much corn. Besides, her nephew David would bring in more corn from his garden on the farm than she could deal with.

Because it was only June, many things weren't yet ready, but she had green onions, bib lettuce, and radishes—all of which were especially good before the summer heat got to them. The beans and the tomato plants were about a foot high and doing well, but so were the grass and dandelions. Esta had gone out with her hoe to set things in order.

Later that afternoon she was sitting on her front porch when Becky and Fred, a niece and nephew from Franklin's side of the family, stopped by for a visit. They lived in Bloomfield, Iowa, just across the state line. They often stopped by Milan when traveling to Grundy County to see Becky's sister.

The three of them had been sitting a while on the porch admiring the late afternoon breeze and chatting before curiosity got the better of Becky and she asked, "Whatever on earth happened to your glasses, Esta?" Her glasses were badly misshapen and sitting awkwardly on her nose.

"Oh," Esta said, "just a bit of foolishness. I was careless and lost my balance out in the garden this afternoon. The ground was soft and there's no harm done. My glasses fell off and I must've fallen on them before I got up. I'll take them up to Roy Perkins in the morning. He'll straighten them out for me."

Though Esta continued to make light of it, Becky prodded until the full story came out.

Esta had just bent over to pull some grass and dandelions that were sprouting among the beans when she fell. The beans were at the edge of the garden near the road, and her fall had caused her to roll down the four-foot bank. When she recovered enough to realize that she had fallen, she was lying in the ditch with her glasses and hoe halfway up the slope.

"Well, there I was in that ditch. I figured I had better try out my limbs to make sure nothing was broken. After all, I am eighty-nine, and I ought to be careful about falling.... But that's just the thing, I am careful! I haven't fallen or even stumbled in twenty years, maybe thirty. It's been such a piece of time I can't remember. Anyway, I figured I'd probably ought to get myself up here to the porch and rest a spell." And so she had—after picking up her hoe and her glasses.

While sitting and recovering, and before Becky and Fred arrived, she had tried to puzzle out what had caused her to lose her balance. All she could remember was leaning on her hoe and reaching for a bit of grass, then she was in the ditch. Try as she might, she couldn't remember the fall. Had she looked up and become distracted? Had her foot slipped?

"I can't imagine what the neighbors would've thought if anyone had come along and seen me in that ditch. They'd think I'd been drinkin'!"

After more pleasant chitchat about how the crops needed more rain, Fred mentioned that he and Becky had been planning to take Esta to dinner at the Paradox restaurant on the levee. Would she like to go? Well, yes, she would, but she still had her gardening clothes on. She would need to go inside for a minute to change into something nicer. Fred and Becky could sit right there on the porch and wait. She'd just be a minute.

And so, they waited. And then they waited some more. After some time, Becky became concerned. Esta didn't come, and she didn't come. Finally, Becky went inside to see what was keeping her. She found Esta on the floor and only semiconscious.

Well, an ambulance was called and it took Esta to Milan's health center, and they sent her in the same ambulance to the hospital in Kirksville thirty miles to the east. Kirksville realized the seriousness of her condition and sent her by helicopter to the state university hospital in Columbia. It was Esta's first time ever off the ground.

THE NEXT MORNING Becky and Fred drove down to Columbia to see how Esta was doing. When they found her in a hospital bed, she seemed in perfect condition, and *she was peeved.* She asked, "What am I doing in a hospital?" followed by, "Where am I?" Becky explained that she had found Esta on the dining room floor and that an ambulance had taken her to Kirksville, and then she had been flown by helicopter to the Columbia hospital. On hearing this last bit about the helicopter, Esta pursed her lips, and declared, "I did not."

HER APPARENT REVIVAL that morning was a false promise. By afternoon she had slipped back into a coma and by the evening of the second day she died of uncontrollable bleeding inside the brain. It may have been this bleeding on the brain that had caused her to lose her balance and fall two days before, or the fall may have caused the bleeding. We'll never know.

She had said wistfully to me one time that she was lonely. "I am the last of my family. They are all gone." Her father had died before I was born. Her mother died of a stroke while we were living together in the Baker house. And her brother Clifford, Reva, and my mother had all preceded her.

I miss them all. And, like many a boy, I miss my mother most of all. But also, I especially miss Esta. She was the last living link to my childhood, and I myself have now grown old and cautious of falling.

32

An Easy Mark

IT IS MY WIFE'S OPINION that remembering and celebrating birthdays, *or not*, is a trait coded differently in the masculine and feminine genes. She may be right—she usually is—but I suspect it has more to do with family traditions. When I was growing up, Christmas and one's birthday were *child-focused* celebrations. Only Thanksgiving was for the whole family, and sometimes the Fourth of July. I cannot recall any sort of gift-giving, card-giving, celebrating or even the mention that the day of their birthday was somehow special for either Mom or Dad. However, Margaret grew up differently. She remembers all family birthdays, and she wants to celebrate all of them.

There is no particular pattern to it, and it does not happen every year, but Margaret has from time to time surprised me on my birthday. I was born in the "Show Me" state of Missouri, and I am usually alert and mildly suspicious of anything out of the ordinary. However, since I also pay absolutely no attention to the annual reoccurrence of the day I was born, I am an easy mark for such surprises.

⸺⸱◦⸱⸺

WHILE WE WERE STILL LIVING in Maryland, I had come home from work one mid-week evening, and, as I often did, I had changed into my bathrobe and settled myself in the living room to read the newspaper before dinner. I had only a moment to glance at the headlines when there was a knock on the door. I greeted the nextdoor neighbors (an older couple) in my bathrobe and welcomed them in. They didn't ask for help, nothing was broken

209

nor did they ask to borrow a tool or anything of the sort. It seemed they had simply dropped in for a visit. I was puzzled as to why they were dropping by on a weekday evening, but felt it would be impolite to ask. Regardless, I offered them a glass of wine, and we sat in the living room chatting about nothing special. I felt there was something odd about the visit, but I couldn't put my finger on it.

Only five minutes or so passed before the neighbors across the street knocked on the door and came in. Nearer to our age, they were really close friends. The four of us often got together for impromptu dinners and movies, and we sometimes helped each other with maintenance projects, but that mostly happened on weekends. They too, seemed to have no reason to visit. It never occurred to me to focus on what day of the year it was. I was just puzzled by their visit on a weekday evening—we all had to show up for work the next day.

I remained puzzled until, even before I had returned to my chair, another couple knocked on the door. It appeared that Margaret had been waiting for this third couple, and just as I opened the door, she stepped from kitchen with champagne and a birthday cake dotted with candles. Suddenly it all became clear as they sang "Happy Birthday."

ANOTHER YEAR, after we had moved to Boulder, Margaret quietly arranged for our two grown sons to fly into Denver on my birthday and meet us at a local restaurant. That evening she told me we were going to have dinner with Elsa, a long-time friend of ours whom we'd often meet when she came to town to visit her son.

As we entered the restaurant and were shown to our table, I saw our two sons already seated. Smiling at me the younger one said, "Hi, Pops." I was so startled and confused that instead of greeting them, I looked around the restaurant and asked, "Where is Elsa?"

FINALLY, THERE WAS THE TIME we were spending the month of February in Costa Rica. We had decided to try to train our ears to hear, and our tongues to speak *Español* and we were trying to stuff our heads full of Spanish grammar and vocabulary. *¿Habla español? No, yo hablo solamente inglese y un pequeño Alemán.* [Do you speak Spanish? No, I speak only English and a little German.]

That month felt somewhat like being back in high school and Margaret and I were going steady. Although we were in separate classes in the morning, we ate lunch together in the *comedor* [the dining room], and we studied together in the afternoons in an open-air bar. (Okay, I didn't say it was *exactly* like high school: We were an old married couple—well past "going steady," and we studied together in a *bar*—something I never did in high school.)

In a way the trip made her surprise easier: no telephone calls from relatives, no TV or radio announcing the date, and no scheduled events—other than the routine sleeping, waking, attending class and studying. Still, I could have been more alert. Our younger son has a birthday the day before mine, and Margaret made sure that I had bought a phone card and remembered to call him on his birthday. The call did nothing to prepare me for the following day.

The first thing next morning as I was sitting down with our host family for breakfast and still oblivious as to what day it was, they all wished me a "Happy Birthday." I was completely surprised. Not only because *they* knew when my birthday was, but because I hadn't yet realized it myself. After breakfast Margaret and I walked together to the bus stop and rode up the mountainside for morning classes. I had become absorbed in learning Spanish and completely forgot about it being my birthday.

At some point, Margaret must have told the other students. When they started singing "Happy Birthday" at lunch, I was not only surprised, but embarrassed by all the attention. As incredible as it may seem, between breakfast and lunch I had started a new day and, again, had forgotten about it being my birthday.

That day happened to be a Friday. After class we joined with some other students and headed for a weekend at the Manuel Antonio beach on the western side of the isthmus. The four-hour bus ride started with a slow crawl through the permanent traffic jam around the San José airport, but once past the airport, the trip became interesting as we traveled through beautiful green mountains and then along an ocean highway with scenic views of the Pacific. We paused at a river to watch the crocodiles, and, as we neared Manuel Antonio, we marveled at the narrow, one-way bridges; temporary, make-do bypasses; and a major roadway crack. A recent earthquake had vertically displaced the roadway a good six inches as the fault line crossed it.

It was enough wonderment that, once again, I completely forgot about my birthday. That evening we had dinner at a lovely, open-air restaurant, and I was completely surprised for a third time when our waiter brought to our table a chocolate cake with a candle while the band played "Happy Birthday."

MARGARET HAS ARRANGED other birthday surprises over the years, but the year in Costa Rica when she surprised me three times in a single day will probably remain the record. However, one cannot be too sure. I am an easy mark, and Margaret is so clever and determined to celebrate birthdays. Who knows, some year she may manage to hit me with four surprises.

33

Anne Marie's Faith

IN MANY WAYS we *homo sapiens* are no different than any other animal species. We may be bigger, stronger, faster than many; and we can see, smell, and hear better than some. But we are smaller, weaker and slower, and we cannot see, smell or hear as well as others. The one area where we are uniquely superior to all other species is our ability to think. However, even here we need to be careful not to claim too much. Many mammals seem to be our equal when intuitively recognizing dangerous situations, distinguishing between friend and foe, loving their mates and offspring, and deciding on immediate action—all things that require thought. The kind of thinking that we humans are so good at is the ability to create realistic mental scenes set in places and times other than the "here and now." And then we can let these scenes play out following rules and assumptions of our choosing.

It is this ability to consider the hypothetical that allows us to reminisce, interpret, and analyze the past, as well as plan for the future. As a survival tool, this kind of knowledge, when coupled with the ability to talk and the formation of cooperative social groups, has proven more effective than all other traits that have evolved in the animal kingdom. It has proven superior to stronger muscles, larger claws and teeth, better eyesight, better hearing, greater speed or size, etc. It is surely the quality that prompted the writers of the King James version of Genesis to assert that "God said unto them [*homo sapiens*]...replenish the earth and subdue it; and have dominion over ...every living thing that moveth upon the earth."

However, this knowledge comes at a price. With painful and vivid clarity, this special ability has brought us the disquieting knowledge (also mentioned in Genesis) of our own personal mortality. Each of us is aware that the world existed before we were born. Each of us is aware that the world will exist after we die. And each of us is absolutely certain we will die.

———————

IT WAS A SUNDAY AFTERNOON in late spring—warm and sunny, but not yet summer-hot. The eighty-foot oaks in the backyard had leafed out, providing shade over the all-glass solarium we used as a dining room. My wife, Margaret, and I were entertaining old friends who had come for an afternoon of food, wine and friendship. We had just finished a simple but elegant meal of broiled salmon.

We had known John and Anne Marie since they had moved to the Washington, D.C., area to pursue professional careers. John was an administrator at Marymount University, where I served as professor and department chair for mathematics. Anne Marie was a nurse who worked in oncology research at NIH (National Institutes of Health). The friendship that developed was one of those happiest of situations where each of us individually enjoyed the companionship of the others, both as a couple and as individuals.

After we finished eating, the lively dinner conversation continued as we sat lounging in easy chairs, enjoying the fresh colors of spring. We explored many topics both global and personal: politics, literature, family, grandparenthood, childhood, work, and so on. We freely shared our thinking on most things—except religion. John and Anne Marie were both devout Catholics and active in their parish. Margaret and I were inactive members of the Washington Ethical Society, a congregation with even less of a traditional dogma than the Unitarians.

I am not sure why it happened that particular afternoon. Perhaps it was as Anne Marie said: She had a simple curiosity about our obvious differences. Whatever the reason, I was caught off-guard when, with her usual infectious enthusiasm, she announced, "You all are such good friends and have such interesting ideas.

We always have a wonderful time when we get together... like this afternoon. We talk about everything. Anyway, I have been wanting us to talk about really deep stuff. You know, like the meaning of life, what is our purpose here on earth, and what happens when we die. I know we are different, but we are such good friends. It could really be interesting to see how we are different and what we have in common."

And so, it might have been. But no one spoke. Our sudden quiet made Anne Marie a little nervous. She began offering random comments, trying to fill the silence and encourage us to join her in this new topic.

For my part, I was too distracted to speak as I frantically assessed the dangers that lay in such a discussion. My hesitancy was prompted by two thoughts: The first, was of real danger: John and I worked at a university run by the Sisters of the Sacred Heart of Mary. These Sisters mostly regarded me favorably, even though I was not Catholic. They may have assumed I was Protestant. They may even have thought of me as Lutheran or high church Episcopalian. However, I was certain they would form a very harsh judgment of me if my true religious thoughts were revealed in any detail. Second, and of only minor concern, there was the matter of our friendship with John and Anne Marie. Before that afternoon, I had not given much thought to whether our friendship could tolerate an honest sharing of religious convictions.

When the subject arose, I felt I had to pause at least for a moment to consider our friendship. In the end, I concluded that our friendship was strong and generous, and it would easily survive such a conversation. My greater worry about the university was resolved when I reasoned that, if I asked them, I could trust John and Anne Marie to avoid speaking of my private beliefs among the people at the university.

Watching Anne Marie for an opportunity, I began cautiously, "Uh, my beliefs are really quite different and uhh...."

Relieved that someone was finally joining the topic, Anne Marie tried to encourage me further.

"Oh, I know you are not Catholic, but that is just what I mean—finding similarities and exploring differences can be exciting. It is boring to talk the 'same old same old' all the time. I need to hear something different."

Then she gave a little laugh and paused. I continued. "Uhh... my problem is I am not too sure how much common ground we have, nor am I sure how such a conversation would go.... You know I was raised a Southern Baptist, but that was a long time ago.... I no longer think that way...." I paused again before finally taking the plunge. "For instance, I don't believe we are part of a universal plan. I don't believe we were put here to play a part in a larger scheme. I believe that when we die that is the end of us. I do not believe there is an afterlife. I am moral and I have ethical principles, but I don't believe these principles come from God. I don't believe there is a God. I don't even believe there is a 'universal spirit.'"

Doubt flickered across Anne Marie's face, but she quickly pressed on. "Oh, I know you are different, and that's good, that's what I want to talk about. All my life I have learned only the Catholic drill on stuff. It would be interesting to learn something new.... For instance, we are so puny and insignificant. We all believe there is something out there that is bigger than ourselves. We can't be all alone. I just think it would be interesting to explore those beliefs. Regardless of what you call it, I just think it would be interesting to hear your beliefs."

"Yes, I agree that we are pretty insignificant; and yes, I am different, though perhaps in ways you don't anticipate. I don't believe in anything spiritual. I do believe we are all alone. And I don't think there is much to explore about my spiritual beliefs other than the fact that I don't have any."

As this information settled in, the conversation struggled along for another few minutes, never getting much traction. Margaret volunteered some things about her own beliefs, which are more spiritual than mine, but it was not enough. Anne Marie was distracted as she processed what I had said. Gradually the conversation began to drift to the president from Arkansas and other safer, more familiar topics. Before we left the subject completely, I asked John and Anne Marie to keep the conversation confidential, and both quickly agreed.

"Of course we'd never say anything."

However, Anne Marie continued, "But I am sure it would never matter. Catholics really don't worry about that kind of thing anymore."

This alarmed me, and I said, "In general Catholics might not think much about it, but it would matter a lot to the Sisters. I doubt that they would ever forgive me were they to learn my true beliefs."

John made a nod of agreement, looked significantly at Anne Marie, and said, "Yes, it would matter quite a bit to them. We won't say anything."

With that I felt safe.

ABOUT FOUR OR FIVE MONTHS passed before the four of us were again in a private setting that allowed for thoughtful discussion. We had met for lunch at the Chart House in Old Town Alexandria. After a pleasant meal we decided to walk south on a path beside the Potomac River that led to Jones Point. (Jones Point is the southernmost point of the original diamond-shaped layout of the District of Columbia before the Federal government ceded the southwestern side of the Potomac back to Virginia in 1846.)

Anne Marie is an aggressive walker, and I used the opportunity to match her pace. It was not long before the two of us were well ahead of our spouses, who were talking about I-know-not-what.

After a bit, I ventured, "I feel kind of bad over our discussion about spiritual beliefs. I never wanted my beliefs to be such a surprise. I feel that I sort of dumped on you and stopped the conversation."

Always gracious, she replied, "Oh, no. It wasn't you... I mean you just said what you believe. It's just...." Her voice trailed off.

We said nothing for a while. Then she said, "It's just that... you know... I grew up Catholic. And I... I guess I have sort of led a sheltered life.... I learned all that Catholic stuff in school, and that's just the way it was. I have never really explored how other people think. In the '50s and '60s, we were told we would lose our souls if we visited other churches. But now that's all changed .... And we know you and Margaret so well. We are such good friends, and we have such good, thoughtful conversations. I just thought it would be fun to, you know, to broaden out a bit."

"Well, I don't really mind telling you anything about myself, but since starting at Marymount, I have become pretty cautious about discussing religious topics. I don't want to offend anyone there, and I don't want my beliefs to interfere with my career. John and I have had several discussions involving the ethics of various university policies on different issues. I think he may have guessed my religious thinking, but he was too discrete to ever ask about it."

As we walked on in silence, I watched the sailboats on the river and waited.

Finally, Ann Marie said, "I just can't see how you can believe in nothing. It seems so awful to imagine that there is nothing out there. You must believe in something.... Aren't you depressed all the time? I mean I would feel so lost."

"Yeah, I understand what you are getting at, but I don't feel depressed. Do I seem lost or depressed to you?"

She answered with a pondering, but firm, "No...."

I continued, "I love my wife, my sons, my friends, my university, and my country. They are all important to me. I often find myself caring about what is the morally right thing for the university to do. John has often said he thinks I care more for such matters than many of those we work with, including the Sisters, who can sometimes be rather materialistic and transactional when deciding university policy and practice.

"I grew up Baptist in rural Missouri and, before she died, Grandma took me to church on Sunday. I heard the preacher preach; he spoke about the most urgent matters; everyone seemed to agree with him, at least on the main points. By the age of thirteen, I believed deeply in a God as the Baptists describe Him. But the next year, when the family moved to the Chicago area and I entered high school, I began to question what I had been taught in church. By the time I entered college, I was pretty much as you see me now—convinced that *Man made God in his own image*, to turn Genesis 1:27 on its head.

"I remember that at first, I was frightened of not believing in the Baptist God. My Baptist experience caused me to worry that God would be angry if I questioned His existence. But then it came to me that, if God doesn't exist, then it doesn't matter what I *imagine* He may think. And, if He does exist, how could He be angry with an earnest young man who makes an honest mistake in his struggle to understand the spiritual world? At the time, accepting a life without a God was the scarier of the two choices I faced. Things would have been easier if I believed, or at least pretended to myself, to believe. But I could not do it. I could not lie to myself, and if there is a God, I could not hide my thoughts from Him—He would know I was only pretending."

We were nearing the point and walked on in silence until Anne Marie said, "Yeah, but...I mean...I think about trying to live without faith. It just seems so empty, so depressing to think that we are all alone.... I've got to have faith in something.... Without faith I'd be nothing.... I wouldn't know what to do."

I responded, "I came to that place as a young man. It took me a long time just to consider the possibility that there was no God. Then, I settled on this fact: Either we are or we are not alone, and no belief, or nonbelief, on my part will change the situation. So I might as well accept it, and get on with my life."

Anne Marie looked out over the water. "But I've got to have faith, or I'd be all alone with nothing...."

WE REACHED THE lighthouse at Jones Point in silence and I said no more, but I was thinking: *Yeah, but if it was only fear of the void that pushed one to believe in God, it is a mighty slender reed to lean one's faith on. Priests and preachers surely have it wrong when they separate the believers from the nonbelievers, asserting that the former are among the "saved from eternal death," and the latter are "damned to eternal hell." A loving God surely would not want believers who believed in Him only out of fear of either the void or eternal damnation. What a petty attribute to assign to a God "who so loved the world that He gave His only begotten son...."*

Anne Marie was bright and quick. She would have understood if I had voiced my thoughts. But I had no heart for it. If she was too frightened to give up her professed faith, it would not matter what I said; and if she decided to face and accept her fear, she was able enough to manage it by herself. I had offered her a living example of someone who did not believe in the existence of God, the existence of a spiritual world, or of an afterlife—and yet, someone whom she regarded to be like herself: happy, caring, principled and moral—someone who had purpose in life and did not drift aimlessly in despair. She would need some quiet time alone to sort out the dissonance.

Jones Point

220

34

Mourning Whiskey in the Morning

I have yet to see anyone
make it out of this world alive.
- J.B. KNIFONG, my father, a digger of earth,
bore witness to this truth on February 13, 1986.

I HAD JUST FINISHED teaching my Wednesday morning class and was checking my mail, when the Dean's secretary noticed me and said that my sister in Chicago had called. I needed to call her back. I asked, "Did Jane say what she wanted?" The secretary said, "Ahh...she said her name was Becky."

This puzzled me. Although Jane, three years younger than I, did call on rare occasions, Becky, five years younger than Jane, never called. It also concerned me because Jane lived with her family. Becky lived with Dad, or rather he lived with her since Mom had died six years earlier. I knew something had happened. Someone needed money or was in the hospital, or something. I never gave it a thought that Dad might have died—until I heard Becky's tear-choked voice on the phone.

At first Becky spoke in simple, short bursts—Dad had gotten up that morning, he'd gone to the bathroom, he'd had a heart attack. When she had come downstairs, he was hunched over on the bathroom floor, "mooning the world." In between the sobs she chuckled a bit at this last part.

"Mooning the world?" I repeated while trying to sort out my own grief and, like her, trying unsuccessfully to ignore the humor.

A version of this story was first published in *The Washington Post*. It appeared 7/18/2004, under the title they chose, "There Was Love All Around: A Drink for Dad."

Had Dad done this on purpose? He had had a great sense of the risible, but…. Becky, sensing my confusion replied, "I am sure he didn't know a thing about it, but it is kind of funny, isn't it? Dad would have gotten a chuckle out of it." As it turned out, it isn't the only chuckle he would have enjoyed over the next couple of days, if he had stayed around to watch.

EARLY THURSDAY MORNING I was landing at O'Hare field. By ten o'clock, I was parking a rental car in Becky's driveway. Entering the kitchen from the back door, I found both my sisters crying. At the sight of them, I, too, began sobbing. For some time, the three of us stood hugging each other and crying.

Now, for those of you readers from other parts of the country, I might mention that there is nothing unusual about Midwesterners gathering in the kitchen in times of trouble. Where else would a family go to mourn the death of a father?

The thing that was unusual that morning was that after a bit, one of my sisters, while continuing to sob, mentioned Mrs. Jarvick. I ignored the comment. I was concentrating on my grief and these words had no meaning. I went on crying. Then, later, the other sister mentioned that they didn't know what to do about Mrs. Jarvick. Again, the comment had no meaning for me. I continued to cry. Finally, after I don't know how long, Becky stopped crying and said explicitly that Mrs. Jarvick had called, and they didn't know what to do.

I remember thinking, *So what's there to do? She didn't lose her father too, did she?* But I said nothing. I was grieving the death of my father. Why did my sisters keep bringing up Mrs. Jarvick?

Twenty-five years earlier when the family had first moved to 247 Allen Avenue, West Chicago, Mrs. Jarvick had been a neighbor. Allen Avenue was a typical small-town street—the street where Becky still lived, though a few doors up. There were the Smallmans, Nicoloffs, Allens, Lockes, Jarvicks, Shultzes, Knifongs, and others—

all raising kids under the shade of tall, stately elms. At that time, Mike and Ellen Jarvick, and their son, Mike Jr., lived two doors down. They were nice people, but not special friends. They were just one more family on the block.

So there I was, standing in the kitchen, grieving for Dad, and with every second breath my sisters kept mentioning the name of this woman I could hardly remember. Then it hit me: *Dad had been seeing Mrs. Jarvick! Not bad for a seventy-year-old man who was overweight, smoked, didn't exercise, had high cholesterol, high blood pressure (only occasionally took his pills), was blind in one eye, and had tunnel vision in the other.*

I stopped crying. I stood back from my sisters and directly asked, "Has Dad been dating Mrs. Jarvick?" Becky nodded and mumbled through her tears, "Only just a little bit."

I went to the phone and asked, "What's Mrs. Jarvick's number?" Becky produced it promptly. Clearly, she had had it in waiting. When I got Mrs. Jarvick on the phone, I knew I was in for another strange conversation, but this time I was ready.

As soon as I identified myself, Mrs. Jarvick began a confused, circuitous rambling. Interrupting her, I cut to the quick. "Mrs. Jarvick, we three kids are here in the kitchen. If you can make it, we would love to have you come up and join us. Do you have the time?"

There was an abrupt silence. She hadn't expected this. Then came a rush of words: Well, yes, she would; well, yes, she could; yes, yes, she would be there right away; oh, she didn't want to intrude at such a time; she could only stay a minute; are you sure it's alright?

Allen Avenue is a short street, and Mrs. Jarvick was prompt. Soon an elderly, short, plump woman was standing with us in the kitchen, and now there were four pairs of teary eyes. Even though it was shortly after ten o'clock in the morning, I went to the cabinet and found Dad's nearly full bottle of Jim Beam. I asked Mrs. Jarvick if she would have a drink with us: Well, she hardly ever, but yes, she believed she would this one time. No, she didn't mind if she did, but only a little one. Finding water glasses in the cupboard, I poured four straight whiskeys, three fingers each, and we drank them down.

It was so much the right thing to do, I poured another round.

With a couple of neat whiskeys, I was feeling some better as I listened to Mrs. Jarvick, who by then was also feeling better. She told how "J" (my dad) had promised yesterday to drive her downtown in his white Chevrolet convertible to do a little shopping. I could not help but think—*this was a man who was nearly blind.* Then, in the morning when he didn't show up, she became worried and called the house. He was never late.

I poured another round and Mrs. Jarvick's words began to ramble a bit. "Your dad and I used to play cards together. There was really nothing much else to do.... The other night, before he left.... He was such a good man. He promised to drive me.... I was so lonely after my Mike died. And then too, his Fay (my mom) was gone.... He was such a good man. There was just the two of us. We were both so lonely and he was so gentle and kind.... He was such a good man. I didn't know how you kids would feel about it. I didn't want to intrude...."

Dad playing with his dog, Cricket

Contrary to what the Temperance League might try to tell you, there are times when morning whiskey—taken in moderation—can be very beneficial. By noon, Mrs. Jarvick had thoroughly unburdened her heart and by doing so had also lifted ours. We reassured her that we were pleased that Dad had found such a good friend. Soon she was trundling her way home, and I was hearing a quiet and seductive call from the living room couch to join it for a little nap.

Before I drifted off, I was surprised to realize how relieved I was feeling. I had worried about Dad's being lonely after Mom died. And I am sure he was lonely, but apparently not so lonely as I had feared. Perhaps there is hope for us all in our old age.

35

"But It Won't Kill Ya"

IN THE FALL OF '94, after reviewing my blood work and doing his hands-on examination, Dr. O'Donohgue settled me in front of his desk for our annual discussion of my health: blood pressure—good, cholesterol level—high, etc. I had noticed it some months before, but it was such a small thing that had it not been for Dr. O'Donohgue's fancy, glass-topped desk, it would have gone unmentioned. However, as I sat with my left leg crossed over my right, I could clearly see the left leg begin a very slight tremor. I pointed to the tremor, and for a moment both of us stared through the glass at my left foot. It would be still, then after a while, it would take up a slight rhythmic movement. It would continue for some time before pausing and then starting anew.

"What's this about?" I asked Dr. O'Donohgue. He replied that he didn't know, but that he would refer me to a neurologist who "was as good as any of them." Since that day, I've thought a lot about our conversation. Technically speaking, he was honest. He didn't know what it was; however, in a broader sense, he was less than honest. We were there to discuss my health, and he did not share with me any concern that my tremor might be something serious. He had been deeply curious about my heart, my lungs, my exercise routine, etc., all things he could fix. He was pointedly *not curious* about my tremor. Instead, he passed me on to another fellow who, as it turned out, was equally not curious.

DR. LOSSING'S CRAMPED OFFICE was strikingly different than Dr. O'Donohgue's spacious quarters. In Dr. Lossing's office I was instructed to sit high on the edge of his wooden desk. (As a permanent fixture in his office, he had conveniently placed a stepstool to help patients climb up to this strange perch.) When I commented on the unusual arrangement, Dr. Lossing explained that he specialized in movement disorders, and he had his patients sit this way so that he could better observe their movements.

During my appointment, Dr. Lossing spent some time asking me about my tremor, other aspects of my health, and the health of my relatives. Despite his many questions, they all seemed rather routine. He didn't seem curious. Finally, after some time, he declared that he, too, didn't know what ailed me, but that he would prescribe a low dose of propranolol, a drug that slows things down.

My tremor immediately disappeared. It worked like a charm—at least for a while.

Six months later, I found myself again perched on Dr. Lossing's desk pointing to the tremor in my left leg. He still maintained that he didn't know what was going on, but he prescribed a higher dose of propranolol, and for a while my symptoms again disappeared. This routine continued for the better part of four years as I gradually took larger and larger doses of propranolol.

Finally, one day it happened: When I returned to my high perch expecting a yet higher dose, Dr. Lossing told me that I had reached the allowable safe limit for propranolol. He could not prescribe a higher dose for fear of causing my heart to stop. This got my attention!

Although he still claimed not to know what was wrong with me, he suggested that I try a low dose of Sinemet. Sinemet (also known as carbidopa/levodopa) is a drug used by Parkinson's patients to make up the loss of dopamine in the brain, but as he wrote the prescription his only comment was, "Maybe this will help."

It didn't just "help." It was great!

Sinemet not only stopped my external tremor, which had been the focus of my concern, but it also quelled an internal feeling I hadn't realized was present—a sort of internal tension I still have trouble describing. In a strange way, it felt like the root cause of the problem was finally being addressed.

Some months later, when I went back to my perch on Dr. Lossing's desk, I asserted, "Finally, this is the right drug. Internally I can feel it hit the right spot." Although I didn't realize it at the time, in effect, I was diagnosing myself with Parkinson's. Even with such an enthusiastic report, Dr. Lossing was still reluctant to tell me what was amiss, though I am sure he knew that I had Parkinson's. Instead, he only *suggested* that I *might* have Parkinson's!

Living in the Washington, D.C., suburb of College Park, I had no problem finding another neurologist for a second opinion. I made an appointment at Johns Hopkins in Baltimore. This time as Dr. Reich did his examination, I sat beside his desk, not on it. Finally, after his examination he declared, "... I concur with Dr. Lossing. You have Parkinson's." Then, urgently leaning forward, putting a hand on my forearm, and with all earnestness, he stressed, "But it won't kill you." Although I didn't say it, I remember thinking at the time, *Why did he say that? There are worse things than dying, which we all do eventually.*

It was just beginning to dawn on me why medical doctors might be so reluctant to make a Parkinson's diagnosis. It's a terrible disease that starts off as not too bad, but then slowly gets worse and worse. If something else doesn't come along to kill me—the flu, cancer, a heart attack, a stroke, etc.—eventually I will become bedridden. There is no cure, and it is not something doctors can fix.

What none of the doctors would tell me at the time was that the drugs would control the symptoms for only about ten years. They were more forthcoming ten years later when it had become obvious to all that the drugs were becoming ineffective. Like with propranolol, there comes a time when larger and larger doses of Sinemet and its ancillary supporting drugs no longer work. After that, Parkinson's patients face worsening symptoms as they gradually lose control of their muscles.

I can be sympathetic to my doctors' feelings of frustration with this disease, they do not want to cause undue alarm. It is true that, had I known what was ahead, I would not have done anything differently. It just would have been good to know what to expect. I was paying these fellows to share knowledge and experience that I did not have, but that they had in abundance. In my mind, they were shirking their duty by not telling me what they knew, or at least what they strongly suspected.

I WENT BACK TO MY LIFE, which, as I just mentioned, I would have done anyway. Over those ten years as I gradually took more and more drugs to control my tremor, O'Donohgue developed Alzheimer's and died, Lossing retired, and Reich began very cautiously talking to me about considering DBS (Deep Brain Surgery). Unfortunately, brain surgery is inherently risky and doesn't work for all patients. On top of this, DBS addresses only the tremor—a major achievement, but not the only symptom of Parkinson's. In this procedure a surgeon implants a battery pack and two electrodes in the brain to turn off the tremor. (Only the electrodes go in the brain, the battery goes in the chest, like a heart pacemaker. A wire running under the skin and up the side of the neck connects the whole affair.)

After moving to Colorado, I had the procedure done in the fall of 2007. By that time the drugs were so ineffective, and I was so miserable, that I told the surgeon, "Bring me back better or don't bother to bring me back at all." Fortunately, the operation was a success that has changed my life. I am still driving and doing maintenance work around my home and for neighbors—though I move more slowly than I used to. The tremors stopped in 2007 and haven't returned, even seventeen years after the surgery. Unfortunately, the other Parkinson's symptoms have slowly worsened. Currently the most troublesome are my balance and speech, which have slowly gone downhill, but then, so have my hair, skin, muscles, eyes, teeth, bladder, etc., etc., etc. It's getting hard to distinguish between what is the Parkinson's symptoms and what is caused by aging. I am getting old.

IT'S BEEN SOME YEARS now, since I attended my fiftieth high school reunion. Even in 2009, I was struck by how incredibly old everyone seemed. They were—we were—all old, and yet we were the lucky ones. About a fourth of the class by 2009 had already died. (Today more than half of us are gone.)

I just turned eighty-four, and my body often reminds me that it is wearing out. It forces me to be physically aware of a simple fact that I have always known theoretically: The human body was not designed to last forever, and I am sure I have lived beyond its expiration date. With each passing day, death becomes a sooner-rather-than-later event. Such is the way things are. From its beginning, life is a terminal condition.

But I've had a good run of it. I have two good sons who are nearing old age themselves. I have already lived longer than either of my parents and at least one of my early Parkinson's doctors (maybe all three). And finally, there is this woman I live with. For some reason I can't quite understand, she makes a point to remind me daily that she is madly in love with me. Fortunately for us both, I feel the same about her. I am as madly in love with her as the day we married forty-four years ago.

Margaret and Dan wedding photo, 1981

For those who are not from Northern Missouri, a word

About Milan and Sullivan County

—— *The Land* ——

AS A RESULT of retreating glaciers, Sullivan County has a number of north-south hills and ridges that stand 100 to 200 hundred feet above the flat bottom land. The county's creeks and rivers flow south toward the Missouri River, which cuts across the state from Kansas City eastward to Saint Louis, where it joins the Mississippi River. The drop in elevation between Sullivan County's waterways and the Missouri River 150 miles to the south is only a few hundred feet. Except when flooding, the creeks tend to move slowly and are muddy.

Before 1820 when Native Americans were living on the land, about half of it was forested, but when the European descendants from the eastern states arrived, the newcomers cleared much of the land for crops. The fertile bottom land will grow most anything and the hillside is good for grazing. The town itself occupies mainly the east side of one of these north-south ridges and extends westward to a second ridge.

—— *The Town* ——

ALTHOUGH I HAVE MADE UP the names for many individuals in my stories, Milan is a real place. It is centrally located in northern Missouri, thirty miles south of the Iowa border. The original town was laid out in 1845. It is the Seat of Sullivan County, and it is farm country. Across from where I lived on Fourth Street was a row of houses, and behind those houses was wooded farmland where cattle grazed.

⸻ *The People* ⸻

DURING THE 1940S AND '50s, the population was mostly of English origin who, after the Missouri Compromise of 1820*, were attracted to the area from Kentucky, Tennessee, and North Carolina hill country. I don't know exactly when my great, great, great grandfather, Martin Jesse Knifong, arrived in Missouri, but it was after the 1820 census where he is listed as a resident of Lee County, Virginia, and it was probably before 1830 where his name is no longer listed in the Virginia records. (I can't be certain because Missouri was too new to have census records for its more isolated parts of the state in its 1830 census.) Martin farmed land about ten miles south of Milan, which didn't yet exist as a town, and he died in 1841.

Armstead C. Hill (1804-1889) was the first settler in the vicinity of Milan. He first visited the area in January, 1840, and erected a log cabin about 200 yards northeast of this site. The original town was laid out upon the farm of Mr. Hill in 1845, but the plot was never recorded. The town of Milan was officially incorporated by the state legislature February 9, 1859. The first courthouse on this site was erected in 1858. The building was destroyed by fire in 1908 and the present courthouse was constructed in 1939. Ancient burial mounds were discovered during the original excavation.

By the time I was born a 100 years later, the town of Milan had been incorporated and had grown to a population of about 2,000. As an adult living in urban areas far from Missouri, I've often joked, with only slight exaggeration, that my hometown was so small and isolated that, as a kid, "every adult I met already knew my name and my pedigree, as well as my shoe size and what I had for breakfast."

---

* The Missouri Compromise was a law passed in 1820 that admitted Missouri to the Union in 1821 as a slave state and Maine as a free state simultaneously, aiming to maintain the balance of power between slave and free states in Congress.

Milan and Sullivan County have changed some since the 1950s. Like most rural parts of America, there has been a general migration to larger cities. My father moved to the Chicago area in 1955, leaving Milan, like many others, largely for economic reasons. The countywide 1950 population of 11,000 has dropped nearly 40%; it now stands at about 7,000. In spite of the county's general population decline, the population of Milan itself has dropped only slightly, in large part because of a meat processing plant north of town, which has attracted a number of foreign-born nationals. Today, Hispanics made up about 22% of the town's population. When I last visited in 2009, I was surprised to see a Mexican restaurant on the Courthouse Square. When I was a child, any sort of special foreign shop was unheard of—restaurant or otherwise.

—— *The Local Dialect* ——

UPON ARRIVING IN West Chicago in 1955, my new high school teachers and classmates thought I sounded like a hillbilly. I still recall the embarrassment I felt when my algebra teacher made me say the word "formula" as "form-u-LA," repeating the word until she was satisfied that I said it the "right" way. I have no recall of how I had been pronouncing it. I only remember saying the "LA" syllable very loudly as I tried to please her.

I speak mostly with the northern Illinois accent I learned in high school, but early childhood remnants still cling. When I was a junior in college, one of my professors went around the room having each member of my English class, say only the single word "just." I was surprised and amazed when he singled me out of the large class as one of two who spoke with a "Highland Southern" accent. I had left Milan seven years before. To this day, I still say "Missouri" as if were spelled "Miz-zur-ah."

And while on the topic of pronunciation, it might help the reader to temporarily forget that there is a well-known city in Italy which the Italians call "Milano," but which is often shortened to

233

“Milan” by English speakers and pronounced as “mih-LAHN.” In Sullivan County the local county seat is pronounced “MY-lun.” An old man once explained to me in dead earnest that the town’s name came from the first settler who came over the top of the ridge near east Locust Creek, looked at the valley and rising ridge to the west, and said, “This is ‘My-Land.’” At the time I was too young to question his wisdom.

The Saturday Afternoon Social Gathering

ALTHOUGH IT WASN’T until 1939 that the current courthouse was built (the first one burned down in 1908), by 1905 the Saturday afternoon promenade around the old Courthouse Square was well-established as a Milan tradition I recall that, as late as 1955, it was much the same as in this old photograph, though—with time

IN TOWN FOR THE HALF-HOLIDAY

Vintage photograph, Poole’s Hardware, 1905

there had been some minor changes. Poole Bros. was shortened to Poole's, women's dresses and hats were a bit different, and the old photograph is missing cars lined up next to the sidewalk—Ford had yet to introduce his Model T.

—— *Milan Today* ——

I TOOK THIS PICTURE in 1991 from 3000' during a visit Margaret and I made to Milan to see my Aunt Esta. The photograph "flattens" the Fourth Street hill somewhat, making it appear less steep than it actually is. The Courthouse Square is centered vertically and about a quarter of the way from the right horizontally. The big backward "S" curve in the upper left, is Missouri Hwy E, known in town as Third Street. It intersects with Market Street at the southwest corner of the Courthouse Square. The corner of Fourth and Painter is mostly

The western portion of Milan, looking to the northwest

hidden by trees, but Fourth Street is one block south of Third, and Painter is three blocks west of Market, which is the western side of Courthouse Square. The east side of town, and beyond that East Locust Creek, are to the right of the picture, and not shown.

MILAN NOW HAS a library serving Sullivan County, established on the north side of the Courthouse Square in the 1970s—long after I had moved away.

Sullivan County Library, Milan, present day

About the Name "Knifong"

—— The Who, Where and When ——

BALTHASAR NEUFANG, my great, great, great, great, great grandfather, immigrated from Steinbach, Germany, to Pennsylvania, circa 1748. Balthasar brought with him a wife, Ann, and two sons, Peter and Martin Jesse Sr. Sometime after Martin Sr. was grown and married, he left Pennsylvania and moved to Rowan County, North Carolina, where Martin Jr. was born in 1774. Martin Sr. stayed in North Carolina until his death in 1786 and never changed his name.

It was Martin, Jr. who changed the spelling of the family name to "Knifong," probably when he married and moved to Virginia in 1800. At the time, German was a popular second language among the Colonists. While living in southern Virginia, Martin, Jr. had eleven children, all of whom used "Knifong" as their last name. After the last child was born in 1818, the family moved from Virginia to Missouri; he was one of the first settlers in the area. He died in 1841 and was buried in the Knifong Cemetery, ten miles south of Milan, on land which he donated for that purpose.

The What and Why

UPON FIRST SEEING the name *Neufang*, English speakers tend to want to pronounce it as "New-fang," which is not even close to the German pronunciation. The German "eu" vowel sound in the word *Neu*, is a sound not used by English speakers. It is somewhat like the English "oi" sound in *oil* or *oink*, but it is shifted halfway toward the "i" sound in *night* and *knife*. The German vowel "a" in *fang* is pronounced similar to the English "aw" combination in *lawn* and *dawn*. It is not pronounced like the "a" in *sang* and *bang* nor like the "o" in *gone* and *song*.

Although it was only partially successful, there is little doubt that the *Knifong* spelling was Martin Jesse Jr.'s attempt to anglicize the name. About the same time another branch of the family changed the spelling of *Neufang* to *Nifong*, perhaps a better choice, though neither *Nifong* or *Knifong*, with its silent "K," fully captures the German pronunciation of *Neufang*.

BECAUSE "NEUFANG" IS SUCH an old surname, there are no records about why it was chosen as my family name. Regardless, we can make a pretty good guess based on its meaning. The German word *neu* translates directly to *new* in English, and *fang* translates directly to *fang* (a long tooth) in English. The word *fang* in German, however, also carries other meanings, such as *talon* or *claw*. Thus, the name could have referred to someone who had rather long teeth or fingernails that were new, but I doubt this interpretation. When *fang* is compounded with other German words (for example *einfangen*, *empfangen*, *auffangen*, etc.), it often takes on a broader meaning, such as *to catch*, *to receive*, *to seize*, *to hold*, *to occupy* or *to fence in*. I believe it is one of these other meanings that was originally intended by the name.

IN 2001 I VISITED the Gastein valley in the Austrian Alps, roughly fifty miles south of Salzburg. It was there my great, great, great, great, great, great, great, great, great, great, great grandfather, Marco Neufang, was born in 1505. There are still *Neufangs* living in the valley, which is surrounded by alpine mountains that are wooded from the valley floor halfway up the mountainside. On the northwest end of the valley, one of these wooded mountains has a shear rock outcropping known locally as the Neufang Wall. The pasture land beneath the wall is surrounded by forest.

I also visited five villages in Germany named *Neufang*. I found no Neufangs living in any of them, but the villages were all in clearings of forested land.

It seems to me that, when *Neufang* was first used as a family name in the 1500s, the name most likely referred the family who occupied the *new catch* or *new holding* of *cleared land* near the wall. The land may have been, perhaps, *received* from a nobleman or Bishop. If I am right, the wall was probably named for the Neufang family who farmed the newly-cleared land at its base.

My Father, James Bradford, and My American Grandfathers

American Generation	First & Middle Names	Surname	Born–Died	Location
7	James Bradford My father, J.B.	Knifong	B. 8/23/1915 D. 2/15/1986	B. Browning, MO D. West Chicago, IL
6	Ester Perry Sr. My Grandfather, E.P.	Knifong	B. 10/8/1893 D. 1/21/1971	B. Browning, MO D. Milan, MO
5	Caleb Bradford Jr. My Great Grandfather	Knifong	B. 11/30/1866 D. 4/19/1953	B. Sullivan County, MO D. Sullivan County, MO
4	Caleb Bradford Sr. My G.G. Grandfather	Knifong	B. 3/23/1818 D. 7/9/1871	B. Virginia D. Sullivan County, MO
3	Martin Jesse Jr. My G.G.G. Grandfather	Neufang/ Knifong	B. 1774 D. 1841	B. North Carolina D. Sullivan County, MO
2	Martin Jesse Sr. My G.G.G.G. Grandfather	Neufang	B. 1745-46 D. 1775	B. Pennsylvania D. North Carolina
1	Georg Balthasar My G.G.G.G.G. Grandfather	Neufang	B. 1718 D. 1787-88	B. Steinbach, Germany D. Pennsylvania

My German/Austrian Grandfathers

Generation	Name	Surname	Born—Died	Location
7	Johann Martin	Neufang	B. 5/3/1680 D. 1/20/1755	B. Steinbach, Germany D. Steinbach, Germany
6	Johann Magnus	Neufang	B. 9/24/1655 D. 2/12/1730	B. Steinbach, Germany D. Steinbach, Germany
5	Ruprecht*	Neufang	B. 1633 D. 2/21/1683	B. Gastein Valley, Austria D. Steinbach, Germany
4	Veit	Neufang	B. 1595-1605 D. 1640-1650	B. Gastein Valley, Austria D. Gastein Valley, Austria
3	Hanns	Neufang	B. 1567 D. 1601? 1645?	B. Gastein Valley, Austria D. Gastein Valley, Austria
2	Georg	Neufang	B. 1545 D. ca. 1620	B. Gastein Valley, Austria D. Gastein Valley, Austria
1	Marco	Neufang	B. 1505?** D. ?	B. Gastein Valley, Austria D. Gastein Valley, Austria

* It is not known why Ruprecht moved from the Gastein Valley to Steinbach, but with the Proptestant movement, there was a lot of intolerance.

** Because surnames were not commonly used before the 1400s, this is about as far back as one can go. For example, consider Leonardo da Vinci (1452-1519): The name *da Vinci* is an indicator of his birthplace. Although today many think of, and use, *da Vinci* as if it were his surname, it is not a family name. During his lifetime, he had only the one name, "Leonardo."

About the Automotive Front-wheel Caster

From Webster's *Third New International Dictionary*

Caster: 3. *a wheel...mounted in a frame free to swing about an axis perpendicular to the axis of the wheel...and used for supporting furniture, trucks, and various portable machines.... 4. the slight backward tilt of the upper end of the knuckle pin of an automotive vehicle employed as a means of giving directional stability to the front wheels.*

FOR THOSE WHO might be curious about the front-wheel casters on a car, think of the front casters on a shopping cart that can pivot vertically to allow the front wheels to turn a full 360°. This vertical pivot always points to a spot on the floor just ahead of where the wheel itself is moving. The offset, which can easily be seen, is what forces caster wheels to swing freely to line up behind where the pivot rod is pointing regardless of the direction the cart is pushed.

It is the same on a car and a bicycle. Although the casters on a car (or a bike) are not vertical—they are tilted slightly backwards—still the (nearly) vertical pivot points just ahead of where the wheel touches the ground. One can see this off-vertical effect on a parked car by turning the wheels all the way to the right (or left) and noticing that the wheels are no longer truly straight up and down but leaning slightly toward the direction of the turn. It is the casters that allow cars to be steered safely at high speeds on smooth highways, and bikes to be ridden hands-free, if conditions are favorable.

If there were only one front wheel on a shopping cart and its vertical pivot rod was long enough to reach above the basket to a horizontal steering wheel, a child riding in the basket could have a lot of fun steering the cart while it is pushed forward.

Though hidden from view on a car, each front wheel pivot also points just a bit ahead of the spot where the wheels rest on the ground. And, like the front wheels of a cart, these wheels try continue in the direction of the vehicle when it moves forward.

However, a major difference between a cart and a car can be shown when a cart is pulled backward. The front wheels of the cart turn themselves 180° around to follow the spot on the ground where the vertical pivot is pointing. If, when the cart were pulled backwards, a child resisted this turning and tried to keep the wheel ahead of where the vertical pivot is pointing, the child would have to fight for control until he or she first let the wheel make this 180° swing.

Unlike cart wheels, car wheels have a limited turning range. None can be turned even close to 90°, let alone 180°. But when moving in reverse, car wheels still try to behave like wheels on a cart and turn completely around. Thus, the front wheels of a car seem to have a mind of their own and fight with the driver for control. As every experienced driver who has backed up too rapidly knows, a car is difficult to control and behaves in a "funny" way.

Acknowledgments

FIRST, I want to acknowledge that I have lived my entire life on land that our ancestors took from the Native Americans. As much as this land has been a blessing and a boon for my people, losing the land has been a curse and disaster for the native peoples to whom it once belonged.

SECOND, like most endeavors, this book would not have been possible without the support and encouragement of many others. I want to acknowledge specifically my good friend, Rahima Dancy, who carefully edited most of the stories and who introduced me to Ann Erwin, who did the layout of the book. Ann also did some of the editing and offered many helpful suggestions. And I want to thank all who read individual stories and encouraged my writing, especially Ann Ryan and Claudia Smith from my days at the Writers Center in Silver Spring, Maryland.

FINALLY, I want to acknowledge my wonderful wife, Margaret Porter, who was most insistent that I publish this collection. Without her persistent prodding and support, these stories would have remained scattered among my other private papers and likely discarded after my death.

About the Author

JAMES "DAN" KNIFONG was born in February 1941, in a Sullivan County farmhouse four miles southeast of Milan, well before electricity made its way to rural Missouri. During his first six years, he lived in Milan and various places in Illinois, as the family followed his father seeking work as an operator of earth-moving machines. During his father's service in WWII, the family lived in Milan. After the war his father used the GI Bill to start a one-man excavating business in Sullivan County. In 1955 his father moved the business to the suburban town of West Chicago, Illinois, where Dan attended high school, graduating in 1959.

Dan married in 1961, and they had two sons. After graduating from Northern Illinois University in 1964, he taught high school mathematics for two years before attending graduate school at the University of Illinois. After receiving a Master's in Mathematics and a Doctorate in Mathematics Education in 1971, he taught at the Universities of Nebraska, West Virginia and Maryland. While living in Maryland, and after seventeen years, the marriage ended in divorce. In 1978 he took his two sons with him to Bielefeld, Germany, for a one-year Senior Fulbright Research Fellowship.

Returning to Maryland, Dan met and married Margaret Porter in 1981. They lived in College Park, Maryland, and he commuted across the District of Columbia to serve as chair of Mathematics at Marymount University, and for a time, Margaret commuted to Baltimore. Both he and Margaret earned their pilot's licenses in 1989 and for six years took many flying vacations in their Piper Cherokee before he was grounded due to the onset of Parkinson's.

Three years after Margaret retired as Chief Counsel for the Food and Drug Administration, they moved to Boulder, Colorado, in 2006. They currently live in Silver Sage Village, a senior cohousing community where Dan is still active doing various handyman projects around the complex.

For those readers who would like to share your thoughts, you may connect with the author by email at dan1941mo@gmail.com.

www.ingramcontent.com/pod-product-compliance
Lightning Source LLC
Chambersburg PA
CBHW060349310726
48976CB00003B/771